I0545436

A Novel by

BETTY OWENS THOMASON

Published by
Sign of the Whale Books™

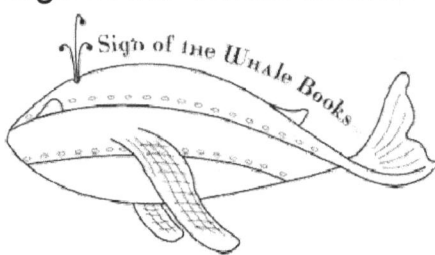

PUBLISHED BY: Sign of the Whale Books™*, an imprint of Olivia Kimbrell Press™, P.O. Box 4393, Winchester, KY 40392-4393
The *Sign of the Whale Books™* colophon and Icthus/spaceship/whale logo are trademarks of Olivia Kimbrell Press™.

Sign of the Whale Books™ is an imprint specializing in Biblical and/or Christian fiction primarily with fantasy, magical, speculative fiction, futuristic, science fiction, and/or other supernatural themes.

Originally published by AuthorHouse March 28, 2007.

Some scripture quotations courtesy of the King James Version of the Holy Bible from the Public Domain.

Some scripture quotations courtesy of the Young's Literal Translation of the Holy Bible by Robert Young Author of the Analytical Concordance to the Bible 1898 Revised Edition from Public Domain.

Original Cover Art and Graphics by Debi Warford (www.debiwarford.com)

Library Cataloging Data
Owens, Betty Thomason (Betty Thomason Owens) 1953-
  A Gathering of Eagles/ Betty Thomason Owens
  xx p. 23cm x 15cm (9in x 6 in.)
Summary: Sent on a mission to reunite the war-torn kingdom, Lady Jael and Prince William will face a darker enemy than either has ever encountered—will their love survive?
ISBN: 978-1939603227 (trade perfect) ISBN: 978-1939603234 (ebook)
  ISBN: 978-1456739799 (Hardcover) ISBN: 978-1456739775 (trade perfect out of print)
1. Christian fiction 2. Christian fantasy 3. adventure 4. love stories 5. family relationships
[PS3568.O3475 O328 2007]
[Fic.] 813.6 (DDC 23)

A GATHERING OF Eagles

A Novel by

BETTY THOMASON OWENS

Table of Contents

Dedication

To Mom

If I take the wings of the morning,
and dwell in the uttermost parts of the sea;
even there shall thy hand lead me,
and thy right hand shall hold me.

Psalm 139: 9-10 KJV

Prologue – The Lady of the Haven

Lady Jael froze. Lord William Prince of Coldthwaite had caught sight of her and was now moving toward her. At once she made to smile but saw no answering expression on his face. As he approached his eyes held hers. The music and revelry faded into the distance as Jael's attention centered on him.

For a moment he stood looking down at her. His next movements were slow – in the way of a warrior – deliberate. His right hand removed his sword from its scabbard. He balanced it with the palm of his left hand – knelt upon one knee before her – all the while his eyes held hers. He laid the sword on the floor at her feet.

Jael had heard of this custom, but had never seen it done. She could hardly believe it was happening now to her.

The noise in the room came to a complete halt as all eyes turned to Lady Jael and Lord William. After he laid his sword down he stood, gazed into her eyes and offered her his hand. According to custom – no word was spoken.

She took a deep breath and exhaled slowly. "Oh dear Lord," she prayed. Her heart beat so strong within her breast, she could hardly breathe. The air flashed and popped with a strange kind of energy as Jael stretched out her hand and laid it in his. He closed his fingers around hers. She grasped her skirt, lifted it to step over the sword and joined him on the other side. He brought her close to his side never taking his eyes from hers.

The silence in the great ballroom was broken. "Who will stand with them?" The question was repeated over and over as the crowd watched in great expectation. Several long moments passed until Young Will, William's nephew, moved forward supported by a cane and carefully lowered himself onto his good knee. He laid the cane aside – retrieved his uncle's sword – balanced it carefully upon open palms and offered it to

William, who took up the sword, placed it back in its scabbard and turned to his lady.

Young Will pushed his way back into a standing position and bowed in reverence before the couple. Afterwards he leaned forward to plant a kiss upon Jael's cheek. The crowd erupted into cheers and loud huzzahs.

William smiled and bowed to his men, Jael's hand still firm in his. She stood in utter amazement, for in the space of only a few moments her sorrow had turned to joy. In the way of the warrior she was now a married woman. In laying down his sword before her, William had offered her his eternal protection. When she gave him her hand and stepped over the sword she had accepted him.

Lady Bethalyn paced about the room too wound up to go to bed. The first rays of the sun peeped through the shutters.

"It is the dawn of a new day," said King George. "Come to bed, my dear."

She perched on the corner of the bed and gazed at him. "Aye my lord husband, it is indeed the dawn of a new day. I suppose I must resign myself to it and be content."

"You will never be sorry for what has happened this even – I can promise you that. There is no better woman for our son." He laid his head back against the pillows and yawned. Within seconds he was snoring.

Lady Bethalyn smiled and shook her head. A moment later she rose, removed her shawl and climbed into bed. When the sun was fully up her eyes were still open but she did not fret. Her lips moved in silent prayer for her family and for their kingdom. "It is the dawn of a new day," she whispered. "Whatever it brings, Lord help me to be ready for it."

– Excerpt from *The Lady of the Haven*

Chapter 1 – Peace Interrupted

Lady Jael rode beside her husband to observe his newest recruits. She thrilled to see the men skirmish amid the rocks and vales of the high reaches of Cragmorton. She had watched them progress from green sprigs to trained warriors.

Jael had not ridden in these parts since her arrival the previous fall. They had come to the high mountain region of Cragmorton on a mission to reunite the provinces under the reign of King George Horatio du Frain, her father-in-law.

It was meant to be a training run – a mere day trip into the outer regions in a time so tranquil that her husband, Lord William Prince of Coldthwaite, felt free to include his lady. Barely two hours had passed since breaking bread, when an uneasy feeling began to scratch away at Jael's insides. She tried to suppress it, tried to quiet its groaning with prayers, but it would not be subdued.

They had traveled nearly half a dozen miles through labyrinthine trails when she reigned in her mount, tilted her head and listened. She was gifted with the unusual ability to hear sounds over great distances.

William turned and rode back to her, his expression troubled. "What is it, my love?"

Her lips quivered as she spoke. "The sounds of suffering … the smell of charred flesh … there are so many – " Her voice cracked.

He laid his hand upon her arm. "Where is this happening? How far?"

"I do not know." She focused on him and stretched a trembling hand toward the South. "Over there, I think, but you must not … I would not – " She crumpled forward in pain from the force of the vision. William jumped down from his horse and lifted her out of the saddle. He held her for a moment against him.

She buried her face in his chest. "I would not have you go," she whispered. "I know you must, but I do not want you to go." She drew her head back to look into his eyes. "It is the price I paid when I married a warrior. I knew there would be times like this."

"We both knew, my love." He kissed her forehead and turned away to look out over the mountaintops. "Peace does not abide forever without exacting a price. I must look after these people. It is a promise made by my father."

"Honored by his son," she whispered. When he turned back to her, she searched his face, memorizing every feature. "Do not take these young inexperienced men with you, my love. Take the older men who have followed you for many years."

He looked out over the small contingent of warriors. "There is wisdom in your words. I will leave these with you, to watch over Cragmorton and their own lands. They will protect it with their lives." He lifted her into the saddle and mounted a beautiful black stallion. Lodan was every bit as regal as the man he carried. They rode to the place where the young warriors waited.

How happily Jael had ridden out compared with what her heart felt now: deep sadness and dismay over what was to come. Her eyes clung to her husband as he rode ahead of her. Within a few hours, he would be gone.

The squadron returned through a narrow passage that opened on the vast expanse of the valley of Cragmorton. Upon a high round hill stood the white stone walls of Wrenook and beyond, pastureland extended to the shores of the Greshne. The lake stretched out in splendorous beauty, reflecting the bright blue sky. Dark green craggy pines lined its northern banks. The town of Cragmorton lay like a patchwork quilt upon the far foothills, its streets all branching out from the gates of the castle, which stood upon the easternmost shore of the Greshne.

The Touri Mountain peaks with their ever present caps of snow, rose high on all sides of the vale, completely enclosing the rich valley. Jael always found its wild beauty impressive, though it was terribly cold in winter.

Soon after their return to the castle at Greshne, William prepared to brief his men. Courin, Captain of the Guard, sent a runner to the holdings and the yard. A hundred warriors assembled within the hour, ready for whatever lay ahead. Jael wondered how they would receive his news. Would he tell them they rode forth on the word of a woman?

Jael couldn't sleep, so she sat near the fire and prayed. At the cock's first crow, she threw a shawl over her shoulders and stepped outside onto the great porch that overlooked the lake. Stars twinkled overhead and a sliver of a moon cast its pale glow on the water. She lifted her hands and sang praises to God – not too loud, lest she wake her sleeping husband. He needed a good night's rest.

A cool breeze off the lake stirred the wistra vines that entwined the portico. The black vision returned, its icy tendrils stealing around Jael's heart, tightening its hold, disturbing her peace. Her voice broke and her song ended.

William lay awake for several minutes before he rose. He donned his leathers, pulled on his boots and cinched his belt. He ran a quick comb through his dark hair, gathered it in his fist and tied it with a leather strap.

In the soft gray of predawn, he stepped through the doorway onto the porch. *Jael.* He knew he'd find her there. She was drawn to the water like a moth to firelight. She cast a glance over her shoulder and then turned back to the water.

He smiled at the soft glow of the moon on her flaxen hair. It shone like a halo or a crown on her head. In his mind, she was worthy of both. Two long strides brought him near enough to encircle her with his arms. He kissed the top of her head.

"I love you more than life itself."

She sighed and turned in his embrace, lifted her lips to his, then buried her face against him.

He caressed her hair and whispered, "You must be strong, my love." His voice was husky with emotion, but there were things that must be said. "I leave you in charge. You must continue what I have started."

"Oh aye, I must carry on," she said, her voice muffled by his shirt. She lifted her head to peer up at him. "I fear they will not heed me. I am not so strong as you."

He chuckled. "In many ways, my dear, you are stronger than I. You are a warrior at heart and there is none braver, not even among the men."

"You flatter me now and preen my feathers. If you truly believe it, then

I am thankful. And you may be assured, I will do my best to be worthy of your trust."

He tightened his arms around her, longing for more time, but there was none. He gave her a kiss he hoped she would not soon forget and parted from her to see to his men.

Not long past daybreak the men set forth. There were no tears, for Jael made sure to show her strength before the warriors. She waved her kerchief as was customary, as all the women did, and she vowed to pray for a good journey. She watched her husband's face, felt his last kiss upon her lips. His hand went up; the men turned their horses. They were away. Dust billowed up from the horses' hooves as they rode off down the valley.

Jael ran to watch from atop the high turret. She loved the heights because she could see almost as far as she could hear. As she watched, a fluttering noise brought her quickly about – an owl came to roost. It had become a friend, and knew that in her pocket, Jael kept small bits of dried meat. She held some out to the owl she had dubbed Isra, and whispered in the ancient tongue. "Were I like you, I could follow and observe from afar."

The owl cocked its head and watched her with its strange yellow eyes. A moment later, it was off soaring across the sky.

As the last of the riders disappeared into the pass, Jael lifted her hands toward heaven and gave praise to God. But she was too troubled in spirit to lose herself in meditation. After only a few minutes, she sat down in the shelter of the balustrade and gave over to grief.

Chapter 2 – Carrying On

Back in their quarters, Jael yearned for time alone to work through the anguish of this first parting. But there were matters of state with which to deal as well as sick to visit and … she swallowed the lump in her throat, William's things to be packed away until his return.

They had been married little more than a twelvemonth. The first three of those months were spent traveling through the Touris, en route to Cragmorton. Jael smiled at the memory of her father-in-law, as he stood and addressed a group of squires and landowners at Castle Coldthwaite.

"Tomorrow I send forth my son, as my representative, as heir apparent, and as an ambassador for Christ. I have ordained him with power to make necessary decisions and to lead in my absence. He will establish our methods of rule in the old country and unite all the provinces."

Jael sat down on the edge of the bed, lost in her memories. King George had gone on to say, "This may sound like a great responsibility – that's because it is – but I have complete confidence in him. He is equal to the task and this woman by his side," here he had given Jael a radiant smile, "with whom some of you are only just now becoming acquainted, is endued with power and great sensibility. She is worthy to reign as the sole surviving member both of the House of Rogan and of the House of John du Frain."

King George had taken hold of Jael's hand then and squeezed it tightly, smiled into her eyes and said, "I do trust in the Lord, fair lady. I know He has sent you to us. Do not fear the future and what it will bring. A blessing follows you and all of those who come of you."

William had advised her to keep this counsel in her heart.

She had hoped to enjoy peace a bit longer. She sighed as she stood up and returned to her work, bundled up William's things and gave the bed one last brush of her hand. She glanced over her shoulder to check on the fire, picked up her shawl and walked to the door.

Jael stepped out into the corridor, where a stray breath of wind lifted a tendril of her hair and blithely whipped it into her mouth. She drew it out and tucked it back into the coils of her hair. Her eyes searched out the small round window just under the eaves. The shutter was broken and allowed air to flow freely. She smiled, for it also allowed Isra to pass in and out. Her gaze shifted to the nest in the corner, well out of everyone's reach.

She descended to the lowermost level of the castle where young warriors worked in lieu of servants. None of the indigenous folk would dare enter the grounds of the castle, for it was believed to be haunted by the former queen.

Jael handed the dirty clothing to one of the men for washing. He snapped to attention and bowed his head. How she longed for ordinary servants to order about, rather than young warriors. They intimidated her, for she always felt they resented their post. No doubt they'd rather ride with their master into the unknown.

"Lady Jael," a man called from the doorway.

She turned to face Brannon, Captain of the Guard.

"My lady I would speak with ye," he said.

She followed his lead to a small chamber across the hall, where several men waited near a table surrounded with stools. She greeted each man with a nod and sat down at the head of the table – in her husband's seat. The men sat down and faced Brannon.

Jael folded her hands in her lap, thankfully hidden by the table. She did not wish for them to see her fidget. "Never let them see your fear," William had often counseled her. She lifted her chin and gazed at Brannon. "What is it, Brannon?"

"My lady, we ask your leave to seek out help for ye here in the castle." He sat forward with his bulky forearms on the wooden table.

Jael's gaze fell from his rough, bearded chin to his big, weather-beaten hands. She drew her head up and scanned the faces at the table. The men kept their eyes averted. Brannon cleared his throat and Jael's eyes snapped back to his. He was waiting for her answer. Not a patient man.

"I think this is wise," Jael said. "If your men are to guard their homeland, they should not be burdened with household tasks. But will you be able to find someone willing to come, Brannon?"

Brannon nodded to another man, who sat on Jael's right, a dark haired, angular man with the clear blue eyes so common in these parts.

"That there's Somwald, my lady," Brannon said. "Somwald, tell her ladyship what ye told me."

Somwald's blue gaze found a spot on the wooden table as he spoke. "There's them in the high villages, my lady what needs shelter and food. Their menfolk is serving Prince William and unable to make sure of their homesteads." Jael frowned at his speech. The mountain dialect was still difficult for her. She raised an eyebrow at Brannon.

"So you think," she glanced at Somwald. "You think these people will come and live in quarters here, be willing to work in exchange for food and shelter?"

Somwald nodded. "There be those, my lady what don't fear the ... Lady – " he cast a glance about the room, as did several of the others. "May she rest in peace – so much as they fear the cold and the want."

Jael suppressed the desire to smile. She had made peace with the *Lady* the first night she slept in the castle. Jael believed the noises she heard throughout the night were more natural than supernatural, made by gusts of wind through the drafty old edifice. Then she'd come face-to-beak with Isra, which confirmed her beliefs.

She nodded to Brannon. "You have my permission to seek suitable servants for the castle and grounds. Now, what other business have you to discuss?"

Brannon's eyes flashed momentarily as he seemed to struggle with amusement. "I have none other ... er ... *household* matters to speak of your ladyship." He cleared his throat behind a fist and looked at Jael. "We have the situation well under control."

Jael did not break her gaze. She understood completely. At her slight movement, Somwald jumped to his feet to assist her. Another warrior opened the door for her. On the way out, she threw a smoldering glance over her shoulder. Barely suppressed anger dug its claws into her chest.

What was it William had said to her? *You are a warrior at heart and there is none braver, not even among the men.*

Ha! – but clearly not a man, and not to be taken seriously. Household matters indeed! Her pulse throbbed wildly in her throat as Jael sped towards the stairs, then stopped so suddenly she nearly pitched forward, her arms flailing the air to catch her balance. After a moment's consideration, she pivoted toward the outer door.

Crispus!

Outside the castle, Jael found the compound filled with activity. Cattle roamed about and a chicken darted between their legs, cackling loudly. She stopped and looked around. Someone really must get things under control around here. Probably a household matter, so would fall into her hands. She gathered her skirt and tiptoed through the yard to a small chapel beside the lake.

Jael would never forget her first meeting with Crispus, a Roman missionary. He'd been staying near the falls of Verani, her birthplace and home for the first twenty years of her life. He'd gone there out of curiosity, after hearing it spoken of as a "cursed place." Jael believed God had drawn him to the place at that exact time. After a short acquaintance, William had asked him to accompany them on their journey. Along the way, he'd taught Jael to read and write and he'd shared his great wealth of knowledge regarding God's word, with all of them.

The chapel was empty. She wandered to the water's edge and sat down on a smooth boulder. The bright midmorning sun sparkled on the ripples stirred by the ever present wind. A large dragonfly danced and swayed over the water, then lit on the surface. Gravel crunched and Jael swung around to see a man of ordinary height, dressed in a light brown robe, cinched at the waist with a leather belt. A scroll was tucked into the belt.

"Crispus, I was looking for you," she said.

He approached and sat down opposite her and rested his hands on his knees. Tight dark curls stood in perfect alignment around his well-tanned face. He had a long thin nose and full lips. Warm brown eyes sparked of intelligence as he spoke.

"How may I help you, my lady?" His speech and mannerisms were exceedingly proper, almost stilted at times. He had learned every dialect of the Anglican language and spoke them all with studied ease.

Jael drew in a quick breath and released it. Her hands still trembled from the anger she'd felt a few minutes before, but Crispus' presence calmed her. Already she began to feel that she had overreacted. She gave her head a quick shake. "I forgot my place, it seems," she said. He cocked his head, and waited for further information. A fish jumped, they both turned to watch the circle of ripples left in its wake. Jael reached down and dipped her hand in the cold water. "I assumed I would be taking my husband's place in the chain of command."

"Ah," Crispus said. "You have spoken with Captain Brannon."

She gave a slow nod. "I have. He has a different perspective."

There was no need for more detail. Crispus leaned forward, his elbows on his knees, fingers interlocked. "You are confused over your role," he said. "I hope you are not at odds with the good captain?"

She turned her gaze to the lake. "I have no argument with him. I only want to clear up a misunderstanding." She faced Crispus. "My husband clearly stated that I would be in charge. I must 'carry on in his absence,' he said. I have no wish to interfere with military matters, but I feel I have an obligation to my husband regarding the welfare of the people."

Crispus nodded but did not speak. He sat upright and removed the scroll from his belt. He twisted it in his hands while he considered her words. Finally, he spoke. "I'm quite certain Captain Brannon meant no disrespect, my lady. My experience of the Cragmortons is that they are a proud people. They have a violent past, and are used to fending for themselves." He darted a glance at Jael. "If you like, I will speak to him."

Jael waved a hand in front of her face to fend off a cloud of midges. "What I would like, Crispus, is for you to find out what orders were given, that I may know how to proceed. Perhaps Captain Brannon was led to believe that he is in charge of more than just the warriors." She relaxed a bit. "I have no wish to engage in a power struggle, Crispus. I've no heart for it. I only wish to know where I stand."

Crispus nodded. "I understand, my lady. I will pay a visit to the men. I bid you good morn." He stood, gave her a quick nod and strode away.

Jael pushed away from the boulder and stepped carefully through the rocks along the shore. She had hoped to feel better after talking to Crispus, but she did not. What must he think of her? She pressed her palms against her cheeks. On her word, William and his men had gone out in pursuit of an unknown enemy and she remained behind to squabble with her protectors?

Crispus sat among the warriors, listening to their banter. Captain Brannon was still in conference with his officers. Nearby, a door opened and a short red-haired man stepped out. Built a bit like a barrel, he moved with surprising agility. He did not look pleased to see Crispus.

"It ain't the Holy Day, Master Crispus, my men have work to do. Your time would be better served among the little 'uns, or alongside her ladyship as she tends the sick."

A few of the men chuckled, but Crispus did not budge. "I'm not here for the men, Captain Brannon. I'd like a moment of your time, if you can spare it."

The captain jerked his head back and focused his full attention on Crispus. "I haven't a moment to give ye, but ye may run alongside if ye've a word to say." Crispus noted the look of discomfort in the man's eyes. Captain Brannon did not hold to the same beliefs as the royal house and he did not like to be preached to.

Crispus had no trouble matching the shorter man's stride. "I was relieved to hear Lord William had left you in charge of the men," he told the captain.

Captain Brannon turned his head to frown at Crispus. "Be ye buttering me up for a fancy dish, young Roman?"

"Nay, Captain, I'm only saying Lord William made a wise move," Crispus said. "The men respect you."

Captain Brannon hooked his thumbs in his britches and strode down the incline toward the stables. "Did her ladyship set ye up for this? Does it goad her that he didn't give her charge of the men?"

Crispus shook his head. "She does not disagree with her husband's decision regarding the men, Captain." They drew near the stables and Crispus knew the captain would cut him off, so he asked him outright, "Will you defer all matters of government to Lady Jael then?"

Captain Brannon stopped so quickly, Crispus nearly plowed into him. "Afore the royals – and ye – arrived, I was chief of Cragmorton," he said. "The natives won't take no orders from a woman, young Roman. Being a man, ye should understand that."

Before Crispus could form an answer, the captain spun about and stomped away.

"Huh!" Crispus said. "So she was right in her assumption." He frowned at the distant mountains and rubbed his chin. She would not like this. She'll be riled. Crispus turned aside to the chapel. This would need a good foundation of prayer.

Chapter 3 – Song and Dance

Jael drove a hand spade into the rich dark earth and uprooted two lindaren bulbs. She would dry them and grind them into a fine powder for tea. Lindaren, sometimes called clear-eye, was used to heal eye infections and swellings. She deposited the bulbs in her sack and cinched it tight, then tapped the spade against a rock to knock off the worst of the soil. She rubbed it clean with a wad of dry grass and gathered her tools, tied the sack to a belt at her waist and pushed away from the ground. Her gaze shifted from the place she had been, to the valley before her. In the distance a flock of sheep grazed and near at hand, a man approached. Jael sighed. If Crispus felt the need to speak with her away from town, it could not be good news. She rubbed her hands together to dislodge any remaining dirt and began her descent.

Crispus halted and bowed. "My lady," he said.

Jael gave him an answering nod. Her eyes searched his face. "What news have you, Crispus?"

He turned sideways and gestured for her to walk with him. She fell into step beside him.

"You were right, it seems," he said. "Brannon has assumed control." They walked in silence for a minute.

Familiar sounds filled Jael's ears and with every step that brought them closer to Cragmorton, came deeper dread. This was not a battle she wished to fight. She looked at Crispus.

"What is your counsel, then? How shall I deal?"

He did not look at Jael, but kept his eyes straight ahead, hands clasped behind his back as they strolled along. "I cannot fault him, my lady. As he says, he was chief of Cragmorton in the absence of the royal family. He says the people will not be ruled by a woman." He cast a sideways glance at Jael.

Jael frowned. "And you think he is right?"

"I think you must tread carefully my lady. Your patience at this time would mean much."

"My patience?" Jael twisted her lips into a wry smile. "You are suggesting I honor his assumption?"

Crispus nodded.

Jael drew in a deep breath of sheep-scented air. "In my heart, I know you are right, but my mind chafes at this counsel."

Crispus chuckled and peered at her. "I am not surprised by that, my lady."

Near the entrance to the castle yard, they parted ways. Crispus went to visit a local family, Jael went to the drying room, where she hung the roots and bulbs to cure. Her heart was heavy. She needed time alone to pray and seek God's will. Her steps echoed through the lonely halls of the castle. Wind whistled through the upper story window as she climbed two flights of stairs and stood upon the place, marked by a dark stain, where the Lady died.

The Magistrate's brutal attack was still spoken of in hushed tones, two decades later. Their lovely queen and all of her children were slain. The northern branch of the du Frain clan had been wiped out in one day's time. Jael gripped the balustrade and glanced heavenward. A few minutes later, she bowed her head and prayed.

"I hear you, Father, I will abide by your word."

Jael watched from an upper story window as Ruda Dungarten and her family moved into the compound a few days later. For the time being, they would live outdoors. They pitched their multicolored tents near the entrance to the city, bivouacked upon the vale like flowers in an open meadow.

That night, there was singing and celebration round the campfire as the townspeople joined in, bringing food and drink with them. Jael cast a cloak over her shoulders and went out to greet them.

She was not really surprised by the cool reception she received. This did not stop her from walking among them with a warm smile for each one.

Ruda, though a bit taller than Jael, was short of stature and plump around the middle. Like many of the northern women, her complexion was ruddy. Her thin lips were set in a perpetual frown and her dark eyes held deep sorrow. Jael could not coax a single word from her, so ended the one-sided conversation with a dip of her head.

As Jael was walking away, she heard a familiar voice behind her.

"Think of your family, woman. Ye'd best remember your place or that one there will have ye thrown out and all o'yorn as well."

Jael stopped and turned about. Brannon stood face-to-face with Ruda, for they were about the same height. Jael bit back a quick retort, pressed her lips together and allowed her gaze to linger on Brannon until the man sensed her there and took a step back. Ruda gave no indication that she was aware of Jael's presence.

On her return to the castle, Jael's path led along the edge of the lake and past the stables, where the warriors were posted. She heard the sound of the flute and timbrel and stopped to watch as a couple of the men danced about and sang. One song ended and another began with a psaltery at the lead, an instrument Jael loved to hear. She stood facing them, one hand holding the hood of her cloak fast in place.

The young dancers began to stomp their feet to the rhythm of the music while another man began to sing. Amazement coursed through Jael's breast as she heard her own name sung to music; the tale of her embattled journey through the Touris.

> *"There's none so fair*
> *Nor none so true*
> *As the Lady of the Haven, Jon Jael!*
> *She donned men's clothes an' cut her hair –*
> *She sat up on a horse and rode – O!*
> *She sat up on a horse and rode – O!*
>
> *A bag o' healin' 'erbs*
> *A brew o' death*
> *That were her tucker and sword*
> *A power so great was ever hers*
> *She sat upon a horse and rode – O!*
> *She sat upon a horse and rode – O!*

This went on for several stanzas, each more fantastic than the one before. The men danced a jig as they sang and ended up with a respectful bow and shy smiles to the subject of their song. Jael returned their greeting with a deep curtsey and a good-natured smile and wished them all good evening.

At least her heart was lighter now, but Brannon's harsh words to Ruda still echoed in her ears.

Chapter 4 – Adrina

Crispus stood in the tiny chapel of the keep, gazing out at the gray peaks on the horizon. "Cold and uncompromising, like the inhabitants of this valley." He spent many early mornings in this way, seeking the Lord's guidance. "You have sent me to a people as rugged as their surroundings. How shall I reach them?"

He sensed a new presence and stepped quietly from end to end of the small sanctum, praying beneath his breath and examining every nook and cranny. A noise at the back of the room drew him up. He stood still a moment then swiveled about slowly. A woman stood there, as though indecisive, her eyes like dark coals in a sea of white.

He thought at first this may be one of the spirits referred to by the townsfolk, but as he moved nearer, he saw she was real – gaunt and thin and dirty – but real. After several long moments, he spoke.

"Have you a need, lady?"

The woman opened her mouth to speak, but was suddenly overcome. Crispus rushed to her before she could hit the floor and do further injury. He caught her in his arms and laid her gently down. He ascertained she was breathing, but from the looks of her, guessed she was malnourished. He lifted her in his arms and carried her to the castle.

One of the local servants, a man named Dobbin, recognized her right away. "'Tis Adrina Grumfeld of Hedda Grumfeld, her who was the midwife for all hereabouts. Ye'd best leave her be."

"Leave her? But she is starving and ill."

Dobbin's square chin jutted out beneath his beard and his eyes became like stony flint. "She brung it on her own self. Ye dunna need to trouble the house of du Frain with her kind."

More curious now than ever, Crispus thought of Jesus and the adulterous woman. "No matter what her sins, sir, she is in great distress. I must do what I can to help her."

Dobbin kicked at ashes on the hearth.

"'Tis on your head then." He scurried away, leaving Crispus openmouthed.

Jael took one look at the young woman with her tangled hair and sunken eyes and was immediately reminded of herself, after her treacherous journey over the Touris.

"I hoped you may give her refuge in the castle, my lady," Crispus said.

Jael made a nourishing tea and fed it to her. After the woman had recovered somewhat, they questioned her.

"I am Adrina Grumfeld and I confess I do not know who my natural parents are," she said. "Hedda would never tell me. She only said my mother died giving birth. No one wanted me, so Hedda kept me with her."

Jael observed Adrina's face as she spoke.

Crispus returned with a bowl of steaming broth and a bit of bread. The woman's hands shook as she broke bread. She closed her eyes as she ate.

Jael gave her shelter for the night and facilities to bathe. She sent one of her own dresses for Adrina to wear. Once she had gained strength, Jael heard her story. Not one to talk overmuch, Adrina had to be prompted with questions.

"**Hedda** Grumfeld was midwife to the last royal family," Crispus told Jael over dinner the next evening. Jael gave him a sideways glance as she dipped a bit of bread in her stew. When she did not respond, he continued, "She came from a long line of scholars and philosophers."

Jael frowned. "Adrina?"

Crispus shook his head. "No, Hedda. She cared for her father until he died and by then, she was too old to marry. She worked as a midwife and became so well respected, her presence was always requested here, by the royal family. I found the records in the archives. Interesting, really."

Jael bit into her bread and chewed thoughtfully. She took a sip of tea to wash down the bread. "I suspect there's a great deal of interest to be found there."

Crispus nodded. "In the archives, oh aye. Apparently, Hedda read to her father all those years, so she was quite intelligent and very well respected."

"Adrina said the du Frain family gave Hedda a small cottage to live in. When she died after a long illness, she left all of her possessions to Adrina. She had only a few weeks after Hedda's death to enjoy sole ownership, since the youngest of the Grumfeld brothers decided it must belong to him, for land can only truly be owned by men."

He nodded. "Aye."

She sat forward to lend emphasis to her words. "He offered to take Adrina on as a servant in his household, but she said she never liked any of the Grumfeld men – least of all Thel, the youngest. He alone had returned from the mines of Touri, to take over the family interests. Adrina thought he seemed a bit too interested in her anatomy." Jael shot a glance at Crispus, who seemed intent on his second helping of elk stew.

He looked up. "The mines of Touri? Is that not the place spoken of by your husband's men? Where the slaves were freed?"

Jael was amused. Was that all he had heard? "Aye," she said, "perhaps he was among those liberated by William's army." She sat back as one of Ruda's girls refilled her cup with steaming tea. After the girl moved away, Jael tilted her head and sharpened her gaze on Crispus. "Adrina found a safe haven in the old chapel. No one ever went there anymore, for as you know, the townspeople feared the castle." She shook her head. "Who knows how long she'd been living in the catacombs, beneath the chapel."

He was thoughtful – she could see – but when he did not immediately respond, she rose from her chair and paced about the room.

Crispus set his spoon down and watched her. "I think I know what you are about. You see yourself in her. Like Lady Jael, Adrina has been driven from her home and left to fend for herself."

Jael nodded. "I confess, I do and am determined to do what I can to help her."

Crispus sat back in his chair, his meal finished. "Grumfeld is completely within his rights to claim the property. Short of changing the laws, I do not know what can be done. From the ancients, it has been so."

Jael scoffed. "And this makes it just?"

"It is unjust," Crispus said, "and unfortunate for the poor woman."

"It is indeed unfortunate, for she is rejected and low and she may not marry a prince."

He grinned at her. "Not everyone can be as blessed as you."

She would not give in to his banter. "It is because I am so blessed I want so much to be a blessing in return. I feel I must help her, Crispus."

She followed his gaze to the open window, where the sky's changing colors signified nightfall.

"She is intelligent," he said with a shrug. "I could use her help in cataloging the library."

Adrina seemed pleased to accept the small downstairs room she was offered, though she confessed to Jael, "The townsfolk will not like that you have given shelter to a … low borne like myself. I do not know but you may someday regret having asked me here. I will no doubt be a burden to you."

Jael could only like the girl more for her honesty and humility. She was a curiosity. In speech and mannerisms she was not unlike the aristocracy Jael had come to know at Coldthwaite, but by her own confession, she was of low birth.

"She is a riddle," Jael told Crispus. "So I will leave her to you, for I know you love a riddle."

Chapter 5 – Cold Comfort

An icy wind pummeled Jael as she crossed the frozen tundra of the upper Touri plateau. Every few feet, she stopped and angled her head to hear whatever sounds rode upon the wind. Voices came from far away, further than her vision could take her, but she could not make them out.

As the sun cleared the mountain peaks, she stood in silent meditation, her eyes lifted to the heavens where they were greeted by a sky bowl of the purest blue. Above her an eagle soared. She lifted a fur-bound hand as if to touch the great bird and spoke in the ancient tongue, *"Mis adone se lunior le amistar."* Watch over my love. She followed its progress until it disappeared below the horizon.

In the next moment, she was caught away to the base of a watchtower. Though she had experienced this before, it still took her breath away. Briefly, she leaned against the stone structure to steady herself.

Upon the heights, a purple and gold standard fluttered in the wind. The sound carried far. It was the only sound. A door at the base of the watchtower stood ajar, and she entered. There she paused a moment, until her eyes adjusted to the deep shadow within. She found the dusty stair and began a climb which ended at the top level, where a narrow ladder of hammered iron led to the roof. On the roof, she stood at the parapet and looked out over the vastness of the northern valley. The Touris where they stood against the horizon on all sides glowed purple in the early sun. The great, wide lake was frozen solid till spring rains washed away the ice.

As she waited, her spirit cried out to God and she prayed for her beloved and the brave warriors who rode with him.

"Six full moons have risen since William and his warriors rode out upon the heels of a dark enemy. How long, Oh Lord, must I wait, without even a word of his whereabouts?"

By now, William would have been joined by his brother-in-law Lord

Toldar, leader of the southern forces at Corwinder. Toldar and Lady Elizabeth had arrived in the fall along with their son, Nathaniel. He'd spent only a few days at Wrenook, his ancestral home, before leaving again to join William.

Jael descended the ladder and then the narrow dusty stairs that wound down the height of the watchtower. She pushed the door open and slipped through, drawing the hood of her cloak down over her eyes to shield them from the brightness of the sun glancing off the snow.

She ran swift and light over the frozen surface of the lake to the foot of the castle, where an age-old doorway opened to a lower level. Here, another ancient stone stair twisted its way up into the underbelly of the castle to a dark wooden door. From there she entered into a vast corridor and padded quietly toward another flight of stairs and the one room on that level where a fire burned brightly, in expectation of her arrival.

Part-way up the staircase, she heard footsteps. She paused and smiled for she recognized them as Crispus'.

"Lady Jael." His voice echoed down the long corridor.

When she turned to face him, he bowed.

"Yes, Crispus?"

"A messenger has come my lady. In your absence, he was sent up to me." He held out a small scroll. Jael descended the steps and took it from him.

"Thank you, Crispus," she said. "Pray, tell me if you knew who rode?"

He touched his fingertips together. "Aye, twas Andor son of Ruda. He sits even now at her fireside in yon kitchen. She meant to feed him well ere he returns."

She looked down at the rolled parchment and then toward the lower end of the corridor from whence came the pleasant smell of baking bread.

Crispus held out the candle he carried. "Here is a lighted candle, dear lady." She drew near and broke the seal upon the parchment, unrolled it carefully and ran her fingertips over the tidy script she recognized as her husband's own hand. She looked up into Crispus' waiting eyes.

"They are forestalled. The enemy has taken refuge in the South, away from the brutal snows of the northern Touris."

"No doubt anticipated by your honored husband."

She glanced up. "It was indeed. The hearty northerners shall give pursuit. They shall find them out and conquer them. We shall see it, Crispus. I only wish it would be sooner, rather than later."

"I too, my lady for your sake as well as my own." His lips quirked. "There are too few ears to hear the great messages I receive."

She gazed at him, saw the mischief in his eyes. "Will you accompany me to Ruda's fireside?"

"Nay my lady, I value the hair on my head too well for that."

She gave him a one-sided smile as she rolled the scroll and set off down the dark corridor. Ruda was not known for her hospitality. She barely tolerated Jael's presence in her kitchen. Jael was not offended since Ruda was so accomplished a cook, but she often wondered what Abigail would think. Jael had never met another who compared to Abigail, housekeeper at Corwinder-by-the-Sea. Dear Abigail, what a good friend you were to me.

The passageway curved around and opened out into a large room where oak beams were hung with an assortment of iron utensils, dried herbs and smoked carcasses. Goatskin bags of wine hung in the cold dark recesses near the outer wall, and kegs of grain stood one upon another in the corner. A huge fireplace glowed at one end, where a small round woman knelt. As Jael entered, a young man stood and bowed from the waist.

"My lady," he said rather loudly, apparently for his mother's sake. Ruda shot a look over her shoulder, but did not immediately rise. She wrestled with a baking pan among the coals. After another moment she pulled it free and stood, holding it carefully with leather grips. A slight curtsy and nod were all she allowed before she ran to the table.

Jael addressed the young man. "I trust you had a good journey, Andor?"

He bowed again. "Aye milady, for the deep, it were a good journey."

Midwinter, the translation immediately popped into her head. She was improving. "Very good," she said to Andor.

Ruda cut off a slab of the hot loaf for her son and ladled up a bowl of stew. She poured out a flagon of strong, dark tea and set these down with a loud clatter on the table before him. Without looking up at Jael, she turned back to the fire to finish her tasks. Andor seemed embarrassed by his mother's flagrant disregard. He glanced at the meal set before him and then back at Jael.

"Do not mind me, Andor," she said. "Please, sit down and eat whilst the food is hot. I will away to my room, but only tell me if all is well at the front."

Andor bowed a third time. "Aye, milady, 'is Majesty, Prince William fares well and afore my leave-taking, 'e did welcome the southern forces." His face brightened. "That Lord Toldar is a sight to be'old."

Jael nodded. The natives were proud of Toldar, claiming him as one of their own.

"He is indeed," she said. "You have lightened my darkness a bit Andor, and I thank you. Come to my door ere you leave and I will send an answer back with you."

"Aye milady, I will do."

She rushed to her room, but a short message was all she had time to set down, as Andor was eager to be on his way. He was at her door before she could finish the first page.

"Weather won't hold, them high passes is a stickery mess in the blains."

She handed him the sealed parchment and pressed a coin into his palm. "For a hot drink on your journey."

A deep blush colored Andor's face as he bowed before her. "Yer kindness is greatly appreciated, milady." His steps were lively and quick as he left her door. At the landing, he paused to push the coin deep into the pack he carried.

Jael shook her head and smiled. He would never spend that money.

It was some time later, a soft knock on Jael's door roused her from a fireside nap. At her answering call, Elayna pushed the door open.

"Tis time fer tea, milady."

"Is it so late already?"

The young servant smiled and placed a carved wooden tray on the table. She poured hot water into a stoneware jug and left it to steep while she stirred the fire.

"Ye was oot so very early this morn, milady. Tis no wonder ye dinna know the lateness of the hour."

Jael smiled as she stirred from her chair and tugged her shawl close around her. She watched Elayna, who was one of the first of the locals to agree to work in the castle. Ruda's eldest daughter Tamara had worked as lady's maid until her marriage. She had managed to persuade her cousin Elayna to take her place. Elayna was tall and angular, a bit too plain to attract an early proposal, but she suited Jael. The girl was fond of sewing and loved nothing better than braiding her ladyship's golden locks.

When the tea was ready, Jael poured herself a cup and sliced off a chunk of Ruda's famous stonebread, a round loaf shaped like a stone and nearly as hard outside, but light and feathery inside. Spread with a generous portion of clotted cheese, Jael thought it was delicious.

Elayna rearranged the logs in the fireplace with the help of a poker and piled on more wood. "Ye did see my cousin return, I ken? What word had he of the warriors?"

Jael touched her lips with the soft towel that had covered the bread. "They fare well for now. The deep cold has stalled the attacks from the enemy. It seems Din Glun's men are not winter-hardy."

Elayna's quick intake of air at the mention of the name caught Jael's attention. These mountain folk were so superstitious. She watched with interest as the girl hurriedly cast ashes about the hearth in an attempt to assuage the evil powers induced by the utterance of the name.

What Jael knew of him, William had written in a letter.

His people call him Din Glun, which means of the sun. Descended of a great family of nomads who made their way slowly across the deepest desert and into the North by way of the Santouri River, it seemed to make no difference to them whether he was good or evil. They worship the sun, so in their opinion, anyone with such strength and power must have descended from there.
"Din Glun has amassed an army of bandits and outlaws; outcasts in their own land. They strike whatever targets promise the greatest return – ships at sea, caravans or entire villages. There seems to be no way to stop him. Even an army pursuing him from the southern cape could not catch him. His army would disband into the foothills and rejoin in the river valley. It seems impossible to follow their trail.

She had been especially interested in the personal description of the man. William knew she would be, so he provided great detail.

Din Glun stands just over five feet tall. He is thin and wiry, but very strong, with long dark hair and a filthy beard that covers most of his swarthy face. He chews a dark leafy substance that blackens his lips and gives his eyes a wild look. Survivors of his onslaughts are few, but those who manage it call him a devil. In those places, the name of Din Glun has become synonymous with the word for "evil one."

She sipped her tea and stared into the flames. The people of Cragmorton never laid eyes upon the man, nor even any of his footmen, but they had heard the tales told and their "livers were full," *worrisome* fears. She returned her cup to the tray and moved to the table where the note lay open. She touched the paper and whispered a prayer. She would not give in to fear. Her liver would not be full.

Chapter 6 – Benabi

𝔚illiam reclined beside his brother-in-law, laying out plans for the journey to come. A map drawn on well-tanned goatskin lay between them.

Toldar's resonant voice sounded. "Are you certain it is wise, brother? Ought we not to wait for word from Rondar? He will surely return soon."

William gazed long at his friend before answering. "Rondar is delayed too long."

Toldar sat up, crossed his legs and leaned forward to trace a line on the map. "Last we heard, he was here. 'Tis a narrow canyon and easy to protect – could be an ambush."

"Aye it could, were they still in place. However, I do not believe they are. If indeed they do run to warmth as we have heard, they certainly will not find it there. This canyon is cooled by a spring and troubled by a northerly wind. It will be quite cold in the deep of winter."

A parting of the tent's door drew William's attention. A young warrior entered and bowed. "Yer pardon, my lords, but a lone traveler approaches afoot."

"On foot?" William repeated as he made to rise. "Can you make him out?"

"Nay, my lord."

Toldar jumped up. "It may be Rondar."

The two men followed the messenger to the edge of the camp, where level ground fell away into a deep valley.

Toldar frowned. "He is in plain sight and unafraid, I do not believe it is Rondar."

"He carries a staff, mayhap he is a shepherd," William said.

As they watched, a rider approached the man. It was Courin, Captain of the Guard. He spoke with the man briefly, then dismounted and walked beside him.

"If it is not Rondar, it is surely no enemy, for Courin walks with him."

William relaxed. "He is only a shepherd then, hunting some lost member of his flock. We will see once he joins our encampment." He continued to watch as the two men drew nearer and began the climb to the plateau.

The newcomer was dressed in sheepskin, covered with a cloak of dark horsehair. A fur-lined cap was low over his eyes, with flaps that covered his ears. He bowed before William and Toldar. When he straightened, he looked directly into William's eyes and then bowed again. "Your majesty, it is good to see you again."

William grinned. "Benabi! I should have known it was you." He moved near and took hold of the man's wrist as Benabi took hold of his in a traditional greeting. "You are welcome here, brother. Come, join me at my fireside. You look as though you could do with a warm drink."

"Aye, you are correct, my lord. I have traveled far this day."

Back inside the tent, William took his place at the fire and gestured to Benabi, who seated himself on William's left, out of deference to Toldar. As was tradition, no warrior sat with his back to the door. A footman appeared out of the recesses and served tea.

"What news of the front?"

Benabi removed his cap and grinned at William. "As the fine people of the North say, 'the blains has taken their revenge.'"

William threw his head back and laughed. "You have that down hard, Master Benabi. Your memory serves you well."

"Aye it does." Benabi ran long fingers through rough, dark hair and allowed the manservant to relieve him of his cloak. "I shall never forget the winter spent among the Mortons of the Crag. It was full on a year before I was warm."

William and Toldar exchanged knowing looks and chuckled. William searched Benabi's face.

"So it is true they scatter to the South?"

Benabi's expression became serious. "Not scatter, my lord, they move as one. I have not seen this until now. They are learning. Do they return, they will be formidable."

Any remaining mirth dissipated. Toldar eyed William, who glanced back at him. "Then we are right to pursue them."

Benabi nodded slowly. "Your men fight well. They are trained and widely known for accuracy with the bow. Din Glun's men have evil on their side. They lose no care for man or beast."

Toldar leaned forward. "You have traveled with them?"

Benabi turned to look at him. "I did, and will again."

"Heard you, of a man called Rondar?"

"A man of the North?" His brow furrowed. "He would not take such a name in the midst. Is he a spy of yours?"

"Aye, since summer last. We've heard nothing from him since snowfall."

"Ye would not now. Since tightening his ranks, Din Glun watches over them with the eyes of an eagle."

Toldar poked at the fire with a stick, sending bright embers flying. "Yet you have come to us."

William grinned. "Benabi blends in with the scenery."

Benabi nodded and took a sip of the tea. "One must in order to survive." His gaze shifted back to Toldar. "Does your man speak the language?"

"Not well, though he understands somewhat. By now he may have learnt it."

"Let us hope he has or he will lose his head, if he has not already."

Toldar's face grew dark. "He knows when to hold his tongue."

"Rondar is Toldar's cousin," William said. He held out the jug of tea and refilled Benabi's cup. "He is a bit like you, a man who could blend into any crowd, dark of hair and countenance and rough chiseled. He would fit in well with the rank and rowdy foreigners."

Benabi drank the tea and wiped his mouth with the back of his hand. His black eyes penetrated Toldar's unflinching ones. "If he lives still, I will find him, I promise you that."

Far into the night, the men talked, until at last they slept. At dawn, Benabi rose and quietly took his leave. William followed and stood watching him descend the heights.

A short time later, Benabi stood upon an outcropping of rock and lifted his staff in silent salute to his comrade.

"I will pray for you my friend," William whispered.

From behind William, Toldar spoke. "There goes a brave man."

"God goes with him." William turned to face his brother-in-law. "In his language, Benabi means, 'like a fox.'"

"'Tis a good name for him."

𝕯in Glun plunged a dagger into the earth beneath the tent and twisted it. He could not understand the attitudes of the men. Certainly it was cold in this forsaken land, but it would only toughen them up, which was exactly what he had in mind. Had he not moved them as far south as he dared? He grimaced and spit into the flames.

His personal servants kept him quite comfortable, housed in his tent with a healthy fire going day and night. There was food aplenty and he had provided diversions. The local women weren't much to look at, but generally the same as any. Still the men complain. He jumped up and paced back and forth, ground his teeth together and kicked at a servant.

He must make a show of strength, but in a way that would not crush them. He was going to need all of them to present as menacing a threat as possible to these northern infidels.

He growled to a servant for help as he donned heavy garments to brave the weather. He strode to a nearby campsite, drew his sword and pointed it at one of the men sitting by the fire. Everyone flinched.

"This one," he said then pivoted on one foot and walked in the opposite direction. He pushed a tent flap aside with the blade of his sword.

"This one."

His first officers took hold of those to whom he pointed and brought them along. After he gathered about a dozen of his men, Din Glun sheathed his sword and returned to his tent. There he greeted his guests and offered them hospitality, fed them and plied them with drink. After they had eaten he raised his cup, "Comrades."

All cups were raised and the term repeated, "Comrades."

Din Glun stood up, stepped slowly around the circle of men until he came to a standstill behind a tall man with a long beak-like nose and full lips. Though tipsy with drink, the man seemed well aware of Din Glun's presence. His eyes, beneath a furrowed brow, darted from one face to the other.

Din Glun laid his hand on the man's turbaned head. "You are well known, my friend. Your complaints have been heard, and you have my full attention." Before the eyes of all present, he drew his sword and slit the man's throat, wiped the blade on the man's clothing and returned it to the scabbard.

There was no sound. No one moved.

"This is my answer to your complaints. If you are men and not whimpering children, you will grow strong from the hardship and you will do it without complaint."

He tossed the body aside and gave orders to his men. "Hang this from a pole at the center of the camp!"

He allowed the other guests to remain, celebrating far into the night. If anyone else was tempted to murmur, they had only to look upon the frozen body of their former comrade.

Rondar looked long upon the grisly scene. Though repulsed by the act, he could admire such a man as Din Glun, for he had found a way to stifle the discord without driving the others away.

From somewhere nearby, a voice spoke. "Come away my friend."

Rondar turned quickly; he could not see the man's face in the shadows, but he knew the voice. He had heard him speaking among the men.

"You must not look too long at that poor cursed one." The man tugged at Rondar's tunic and nodded toward his tent. Rondar hesitated only a moment and then followed. He must be careful, but at the same time, it was just possible that he could glean more information from a friend. Inside the man's tent, he was offered steaming hot, buttered tea. He accepted it gladly, taking a seat across from his host who removed his hooded cloak and laid it aside.

"You are from around here?" the man asked, sending cold chills through Rondar.

"No, I … I'm from … west of here."

The man smiled and leaned forward. He spoke softly, "If this is what you wish to be believed, then you must not speak, my friend."

A shock wave coursed through Rondar as he realized that the man had spoken in the forbidden tongue.

"My words surprise you? I know you understand me. You will be wondering who I am, so I will tell you. I am a friend. Not all of my brethren are evil."

Rondar still had not spoken, though he understood the man quite well. Should he trust him?

"You do not trust me – I understand. We are in a hard place. I have watched you, my friend. I know you report to others. I saw you go to the mountain. You did not know, but I followed you there."

Finally, Rondar spoke. "What is your purpose?"

The man smiled again, revealing straight white teeth. "It is good to know that I am understood. I was beginning to wonder. As to my purpose, I am not unlike you, though I work for others. The evil one has done much destruction, even in his own country. He has many enemies there. He has bruised them, but they are not finished with him. They have sent me to keep a track of him."

Rondar still hesitated. The man's speech, his demeanor, all denoted gentility. Far different from the way he spoke to the rabble outside. Who was he?

"If all of this is true," Rondar said, "how is it that you know the tongue of the ancients?"

"Ah, you have come to that at last. I was hoping you would. It was learned many years ago by my father. He had a friend in these parts – of whom you may have heard – by name of Rogan."

Rondar shook his head.

"You do not believe me? Well, I have proof." He rose and crossed to a bundle of furs. After digging down inside, he drew out a small leather packet and returned to sit across from Rondar. He opened it out and held it up for Rondar to see. There were few men who would recognize what he held up, but Rondar was one of those. It was a crest and a seal. The crest of the house of Rogan and the royal seal of du Frain, and it was signed in the King's own hand. It contained an edict written in the forbidden tongue.

Still, Rondar hesitated. Any one of Din Glun's men would certainly be capable of securing such a document from the person to whom it was given, but that would not explain the use of the ancient tongue.

Should he choose to trust this man, he would be placing his life at risk as well as those of his countrymen. Unless he cut himself off from his contacts for a time … this was a definite, though dangerous choice. He looked at his companion. "May I at least know your name?"

"I regret that I cannot give you my real name. I am known here as Benabi." Benabi sat back, his face relaxed, watching Rondar. "Someday perhaps, if we are successful, we will know one another by our true names."

As he sipped his tea, Rondar studied Benabi. Then he set his cup down and crossed his arms over his chest. "How can we assist one another?"

Chapter 7 – Lost in Translation

Restless, Jael rose from her chair and crossed to the window, where she pulled the iron shutter aside just enough to gaze out upon the frozen lake. She blinked her eyes against the cold. The brutal winters of Cragmorton would seem to discourage outdoor activity, but the natives had no fear of it. Indeed, they seemed to revel in it.

Even now, she heard their joyful cries and leaned further out to see them skating joyfully over the solid surface of the lake. She had tried it on several occasions and found it to be fun, but the frigid air forced her inside too soon. Jael pushed the shutter closed and latched it, then held her hands near the fire.

Oh, for the warmer days of summer, when the sun would cast its spell upon the valley. She sighed and sat down on the edge of the chair. Without William, would it seem as warm? A single tear ran down her cheek. She brushed it away and threw on her warmest shawl.

"Pointless to stand around feeling sorry for myself." She strolled to the royal library, where Crispus and Adrina were hard at work. They had almost completed an ancestral log, from the contents of a family register.

Crispus looked up as she entered. "I was just speaking of you, my lady."

She arched her brows. "Oh? Have you nothing more interesting to speak of?"

"I find it quite an amazing thing that you and Lord William found each other as you did. God surely directed you that day."

"It was miraculous, not just in meeting, but that he survived at all." She turned to Adrina. "He was wounded in battle, fell into the river and was swept downstream."

"Over a waterfall." Crispus nodded. "A fifty foot drop, if I am not mistaken."

Jael smiled. "You are not mistaken. He survived the falls, and I managed to rescue him from the flood-swollen river."

Adrina abandoned her work. "He fell into the hands of a gifted healer."

Jael glanced at her. "It was not his time." She carefully unrolled an ancient parchment.

Adrina returned to work and after a few minutes, Jael began to hum and then to sing her favorite psalm.

Sing to 'Vah, ye sons of the mighty,
Sing to 'Vah honour and strength.
Sing to 'Vah, praise ye His name,
Bow yourselves to Him,
In the beauty of holiness.
The voice of 'Vah is 'pon the waters,
The God of glory hath thundered,
Je-ho-vah is on many waters.
The voice of 'Vah is filled with power,
The voice of Je-ho-vah is majestic.

As the song ended, Crispus called to her. "Here is another name, my lady, an infant – perished at birth. It is as well, I suppose, since all of them died so soon thereafter."

Jael approached the table where he sat surrounded by parchments. She squinted at the fancy print adorned with emblems and caricatures. "What name?"

Crispus slid his finger over the document as he read, "Lura Corina, born midsummer's eve, drew no breath," he met Jael's gaze, "is what it says here."

She studied the entry. "How very sad – words upon paper – that's all this one would ever be."

"At least she was given a name," Adrina said. Jael and Crispus glanced at her.

Jael nodded. "Aye, and Lura is a good name. It must have been oft used by the du Frains, for it was the name of my grandpere's mother." She ruminated over the small details given. Here was the last of that strong family, and she was not killed by the enemy, at least not directly.

Something tugged at her memory.

She walked straight out into the main hall and stood upon the place where the lady had died. She did this often, but now it seemed as if she were drawn here, to the dark stain, so deeply ingrained in the stones of the floor that it could not be scrubbed away, though many had tried. She crouched low, touched the spot with her fingertips. At that moment, a piercing cry assaulted her ears. It was soon followed by a shout and so much noise Jael thought they may be under attack. She jumped up and ran to the landing.

From the vantage point of the upper balustrade, she peered straight down into the foyer. There was such a clot of servants she could not see what had happened and though she called out to them, they could not hear her in the din. Finally, she discerned Ruda, bent double in grief and caught a glimpse of a small limb, lifeless upon the floor. Jael rushed toward the stair and in the next moment appeared in the midst of the servants at the bottom of the stair.

No! I did not think to do that in the presence of all these. Her face burning, she gazed about. Had they seen her? A quick glance to the place where she had been standing only a moment before sent a shockwave through her. Crispus stood there looking at her. From his expression, she had no doubt he had witnessed the event.

She knelt quickly beside the child – Tessa – one of Ruda's youngest girls and gave her full attention to the task at hand, though her mind was reeling. Ruda pressed against her shoulder as Jael tried to determine whether the child breathed. The presence of a quick pulse beneath her fingertips reassured her and she began to check for broken bones. She threw several orders over her shoulder, sending servants scurrying for this and that and finally brought order to the chaotic situation.

Tessa was removed to a bed in the corner of the big kitchen where Ruda could easily keep an eye on her. The child awoke to pain which quickly receded into something else.

"Hungry, Ma!"

"She has a large lump here, beside her ear," Jael told Ruda. "Other than that, I see no sign of injury, which is nothing short of a miracle. I will make a poultice to bring the swelling down. You must keep her quiet, but awake."

"Hungry, Ma!" Tessa's lower lip trembled. Ruda turned away to wipe the tears of anguish from her face.

Jael spooned broth from a pot and handed it to her. "She will be well and running about again in no time at all."

Ruda nodded as she took the bowl and turned away to feed the child.

𝔚𝔥𝔢𝔫 Crispus returned to the library after the scene at the base of the stairs, he stood for several minutes at the window peering out at the adjacent mountain peaks. What had he witnessed? He was aware of Lady Jael's gifts, though she believed they were hidden.

He would not soon forget that first morning he had seen her worshipping God upon the high reaches. He was just going to raise his hand in salutation, when she suddenly faded into nothing. He had rubbed his eyes, even slapped his own cheek. He thought perhaps he slept and still dreamt. But no, he was not asleep. He was not dreaming, for as he approached, she reappeared and as she did he quickly ducked behind a corner of the wall.

His heart felt as if it would break out of his chest. Was it magic? Black arts? Yet clearly, she worshipped. Her face as she drew near, was radiant.

He did not pretend to understand it and now, this one incredible gift, how could it be explained?

"Crispus? Are you well?"

He whirled about. The brightness of the outdoors clouded his vision for a moment and he almost believed he looked at Lady Jael. Until she spoke again.

"Crispus?" Adrina edged closer. "Are you well?"

"Ah! Adrina, I … yes, indeed. I am well. Preoccupied, you might say."

"I thought perhaps the news was not good."

Crispus was puzzled. "The news?"

"The little girl, she is well?"

Perhaps he should stick his head outside the window to shake off the confusion. He gave her a half-smile. "I apologize, Adrina. The girl will survive, is what I heard. A bump on the head is all."

"Ah, that is good. You seemed so distant, I was afraid she had …"

Crispus nodded his understanding and moved away from the window. He reached for a scroll and laid it on the table. She returned to her work. It was not long before his mind had returned to its former occupation. He could not seem to stop thinking about what he had seen. *Shall I confront her?*

𝔍𝔞𝔢𝔩 found Crispus waiting for her in the small dining room. She nodded a greeting. "Good evening, Crispus."

"My lady." He stood until she was seated. Then he sat down also while

Denys moved about the room, serving the food.

She would behave as though nothing had happened. Perhaps he would not broach the subject. "How goes the research?"

"Very well, my lady," he said. "Adrina has catalogued all the scrolls from the tenth year of the reign of John Twain."

"Wonderful! You've accomplished so much in my absence, I shall have to stay out of the library more often."

They were quiet for several minutes as they enjoyed the hot food. Ruda had made Jael's favorite bread and a thick stew of elk meat and parsimony root.

Afterwards, they sat near the fire, sipped rich dark tea and nibbled sweet biscuits. Jael puzzled over Crispus' silence. *Highly unusual!* "Are you ill, Crispus?"

Crispus answered with a wry smile. "Second time today I've been asked the same question. I thought perhaps you may be interested in hearing a story, my lady."

"I am always ready to hear a story from a fine storyteller such as yourself."

He smiled at the compliment, drained the last of the tea from his cup and set it aside. Then he leaned forward, rested his elbows on his knees and peered into the fire. "Are you familiar with the story of Philip, the evangelist?"

Jael picked up a second biscuit. "I do not believe I have heard it."

"It was not long after the ascension of Christ. Philip – one of the original twelve disciples – went about preaching the gospel. An angel of God spoke to him and sent him to the desert and there he met a eunuch of Ethiopia."

Jael frowned. "Of where?"

"Ethiopia. It is a region south of the Holy Land, my lady."

"I see. Please continue, Crispus."

"This eunuch was reading from the prophet Isaiah, but could not understand what he read."

She nodded. *Somewhat like me, right now.*

"He invited Philip to come and sit with him in his chariot. Philip began at the scripture the eunuch had read and preached Jesus to him. The eunuch then asked to be baptized. They were near water, so Philip baptized him." Crispus paused and peered at Jael.

She met his gaze. "I am paying very good attention, Master Crispus."

He smiled. "I see that you are. I only wished to be certain."

"Is this the end of your story?"

"Nay, my lady. I've a bit more to tell. When the eunuch raised up from the water, Philip had gone."

She raised her eyebrows. "Gone?"

He splayed his fingers in the air. "Poof! Gone, my lady. Disappeared. The eunuch went away rejoicing – Philip was found in Azotus – far away from the place where he baptized the eunuch."

Jael's breath caught in her throat, and her heart beat like a kettle drum. She could not bring her eyes to his. He had seen her!

Crispus sat back in his chair. "This is not the only time such a thing occurred. In like manner, Jesus walked undetected through a mob of angry dissenters who meant to kill him if they could find him." He looked up at her. "Undetected, my lady."

"I cannot speak of it, Crispus." She kept her voice just above a whisper.

Crispus lifted his head. "I understand. I only wish to caution you. Take care, my lady." He pushed away from the chair and bowed. "I wish you a blessed night."

"And you, Crispus."

The wood on the fire cracked and the sound echoed in the quiet room. A door opened somewhere and footsteps sounded. Jael rose from her chair. *Denys will want to clear the room and go to his bed as well.* She ascended the stairs and was greeted by Elayna, who waited to assist her. As the girl brushed her hair, Jael allowed her mind to wander back to the first time she had … traveled.

She'd made the discovery quite by accident as she meditated after an early morning prayer. She had actually moved from one place to another. Even now, at the remembrance of it, chilblains rose on her forearms. It was not something she could force and sometimes it seemed to happen quite by chance, but as Crispus had intimated, it was not random. She went where she was needed. She sighed. If only the Father needed her at William's side.

Long after Elayna had gone, she lay in her bed staring up at the ceiling and wondering. She had never been one to waste time questioning God's purpose. In the past, she just accepted it and moved forward, but there was something ominous about this gift.

Chapter 8 – Yellow Cat

Jael was edgy, as she often was upon too much confinement. The cries and playful screams from outside seemed to beckon to her. Dressed in several layers of warm fur-lined cloaks, she stepped out into the bright afternoon sunlight. She moved quickly, to warm herself, and headed at once for the cozy stables where her horse, Sandelstar would be glad of a visitor. After a few moments with the drowsy steed, she set off down the well-kept path to the lake shore.

Here she found many of the village children sent out to get their exercise. They played at a game with sticks upon the ice. She stood for a moment in the shelter of a rock and watched. Then she made her way off across the frozen ground, intent upon breaking off a branch or two of fragrant pine for her fire. Its glow and aroma upon the hearth warmed her heart and reminded her of the haven and her father. It was an old family custom, to scent their home with fresh pine.

The whispering pines shielded her from the icy wind. For a moment, she savored the shelter and the aroma. When she reached up to take hold of a fine bough, a light flashed before her eyes and pain shot through her arm. She blinked her eyes and peered into the depths, where she saw something strange. It was not unlike a serpent in appearance, though she had never seen one in these parts, especially not in the deep of winter. Its head was raised up and fanned out in a strange way. She withdrew her arm and rubbed it, realizing that what she had seen was not reality, however real the pain of it. *What magic is this?*

She turned to look out over the valley and saw no motion other than that upon the lake. She turned back and saw this time not a snake, but a yellow cat, crying as if hungry. Empty-handed, she stumbled away from the pine grove to the door of the castle. She was met by Elayna, who took her things and helped her to her room.

"There, there milady, didn't I warn ye not to stay overlong in the cold?

Ye are not so used to it as them young ones." She helped Jael to the big chair next to the fire, rubbed her feet and set about making a pot of tea. "I seen ye out there and I says to myself that ye would be returning near froze to death. Now what will His Majesty say when he returns and finds ye lookin' as ye do?"

Jael's eyes snapped to hers. "Does he return?"

Elayna's face fell. "Nay, milady. It is just that he could, at any time."

Jael sighed. Elayna left her all tucked up in furs and drowsy from the warmth. When the door creaked open a few minutes later, she ignored it, thinking it was Elayna returning. Her head swiveled back when she heard a soft sound. The same yellow cat she had seen earlier sidled over and sat down near her. It began to lick its paw as if quite at home.

"Who are you?" she whispered and laughed at herself, for she had spoken as if expecting an answer.

Elayna pushed open the door. "Oh I see you have met our new friend. One can always use a good cat, you know. They help keep the house free of vermin and a yellow one like this is good luck."

"Is it now? Well, it had best stay clear of Isra's territory. That regal lady is very protective of her own."

"Aye and she is. I had a time getting used to her, winging aboot." She shook herself, then shrugged her shoulders. "Her's another good luck charm though. None so good as a hooty-owl." She lifted the pelts from Jael and stepped aside so she could rise.

Through the open door, the sound of footsteps echoed. It was Crispus, followed closely by Adrina, their faces alight. Jael glanced from one to the other. Crispus beckoned to her.

"My lady, come – see what we have found." He held out a parchment. "Signed and sealed by the late King Richard Rendwick du Frain. You must see it for yourself."

Under the light of a candle, Jael read the words. She lifted her eyes to Adrina's. "This is good news. Do you know what this means?"

Adrina's eyelids swept low and she dropped her head. "I am hopeful, my lady."

Crispus was cautious as well. "I do not know whether we may enforce it until His Highness returns."

Jael immediately thought of Brannon. She nodded her agreement. "Aye, you are right." She met Adrina's gaze. "Do not doubt, my friend. Once my husband returns, we *shall* enforce it."

After they had gone, she took the parchment and sat down at her desk to read through it again. With many flowery phrases and legalities, this document gave Hedda Grumfeld the right to live in the cottage by name of *Greshne Green* for as long as she lived and when she had "been gathered to her Father in Heaven," the edict declared, "this parcel shall revert to the Royal House of du Frain, to do with as they will."

She gazed at the glowing coals in the fireplace and whispered, "Here is power to give back to Adrina what has been wrested from her." She rolled the parchment and tied it with string. There was more to this story, of that she was quite certain. She rose from her chair and crossed the room to the door of the great porch. It was cold, but she had been cooped up too long. She pulled on a sheepskin coverlet, stepped outside and watched the sky as the sun set behind the mountain peaks.

Adrina puzzled her no end. The woman had blossomed since her arrival. Not only was she intelligent and well-spoken, but beautiful as well. She was not tall, just an inch or so above Jael's height and spare of body and build. Her hair was nearly the same pale golden color as was her own and her eyes a gray-green changeable color, depending on her surroundings. The shape of Adrina's face was not unlike hers as well and more than once, someone had mistaken one for the other.

Adrina seemed unfazed by the attitudes and opinions of the other servants, who merely tolerated her for Jael's sake. She worked with diligence and never complained. If she was someone's "natural child," was it possible she was part royal?

Jael was working at her desk with the yellow cat curled up at her feet when the door opened and Elizabeth entered with her son Nathaniel. Jael stood up so quickly she startled the cat.

"Elizabeth!" They embraced and kissed each other's cheek.

"I hope you do not mind my coming," Elizabeth said to her sister-in-law. "I am bored beyond endurance at Wrenook. Aunt Blessingstock has taken to her bed with a cold and does not wish to see anyone."

"What a wonderful surprise!" Jael and William's sister Elizabeth had been fast friends since their first meeting. Jael bent to scoop Nathaniel into her arms. She kissed his cheeks and hugged him so tight he squealed. She chuckled and glanced at Elizabeth. "I hope you have come to stay a few days at least."

Elizabeth grinned. "I will if you will ask me."

"Do stay!" Jael gave orders for rooms to be made ready. The fire was built up to add warmth and Elayna brought tea and an appetizing array of sweet breads. Ruda had already begun her baking for Holy Day.

Nathaniel, distracted by the cat, climbed down from Jael's lap and sat cross-legged on the floor near the fire.

"He's grown half a span since last I saw him," Jael said.

Elizabeth laughed. "He's adapted well to his new home and he adores Aunt Blessingstock."

Jael smiled as Nathaniel stretched a tentative finger towards Yellow Cat. The creature rolled over and thumped its tail on the floor. Nathaniel glanced up at his mother and giggled. He had a dimple just like his mother's, but in every other way, he was Toldar's image. Jael sighed. How comforting his presence must be, while Toldar is away.

After Nathaniel was sent to bed with his nurse, Elizabeth sat down next to Jael. She rolled and re-rolled the end of her sash. "I had another reason for coming, Jael. I believe … I am with child again."

"That's wonderful news," Jael said as she forced her lips into a smile that she did not really feel.

Elizabeth watched Jael's face. "Perhaps this time my husband will be nearby."

Aware of her scrutiny, Jael turned her face toward the fire. "That would be a good thing."

Elizabeth laid her hand on Jael's wrist. "I would have hoped for you to have similar news by now. I must say I was quite surprised when we arrived here, to find you much the same as you always were."

Jael turned to look at Elizabeth. After a few moments she looked back to the fire. "As you know, upon my journey through the Touris, I was forced to travel as a man. I could not take a chance on … being found out." She raised her eyes to gaze into Elizabeth's. "I chewed Bloodwort to stop my flow."

Elizabeth's beautiful dark brow knit together into a frown. "But surely by now – "

Jael shook her head. "Bloodwort is quite potent and should not be used overlong. I may have done permanent damage."

Elizabeth covered her mouth with her fingertips. "Oh no – surely not."

Jael saw the tears that started in her eyes and quickly looked away.

After a moment, Elizabeth continued. "Does my brother know?"

Jael slowly nodded. "I told him. It would not have been right otherwise."

"And? What did he say?"

"He believes that in due time, we shall have children," Jael said.

Elizabeth dabbed at her eyes. "My brother has a strong faith, Jael."

Jael smoothed her skirt and sighed. "He does indeed."

"I am weary, will you walk me to my room?"

"Of course I will." Jael rose and signaled to Elayna to clear away the tea. Together, they strolled out into the corridor.

"I confess, I feel a definite chill in this place," Elizabeth said. "Do you ever hear her?"

Jael's laugh echoed in the hall. "Do not say you are frightened of ghosts, dear Elizabeth?"

Elizabeth looked askance at Jael. "She died so violent a death, I do wonder whether the stories are true. Perhaps she seeks justice."

Jael tightened her grip on Elizabeth's arm. "Have no fear, sister. She sleeps in peace. The only noises I have ever heard are the wind and Isra." Elizabeth chuckled.

"Isra – you have such a droll sense of humor, sister. Such an apt name for an owl – *night-traveler*." Jael stared back at Elizabeth.

"I'd no idea you spoke the ancient tongue!"

Elizabeth cast her a wry smile. "I am a royal, am I not?"

"You have truly surprised me. However, I have it on good authority, 'tis dangerous to speak it." She grinned as she pushed open a door to reveal soft light from a fire and numerous candles. Elizabeth's maid rose from her seat by the fire and bowed her head.

After leaving Elizabeth, Jael roamed the upper balustrades and prayed until she was tired enough for sleep. Tonight she did not want to think.

𝕬t long last, the harsh winter gave way to the softness of spring. Here and there shoots of green appeared and lifted up colorful blooms to the pale spring sun. Each day the snow melted away a bit more, but the dark cold remained around Jael's heart. How long must she wait? She sat upon the wall of the turret, watching the western pass, her hair loose and billowing lightly on the wind. The glow of the early morning sun was like balm for her soul. She hoped its warmth would still the ache within.

From far off in the distance came a sound – the sound of many horses. She lifted her eyes, barely breathing. Horsemen approached and as she watched, her heart nearly stopped. The men rode to Wrenook and halted for a time. As she waited, one rider broke away and rode hard for Cragmorton. She could not quite make out his identity and did not wait to see. She climbed down the turret and ran out upon the hillside, not stopping to speak to anyone. As the gate opened, she stood breathless, waiting. It was Lodan and his rider. She ran forward into William's arms.

Chapter 9 – Bittersweet Reunion

William was weary and filthy, that much was certain. He was wounded too, but not badly. "The other men follow," he called to the gatekeepers. "Hold the gate open for them." He dropped Lodan's reins and walked arm-in-arm with Jael to the castle.

She could not tear her eyes away from his face. Once inside, she gave orders for water to be brought at once for his bath and helped him to their fireside. She brought herbs and bathed his wounds as he talked of their ordeal.

"Many times we came upon them, within sight and sound of them, but they are canny and seem to disperse into the rocks. We engaged them several times in battle, but for every one we kill, they seem to return fourfold." He stopped to catch a breath, watched her with hungry eyes as she worked. For the most part, she ignored him, intent upon dressing his wounds. He smiled. "Finally, I decided we must draw back and take time to formulate some plan. My brother-in-law has returned with me. He stays at Wrenook."

"Did he say that your sister carries another child?"

"Aye and he is that happy to have her near you for the birth. You have no news to share, I ken?" His eyes were hopeful.

She paused a moment and then returned to cleansing his wounds. "After so many months, since last you saw me, you need ask? I would be well swollen with child by now."

He grinned.

She shook her head. One hardly spoke of such things. "I am much the same as when you left. You know how it is with me."

He leaned forward and kissed her cheek. "Yes, I do my love, but I never give up hope."

She blushed and smiled at him, but continued her work until satisfied that the wounds were clean. "You are not in such bad condition. I hope no one is more so?"

He leaned his head back and sighed. "I wish I could say no, but we have lost a number. It is why I have returned. I could not risk more until I had formed a strategy. I do not like to leave you again, but we will not be here long – a few days only – no more."

Tears started, but she blinked them away. A knock at the door brought the servants and a great bustling about to prepare the bath. His eyes did not stay open long after the hot bath. After she had seen him safely into bed, Jael spent the time ordering his food and repairing his clothes. When he awoke he would be hungry and ready to work. Since he would not be able to stay long, she meant to be by his side every possible moment.

William slept all night and when he awoke, found himself face-to-face with the yellow cat. From her place beside his bed, Jael laughed.

He grinned back at her. "This creature has come to claim its place, no doubt."

She raised her brows at him and shooed the cat away. "Nay, she does not sleep there, I would not allow it. She is a vagabond and most of the time, an uninvited guest, but she has attached herself to me it seems."

He took her hand in his and chuckled softly. "I do not wonder at that. No doubt you've spoken to her. Has she a name?"

"Yellow Cat."

He laughed out loud as he pulled her to him. "I see you have not lost your humor."

Jael was just returning from a ride on Sandelstar, accompanied by her groom, a young man named Conor. In the town, the sound of metal on metal could be heard as craftsmen went about their duties, fashioning weapons of war. So many arrows were produced Jael began to worry lest they run out of wood for winter fires. She passed the farrier's hut and continued to the gate where a young page ran forward to hold onto their horses' bridles as Conor helped her to dismount. As she handed him Sandelstar's lead, a new sound caught her attention. Her head pivoted slowly, seeking the source. She tugged distractedly at the strings of her cloak as she walked across the courtyard to the chapel. Conflict? In the house of prayer? She hesitated near the door, much too distracted to fade.

She had never heard her husband so enraged.

A moment later, a man rushed from the small chapel, red-faced and so preoccupied, he did not even notice her standing beside the door. She was relieved that he had not, for she recognized him at once. Lord Grumfeld. Shortly thereafter, William exited the building. His face was flushed, his expression, grim. At sight of her he softened, drew a breath and pulled her hand into the crook of his arm.

"Lord Grumfeld refuses to take part in the present battle. He will neither give his own time nor will he allow a member of his household to go."

"That seems rather strange."

"It is an open defiance and I do not understand the reason for it. So I shall suffer no qualms about tossing the man off of royal property!"

Jael stood still and looked up at him. She had just been wondering whether now would be a good time to tell him about the scroll they'd found. Apparently, he already knew.

"So you know of the scroll?"

"I spoke to Crispus early this morn. He thought perhaps you had shown it me." His eyes found hers as he spoke.

She shook her head. "You've been so busy, I did not want to burden you with domestic disputes."

He dropped her hand and stepped away, his back to her. She wondered at his mood. She had never seen him thus.

Alone in their room, he confessed his frustration. "I'm not the sort to treat men as cattle. Each individual is important to me. I am haunted by their faces." He dropped his head into his hands. Jael knelt before him.

"You treat them as friends and brothers. You are the best kind of leader."

He lifted his head and looked at her. "I think of how we rode out, so confident, so prideful – I'm afraid we all but fell on our faces."

She lifted his weather-roughened hand to her lips and kissed it. "Nay, my lord, do not say it. You are always so full of faith, I never thought anything could defeat you."

He turned his hand to engulf her small hand. "You see me now for what I am, my love. A mere man, empty of my pride."

"I believe Crispus would say that you are 'fully at a place where God can use you.'" She mimicked his proper accent so well, she made William laugh. But it was not his usual full-out guffaw. She resumed her usual tone.

"I would not like to have you return to battle in your present state, my love."

He let go of her hand and stood. She leaned against the chair he had abandoned and watched as he paced about the room.

"I have decided that I need to spend some time on my own before the Lord."

Her eyes snapped to his.

He held her gaze. "I shall fast and pray and seek God's face."

She nodded. "Many fine men have done the same in similar circumstances."

He drew near and opened his hand to her. She placed her hand in his and allowed him to help her rise. He pulled her into an embrace. "You do not mind then? We have so little time to be together."

She laid her head against his chest and listened to the beat of his heart. "Am I to be jealous of God? Nay, my lord, I will join my prayers with yours."

The moon was rising over the Touri Mountains when William left her to sequester himself in the chapel. For three days, he lay on his face before the Lord.

The men spent only a fortnight at Cragmorton. Jael rode along with them as far as Wrenook, where she would stay for a while. She sent fresh herbs and as many lengths of clean cloth as they could carry for the battles ahead. More poignant moments passed as the two couples made their farewells. No one knew how Jael wished to follow her husband into battle, for she had the heart of a warrior as well. Instead, she must use that strength and courage to stand proudly as he rode away.

At the entrance to the pass they paused and lifted up swords to the families that stood waiting. "To conquer," William shouted.

"To conquer," the men echoed, their swords flashing in the sun.

Jael drew in a long slow breath and held it. In her heart, she wanted to believe it, but the dark curling tendrils of evil continued to trouble her, and she could not forget the strange serpent which struck at her in the midst of winter.

For several long slow hours Jael and Elizabeth sat upon the flagstone porch beneath the vine-covered trellis. Nathaniel played with small wooden toys fashioned by ancient woodcarvers. Aunt Blessingstock had informed them that these were the same toys his father had played with as a child.

No words now passed between them, so heartsick were they. After a time, the silence was broken by the approach of a rider. Crispus had come. Jael found that she was glad to see him.

"I felt that you would be wanting a bit of company about now," he said, by way of introduction.

Jael smiled her welcome. "You reckoned rightly sir. I am afraid you have found us feeling quite sorry for ourselves."

"Ah well, that is certainly within reason and right. I come with good news that may lift your spirit a bit at least."

"Tell me it at once then."

"I have taken the edict written by His Highness to Lord Grumfeld and he immediately acquiesced, not wanting to 'bring down the King's wrath upon his lowly head,' to put it in his words. He has given over without a fight, it seems."

"I must confess I am somewhat surprised by so short an end to what I thought would be a long, drawn out affair."

Crispus nodded his agreement. "I was of the same mind, my lady. I do not know what caused the change in him, though …"

"Though what, Crispus?"

"The rumors, my lady … are rampant throughout the district, of the devastation, the abject brutality of this new enemy. Perhaps Elder Grumfeld feels that now is not the time to alienate the crown."

The darkness around Jael's heart increased at his words. She drew in a long, slow breath to calm herself. "You are probably right, Crispus. He will do well to support the men who made his return to Cragmorton possible."

"What are you two talking about so earnestly?" Elizabeth asked, as if waking from sleep.

She filled Elizabeth and Aunt Blessingstock in on the details, but could not seem to gain Elizabeth's full interest. She was too apt to sit in dark silences for several days after her husband's leave-taking.

"Do join us for tea, Master Crispus," Aunt Blessingstock said. Crispus bowed with such exuberance that the old lady giggled and the mournful atmosphere was broken.

Immediately following tea, Crispus got down on all fours to play with Nathaniel, whose excited squeals and laughter echoed throughout the courtyard.

Aunt Blessingstock leaned forward and touched Elizabeth's knee. "There is naught so cheering as the joy of a child."

Elizabeth nodded, laid her hand upon her swelling middle and gave her a wan smile.

By the time Crispus was ready to return to the castle, Nathaniel was fast asleep and Elizabeth was a regular chatterbox again.

"I do not know how to thank you, kind sir," she said, "for what you have done. You have lifted us all out of our doldrums. Do say you will return, and often."

"Of course I will, and gladly. I hope to see you at chapel, dear lady and when the little one is ready, I would be honored to begin his lessons."

"Oh well, as for that … he is only … " she hesitated a moment. "But, I suppose it depends on how long we shall be in residence here. Nothing is certain, is it?"

"It is all a mystery to us, but do be assured, the Father knows."

"Therein lies our hope," she said, looking to her sister-in-law for assurance.

Jael forced a smile, the all-too-familiar sense of dread returning. Whenever she was free to do so, she intended to ascend to the tower and take a few minutes to assess her feelings and to worship in private. Surely time alone in the Lord's presence would mend her heart and restore her soul.

On the second day of her sojourn at Wrenook, Jael visited with Lady Blessingstock, thrilling at the stories she told, for this woman of nearly a hundred summers had seen a good deal.

"How did you manage to survive the reign of the Magistrates, dear lady?"

Lady Blessingstock covered her mouth with her fingertips and giggled like a young girl. "It was ingenuity, dear. I dressed as a servant and worked among them day after day. It was not so different from the way I'd always done." She bent near to whisper, "I did not come from aristocracy."

Jael opened her mouth in mock surprise. "So we are on equal ground, as I have not lived as aristocracy."

Lady Blessingstock's wizened face sobered at once. "But thee are and never doubt it, fair lady." She sat back and sighed softly. "I remember Justus Drudan well – who was thine grandpere – he was the image of the original Rogan, they say."

A thrill ran down Jael's spine. "You knew my grandfather?"

She gave Jael a mostly toothless grin and nodded her head. "I did, for he would journey here from time to time. Here it was, he would bring the freed slaves for safe harbor." She sat lost in thought for a moment. "The Rogan was mythical in these parts. Oh, I never laid eyes upon him, but my mother's eyes would go all dreamy when she spoke of him."

Neither spoke for several minutes, but sat in companionable silence. A shaft of light shone on Lady Blessingstock's face and she settled back and closed her eyes. Jael thought she may be asleep, but then she sat forward, opened her eyes wide and said, "Thine golden hair must come from the du Frains. They all had fine pale hair and eyes like the sky above. Oh, so many things I remember. So many years have come and gone." She sat back again, and gazed out of the window. "I only hope to draw breath long enough to see my dear nephew come home in peace to his beloved Elizabeth."

Afterwards, she took Jael outside and together they walked around the walls of her great house. They sat beneath the blossom covered arbor and watched the hummingbirds at work.

Chapter 10 – Visitors

Early morning of Midsummer's Eve, Jael was awakened by the distant sound of hooves upon stone. She threw on her cape and ran to the steps of the turret. Seven days had passed since her coming to Wrenook, and the tower guards had grown accustomed to her visits. They took a position below stairs to give her privacy. She hastened up the stairs. Had they been able to hear the distant hoof beats, would they have been so amenable?

In the open, Jael gripped the wall and leaned out to see who was riding. Faraway down the valley, she could see them. They were a strange lot, so she called to the guard. The door opened and the sentry reappeared, much alarmed.

"Make haste," she said, "and see what you think of these."

Together they watched as the strangers rode on towards Greshne. The horses were not of the rough northern sort, but were smallish and fine-boned. The men's apparel, though not too outlandish, was definitely foreign. What she could seen of their countenance showed too much brown skin for the northern regions.

Jael turned to the young man beside her. "What shall we do? What alarm do you give to the castle?"

The sentry moved quickly to take down the pale blue Wrenook flag and replace it with a large red flag, signifying danger.

"If the man upon yon Cragmorton's tower is on guard, he will see it and take care."

He called down the stairs to another guard within. "Send riders to the hill yon, we've strangers abroad!" He dipped his head to Jael. "Now, milady – if ye please – do go down and find shelter fer yerself."

She started to protest, for she wanted to watch, but thought better of it. Instead, she allowed him to assist her down the steep steps to the top floor of Wrenook. When he had returned to the turret, she did not go to her room as he had ordered, but to the gallery whose windows offered a full view of Greshne and beyond to the castle. She closed the door and stood there in the window, longing with all of her heart to see what was happening.

Five miles of distance meant little to her, so keen was her vision. As the riders approached the gate, they were challenged by sentries alerted by the red flag of Wrenook. The foreigners gave no offense, but turned away to the northern track and made for the mouth of the river. She was happy to note that they were followed at a distance by several castle guards.

"Good men of Cragmorton," she whispered. She closed her eyes and offered up a heartfelt prayer for their safety. Then she lifted up her voice in praise to God for His divine protection. In a moment, she was whisked away to another place where she had never been before. Beside her the water crashed loudly over rocks down to the Greshne. Before her, the green valley of the Greshne fell away, its moss-covered rocks scattered all about.

Why had she been brought to this place? Among these very rocks only a few moments before, she had seen the foreigners climb. Now the men of Cragmorton followed stealthily, to make certain the strangers had gone away.

She turned aside, assured the men could not see her and cast a look over her shoulder. On the other side of the pass, unseen by the men below, the foreigners had laid a trap, meant to overtake them. She had no doubt they planned to double back and accomplish whatever evil purpose they had in coming here. She must warn the men, but could she move quickly enough? If she suddenly appeared, what would they say? To give her secret away at such a time as this was most unwise.

Resolute, she pulled the hood of her cloak over her head and held out her arms. She began to pray in the ancient tongue but lost account of her words. She did not understand the sounds that flowed from her lips.

The men of Cragmorton, momentarily stunned, were forewarned of danger and drew their swords. Jael glanced over her shoulder to see what had happened to the intruders. She was astonished at their reaction, for they behaved as though they had seen a ghost. Only one brave soul ventured nearer and reached out his sword to try to touch the apparition. Jael swept aside and as she did, the men of Cragmorton charged forward, overtaking the foreigner. In obvious panic, his comrades mounted their horses and got quickly away.

She stood silent, invisible to all until the entire scene had played itself out. After everyone had gone, she picked her way along the rock-strewn banks of the Greshne. There in the shelter of the pines, she stood and worshipped God for His protection.

"Thank you for the gift that you have seen fit to give," she whispered and as she did, found herself back in the gallery at Wrenook.

The appearance of the strangers in the peaceful vale set everyone on edge. Jael was no longer free to go about as she pleased. They were under guard day and night. After her return to Cragmorton, she found her liberties almost completely taken away.

"I see no need for such stringency," she said to Crispus, who did not share her tranquility.

"You must allow the men to do their duty, my lady. After what I heard." He grinned. "The tale is told with such gusto – how the late and former Queen made an appearance in the high crags, warned them of danger and frightened off their enemy." He looked askance at her.

Jael dropped her eyelids and examined her fingernails. *He knows it was me.*

"They call her their guardian angel." She lifted her eyes to his and he pressed his lips together and lifted his dark brows. "What I found most interesting about the narrative was the fact that she wore a dark blue cloak … not unlike yours."

Chapter 11 – The Enemy's Camp

Toldar stood looking over the camp of the enemy, far below. He remembered the words the mayor of Tetris had written in his plea for help.

Their camp sits like a festering scab upon the mountainside. Their numbers are vast, with more coming every day.

Indeed, it did look like a festering wound and the stink of it rose even to the heights. He shook his head. What kind of man must this Din Glun be?

He stepped back into the shadows to ruminate on the scene before him. It seemed as though they would be sorely outnumbered, though Benabi had assured them that the Northern warriors were far more skilled in battle. He signaled to the scout whose post he had assumed. "They are settled in and seem to be in no hurry to depart. I will send Dawkins so that one of you may leave to bring word, should the need arise."

"Aye, sir."

Toldar climbed down to the shelter on the lee side of the mountain where their horses were tethered. He did not delay, but rode quickly back to the warriors' camp.

William waited in the shelter of a large outcropping of rock. At sight of Toldar, he stepped out of the shadows. "What news have you, my brother?"

Toldar drew up and jumped down from his horse. "They do not depart for the southern banks. I believe it may have been wishful thinking on our parts."

William hooked his thumbs in his belt and walked beside Toldar. "It would have been better had they scattered. Instead, they nest together in a great hive. We will approach this carefully." He gazed at Toldar. "But approach we must. We cannot allow them to go on the attack. They would infiltrate my father's kingdom and wreak havoc."

"We'd best be quick about it or we will have water to contend with." He nodded to the bank of thick, dark clouds on the horizon.

"Aye." William craned his neck to look at the western sky. "I have seen it. It may work for us, accustomed as we are to hardship in all forms."

William addressed his men. "Take what rest you can for we ride at daybreak." He took to his tent and composed a letter to his wife, whose countenance was ever before him. Whatever decision he made, he knew it would have its effect on her. He longed to crush the enemy in one fell swoop, more quickly to return to her side. But he must face the bitter reality that this could be a long struggle. Sheer numbers were against them.

The letter finished, he rolled the parchment, tied a string around it, dipped the knot in hot wax and pressed his seal into it. The parchment went into his saddlebag. He sat down and removed his boots, then lay back upon his pallet and covered himself.

Someone in the camp strummed a lyre and began to sing a familiar psalm.

> *"I exalt Thee, O Jehovah, for Thou hast drawn me up,*
> *And hast not let mine enemies rejoice over me.*
> *Jehovah my God, I have cried to Thee,*
> *Thou dost heal me.*
> *Jehovah, Thou hast brought up from Sheol my soul,*
> *Thou hast kept me alive, from going down to the pit.*
> *Sing praise to Jehovah, ye His saints,*
> *Give thanks at the remembrance of His holiness,*
> *For a moment is in His anger, Life is in His goodwill,*
> *At even remaineth weeping, and at morn singing."*

Sleep evaded William for the greater part of the night. He heard every sound. Near dawn, he crept from his tent, roused by a small commotion.

The sentry turned at his approach. "A rider, milord."

William searched the mountainside until he found the solitary rider threading his way through the rocks. He smiled as he recognized the horse and strode forward to greet him.

"Young Will, how have you escaped my mother's clutches?"

The young man threw him a jaunty grin. "Ingenuity and grit my dear Uncle." He jumped down from his weary horse and handed the reins to Roy. "How goes the journey?"

William gripped his shoulders. "Well enough. Now tell me how you managed to get away."

"Grandfather took pity on me." A broad smile lit his face. " He sent me to gather intelligence, told me not to hurry back."

William chuckled. "And my mother did not object?"

Young Will shrugged. "Once I had secured permission, I took my leave."

William looked askance at him. "You slipped away? I never took you for a coward, Nephew."

"Oh, well, I am quite certain Grandfather had his fill of her objections. There was a fete planned and ..."

"Hah! A fete – by chance was there a certain young lady included in this gathering?"

Young Will scratched his head. "Well, uh, Lady Euthagenia was unable to secure you – "

William gave a loud guffaw. "And my mother is determined to have her in the family. Ah, it is too much, think how Lady Jael will react to this news."

"Aunt Elizabeth as well. I daresay she will have nearly as hearty a laugh as you."

Their conversation turned serious as William related the events of the past few days. "We ride today."

Young Will frowned. "I hear they're a dark army, filled with outcasts and the dregs of humanity."

"You heard right."

"I hope your lady was not subjected to any of it?"

"No thankfully, but it was she who gave us the first warning of their presence. She heard them afar off and caught the scent of charred flesh in the air."

"She is an amazing creature. You are fortunate to have her. She waits in Cragmorton?"

"Aye, we left her safely put up at Greshne, within the fortress. The natives have outlived a deal of brutality. I am confident they will keep her safe in our absence."

"Uncle, she is quite capable on her own."

William smiled his agreement. At the campsite, Young Will was greeted by those of the men who knew him well. Here Toldar joined them, and his affectionate slap on Young Will's back nearly sent him flying into the fire.

After a quick repast, the lot of them descended to their horses. William drew near Young Will's horse, gripped his nephew's shoulder and spoke in a low voice.

"I would that you proceed at once to Cragmorton, Nephew."

Young Will's expression registered surprise and dismay. "I am well able to fight, Uncle; my leg is completely healed."

"I do not doubt that you are, but I would prefer to have your leadership at Greshne. I will rest easier knowing you are there." He released the young man's shoulder and stepped back as Toldar drew near.

"I know you are disappointed, Young Will, but it will not be an easy task. The young warriors of Cragmorton are green and untried. 'Twill be a challenge."

William nodded. "'Tis a grand landscape, as well. There is none so fair, even to the coastal regions."

Young Will gave his uncle a sidelong glance. "Nor so fair a face as awaits you there, by the look in your eyes."

"I am found out."

Toldar mounted his horse and leaned forward. "Take care, Nephew. 'Tis a difficult road through the upper passes."

"Aye," William said, "and winter can be long and harsh in these regions."

"It is beautiful," Young Will said. "Once you grow accustomed to the pain and the chill." He drew in a deep breath and squared his shoulders.

William knew he struggled, he was a warrior after all, from a long line of warriors.

"There's one more thing I need to tell you," William said. "There is a Roman staying at Cragmorton, a missionary sent into the Northern regions by the Apostle. We came upon him in the Haven, where he was breaking his journey for a spell. I think you will like him, he is a man of intelligence and wit."

Young Will seemed surprised. "And you have left him alone with your lovely wife of intelligence and wit?"

William threw his head back and laughed. "It is good to have you among us again, Young Will." He took the scroll from his saddlebag and held it out. "I was going to send this by courier, but you are much better. Her ladyship will be overjoyed to see you."

Young Will bowed his head. He stowed the letter in his saddlebag and glanced about.

Toldar's horse, eager to be off, jumped and skittered about. He reined him in and drew alongside Young Will. "I am not much for writing, as you well know, so I ask that you convey my greetings to your Aunt Elizabeth. I pray she fares well."

William and his army camped at the base of Mount Ishcairne, within half a day's journey of the enemy camp, where they took shelter among a stand of coney pines. Young Will rode with them as far as the Ishcairne River where he turned north to the high mountain pass.

"I do hope Young Will has better weather," William said to Toldar, "but there is not much hope of it." He looked off toward the high mountain peaks, the tops of which could not be seen for the lowering clouds. Here and there a forked tongue of lightning struck.

Toldar gazed out into the pouring rain. "He is young and hearty and well able to contend. There is not a better one for a solitary journey." He turned to look at William straight on. "He learned those skills from two great warriors, you know. I, for one will sleep easier, knowing he is in Cragmorton. Though your lady is full able to protect herself, I fear mine is not."

William was confident that his lady was self sufficient and more brave than most, but he also knew that she would be pleased to see his nephew. There was a close bond between the two since she had saved his leg and probably his life.

An advance scout delivered a message from Rondar, which had been pushed into the hollowed-out shaft of an arrow. William twisted the arrow between his fingers. There was nothing to lead anyone back to Rondar, save the feathers. Among them was one of a pinkish hue from the underbelly of a loon.

"What think you of this message?" William asked Toldar with a mischievous smile. Toldar looked at the scrap of parchment on which several flasks and a straight line had been drawn and he grinned.

"Not much of an artist, is he? But the message is clear enough." He pointed at the flasks. "They celebrate tonight, eating, drinking and making merry." Their eyes met.

William nodded. "They'll be fuzzy-headed at dawn."

William stood on a rock to address his men. "The armies of Israel encircled the enemy camp, lit torches, broke their clay pitchers and blew ram's horns. They created such a tumult that the enemy's hearts failed them, thinking they were vastly outnumbered." He stepped down, walked slowly through their midst and made eye contact with many of them.

"In just this way, we will confuse our enemy. Their numbers are great, but we can overcome them. We must use whatever means is available to us." He gave orders to the captains to scatter their men upon the mountainsides. "We will surround the slumbering enemy camp."

Just before dawn, the warriors blew upon ram's horns and shouted. They beat upon their shields with swords and lances.

Benabi stepped outside his tent at the sound of the ram's horns being blown. The commotion caused pandemonium in the camp. Men shot forth from their beds, confused from slumber and strong drink, still pulling on their clothes and fumbling for their weapons. They crouched beneath their shields as arrows beyond number fell from the sky. Benabi sought Rondar and the two men took cover in the rocks.

From this vantage point, they observed Din Glun emerge from his tent, fully armed and ready. He gave a shout out to his men as Toldar's battalion ran upon them, swords drawn.

"What are you? Sniveling infants? If the enemy's arrows do not kill you, I will kill you myself! Take your positions!"

He mounted his horse and rode to high ground to observe the fray. Once he reached it he held his battle standard high in the air.

Benabi took hold of Rondar's arm. "I think it will be best if I join the fray. You stay here as long as you can, my friend. I would not have you killed by your own men."

Benabi soon found his mount and rode into the midst of the battle. He worked his way around to join the other leaders directly behind Din Glun. At the fullness of the dawn, another trumpet sounded and the northern army retreated. Din Glun turned his horse about and looked directly at Benabi.

"Search among the dead for any infidels who still breathe and bring them to me." Then he leapt from his horse and returned to his tent.

Benabi rushed to do his master's will, stopping only for Rondar. He gave orders to the others of Din Glun's men to assemble the dead.

Benabi was relieved to see that Toldar's men had been able to evacuate most of the injured. Rondar was able to assist the remaining few into the rocks where they could be rescued.

After all this had been accomplished, Benabi dropped upon his knees in Din Glun's tent. "Master, there were none found alive."

Din Glun's eyes still burned with murderous hatred. "None – how can this be?"

Benabi faced the tent floor. "Any still able killed their comrades and then turned their swords upon themselves."

Din Glun tossed his head back and let out a bloodcurdling yell. Then he stood up and strode quickly from the tent, barking orders as he went.

"Sever the heads of the enemy dead! Mount them upon stakes and leave them as a token. Toss their vile bodies into the river to poison its flow. We shall desecrate this valley so that no one will ever dwell here again."

From the safety of Benabi's tent, Rondar watched in silent horror as the bodies of his countrymen were defiled and tossed into the river. His eyes rose to the heights, where he knew Lord William and Lord Toldar would be watching. Within the hour, Din Glun gave orders to break camp and they made their way down the valley and out upon the plain of Inglethwaite.

Rondar sought out Benabi's company upon the trail. Benabi spoke to him in hushed tones.

"Din Glun means to wreak havoc upon the Village of Inglethwaite in return for the brutal raid by the northern army."

As they rode from the valley, Din Glun threw back his head, raised his staff, and released a raucous laugh. The sound echoed in Rondar's mind. He lifted up his eyes and prayed for a miracle.

It was a long and difficult journey through the eastern pass out into Inglethwaite. The canyon was narrow and treacherous and the sheer numbers left to Din Glun rendered their progress annoyingly slow. As they emerged from the pass, dark and ominous clouds descended upon the plains. A great storm threatened. They advanced into a wide valley as the weather broke and loosed its fury on the weary travelers.

Lightning crashed down upon the rocks and thunder roared while hailstones fell so densely it was impossible to see. They took cover wherever they could find it. There was no time to set up tents, which was just as well, they would have been shredded to pieces by the falling ice. Three men were struck down by lightning bolts while trying to set up a shelter for Din Glun.

Rondar heard the murmurs among the men, of a curse on them because of the desecration of the dead. He fed that fear. "Those people serve the God of the Jews," he said. "He will not tolerate what you have done this day."

When the hailstones ceased, the air was filled with arrows from the heights as William's famed archers troubled the outer ranks. Din Glun shook his fist at them and shouted orders to his men to attack the archers, but by the time they were able to get near, their attackers had gone, just as Din Glun's own army had done in previous battles. They left many trails like little rivulets running amidst the rocks; impossible to follow.

Rain continued throughout the night. Din Glun took shelter beneath a great overhanging rock. By the light of a large fire, he consulted with his cronies. Rondar drew near, hoping to hear the dark leader's strategy.

"These heathens taunt us. They are like so many fleas on a dog. They are mere pests – nothing more." He stood up and strode back and forth, his hands behind him. "We will wait them out. We will attack when they least expect it."

He turned to glare at a man called Ari. "Have the men returned from the North?"

Ari bowed his face to the ground. "No, Master, they have not."

Din Glun kicked at the stones beneath his feet. "It is time they had. Take more men and if you run across those dungbearers, kill them! Do not bother to return until you have what I need, lest you meet with the same fate."

Chapter 12 – Rose of Wrenook

𝔄 bell sounding below brought Jael to her feet. She ran to the door and then out upon the landing, to see who had come.

"My lady." Darien stood below stairs, looking up at her. "Lady Elizabeth calls for you. Will you come?"

"Of course, I will come at once."

Denys, who had been standing near the door, moved forward and bowed his head. "I will make the necessary preparations, milady."

Jael hastened to gather what herbs she would need. When she emerged from the castle, she was surprised to find a small party of horsemen.

"What is this?"

Denys stepped to her horse. "You may not travel alone, milady, by orders of Captain Brannon."

She raised her eyebrows. It was the first she had heard of this, but she had not done any traveling in a while, since the incident at Greshne. She allowed Denys to lift her onto her horse and hung her bag of herbs on the saddle horn. She looked up at Nolan, who was obviously in charge of this excursion. "Lead on then, Nolan. I will follow."

Nolan nodded and turned his horse. Two men rode before her and two after. Jael felt safe and relaxed in their company.

The day was overcast, the air heavy with rain. Just after they set out, the sky loosed its burden upon them. This made for a long and arduous five miles through deep mud and swollen brooks. Jael wished again that she had been able to persuade Elizabeth to come stay with her at the castle, but she would have none of it. She loved Wrenook, which surprised everyone who knew her. Besides the staff and Aunt Blessingstock, she and Nathaniel were quite alone.

Nathaniel was three years old now and running about whenever he was let alone to do so. Jael smiled as she thought of him. She did love him so and had missed him terribly while they had been parted. Finally the walls of Wrenook loomed up before them, alive with the deep red blossoms of the climbing roses. The waterlogged air was full of their scent. Nolan dismounted and knocked upon the wooden doorpost, calling out to the guard within. The gate creaked open and once inside, Darien helped Jael dismount and led her to his mistress's rooms.

"Thank the good Lord ye've come, milady for her is in a bad way. My wife is with her, but the Lady will not settle till ye've come."

Jael was not unduly alarmed, knowing how dramatic Elizabeth could be. She opened the door and entered without waiting to be announced. She set her things down upon a nearby table and crossed to the bed where Elizabeth lay with her eyes tightly closed and her face screwed up in silent pain. Jael stood silent for a moment looking at her. A maid brought a bowl and filled it with warm water for Jael to wash her hands.

"Where is the child?" Jael asked.

"My sister cares for him in his quarters. She has fed him and will soon have him asleep for the night."

"How long has she been like this?"

Elizabeth groaned. "There is nothing wrong with my hearing." She took a deep breath and exhaled. Her eyelids fluttered open. "The pain has passed for now. It has been most of the day, my good friend." She leveled her gaze at Jael. "I thought you said this one would go easier."

Jael smiled. "And it shall, do you give it a chance. Here, let me help you up. You are stifling the child, lying there like that. Why did you not call me sooner?"

Elizabeth sighed. "It would start and stop, all day long." She allowed Jael to assist her in sitting up. "I care not what you do with me as long as you've brought herbs. Have you then, or came you away too quickly?"

"Nay, my sister, I would never come without them, but you know you cannot have them yet. You would not have me slow the birth, surely?"

"When it is your time for this, do not expect sympathy from me. Should you not check the position of the child? Perhaps it is turned wrong again."

"I will check it if you like, but I do not think it is turned wrong." Jael laid her hands upon Elizabeth's round belly and closed her eyes. After a moment, she opened them again and looked at Elizabeth. "All is well and good. In due time, the child will come."

Elizabeth offered her most engaging smile. "You will not say whether it is male or female?"

Jael shook her head.

"You are too cruel, sister."

"Sometimes you remind me so much of your brother. Neither of you has any patience. Within the hour, you will see whether it is a boy or a girl. Have you a name this time?"

"Only if it is a girl … " Elizabeth's voice broke as another pain wracked her body. Jael sat down beside her and held onto her hands. "Try to relax and think of the roses in bloom."

"They are lovely!" Elizabeth breathed. "I do miss the sea, though. Do you not also? I know how you … " She gasped. "Loved it."

Jael mopped Elizabeth's face with a cool rag and helped her to sit back. "Someday we will walk upon its shores again. At times I feel that I can smell its scent upon the wind."

"You probably can. I believe you may at least be able to see that far and hear the waves crashing upon the rocks. Would that I had your powers, I would call out to my husband and have him here with me, to see what pain he causes me."

A soft chuckling sound behind them reminded Jael that Darien's wife was still in the room. "Here Luxa, help me move her to the birthing stool. I do believe she is ready."

"Then prepare that wonderful tea for me if you please," said Elizabeth to her maid.

Jael nodded to the maid. "Hilda, bring boiling water for the tea. No harm in having it ready." When Elizabeth was safely on the birthing stool, she went to measure out the herbs. A moment later, Luxa called out to her. "My lady, come at once. It is here already."

Jael dashed to Elizabeth and dropped down upon her knees just in time to catch the infant as it was expelled from the womb.

"She is smallish, but quite healthy, I believe," Jael said to the surprised women looking on. "She was only tired of the fight and in a rush to get out."

Tears ran down Elizabeth's cheeks as she reached for the child. "A girl – oh Jael – how happy I am to see her. I have longed for a girl."

Tiny cries eschewed from the rosebud lips of the infant as Elizabeth caressed her. When Jael was satisfied that all was well, she and Luxa moved the two back into the bed and Luxa went to work cleaning Elizabeth up. Jael took the baby and rubbed her down with sweet oils as the maid served the tea to Elizabeth. Soon mother and baby were both sleeping peacefully and Jael had a moment to sit down and catch her breath. Luxa went away to make a quick meal for her while Hilda built up the fire for the night. "Will ye sleep here, my lady?" she asked. "Or shall I make up a room for ye?"

"I will sleep here, this chair is fine." The big one-armed chair reminded her of the one in her room at Corwinder where she slept for nearly twenty-four hours following her arrival there. Soon after Hilda left, Luxa returned with a bowl of steaming tea and another of thick soup topped with a slab of bread. When she had eaten, Jael leaned back on the chair and promptly fell asleep.

She awoke feeling cold and drew the furs up from the place where they had fallen. The fire had died down, so she went and threw on a couple of logs. She placed her palms on the small of her back and arched it to relieve an ache there, then glanced to the bed. Elizabeth and the child were still asleep.

Back in the chair, bundled in furs, she looked up to the top of the walls, where scrollwork joined the ceiling. In her opinion, it was pure foolishness to build such great hulking edifices in such a place. Just like Cragmorton Castle, it was drafty and so cold – almost impossible to heat well in frigid weather.

A tiny sound emanated from the bed, so Jael got up and lifted the child into her arms. She kissed her forehead and looked into the beautiful little face. For the first time in her life she experienced a desire that she could not quell – almost overwhelming.

Would this ever happen to her? Would she ever hold her own child in her arms? How she wished to give her husband a child. He so longed for an heir. She sat down in the chair and held the baby until she slept again.

"Elizabeth Rose," Jael whispered as she nodded off.

Chapter 13 – Happy Reunion

Jael's eyes popped open at the sound of Elizabeth's voice.

"Elizabeth Rose." Her eyes danced with mischief. "I've been sitting here waiting for you to waken, sister. You see, you no longer hold my child. Thankfully Luxa came to check on us. How deeply you sleep, dear friend."

Jael sat up with her heart thumping. "I did not drop her?"

"No of course not, silly." Elizabeth gave a dismissive wave. "She was crying for her breakfast. Did you hear what I have called her? Since she is a girl, I feel quite confident in giving her a name without her dada's help. He would only think of something hideous anyway."

Jael decided not to tell her that she already knew the child's name. She would only wonder at it, and Jael could not explain. She sat forward in the chair and moved the heavy furs aside. "Elizabeth Rose is a very pretty name. It suits her, I think. Will you call her Rose?"

"Most likely, not to confuse everyone, and she will be as lovely as the roses upon the wall outside." Elizabeth's adoring eyes watched the child's face in repose.

The last few miles of his journey sent Young Will through a treacherous and narrow ravine with great towering cliffs on either side. Finally he emerged from its close walls and looked up into the full day. Another late summer storm had subsided for a while at least.

A vividly beautiful scene greeted him as the pass opened out to the high mountain vale of Cragmorton. For a moment he could only stand and gape. The sheer vastness of the landscape took his breath away. Less than a mile's ride would bring him to the round hill of Wrenook where he could break his journey. He climbed upon his weary horse and pressed forward through the thick dirt and mud.

Jael awoke to a tumult below. She rose slowly and pulled her shawl over her shoulders. After leaving Elizabeth's room, she had slept again, making up for lost time. At the window, she looked out upon the courtyard. One man was leading a horse to the stables as another led the rider towards the house. The newcomer was tall and slender and had a slight limp. A smile curled Jael's lips as she closed the shutter and went to splash water on her face. A light knock upon the door brought a maid who set down a tray and came at once to assist Jael with her garments.

"William the Younger has come, milady and desires an audience with ye."

Jael nodded. "I have seen him and was just planning to go down."

"He waits in the hall. I have brought tea."

"Make ready in the parlor then."

The room Elizabeth had given her held a separate sitting area where a low fire was burning. Jael moved to it at once and stood waiting for her visitor. The door soon opened and Young Will entered and bowed.

"Dear Lady Jael, I hope I do not disturb you at so early an hour."

She crossed to him and took his hands in hers. "Nay, dear nephew think nothing of it. I am so pleased that you have come. Sit beside me and take your rest. You look so tired."

Young Will lowered himself carefully into the proffered chair. "Aunt Elizabeth has not yet risen, for I hear that she was delivered of a child a short while ago."

"Aye, a girl child aptly named Rose. She is a beauty. Now tell me, Young Will, why you have risked life and limb to come to us in Cragmorton?" She poured out a cup of tea and handed it to him. He took it and settled back in his chair, crossing one leg over the other.

"I went to gather intelligence, but my uncle sent me onward to guard the women."

Jael set the tea jug down. "You have seen my husband? How does he fare?"

"As well as can be expected, apart from you my lady." Will drew the rolled parchment from his pocket. "I bring a letter."

Jael took it and tucked it away into the folds of her garments. She bit back a smile and fought the temptation to bring out the scroll and crack the seal. She took a deep breath and finished pouring her tea. As Will related the events leading to his departure from Coldthwaite, she began to waken and so did her stomach. When Denys entered with a fragrant tray of freshly baked bread and a variety of cheeses, she shot from her seat like a stone from a sling.

Young Will chuckled as he followed her to the small table. "How long since you have spoken with my uncle?"

Jael smiled into his eyes as she settled into her chair. "It is not so long ago, dear Will. Your concern is noted and appreciated."

After several bites of bread and cheese, Jael sipped her tea and observed Young Will. His long legs did not really fit beneath such a small table. He looked a bit like a giant taking tea with a mouse. She smiled at the memory of the children's tale Crispus often told Nathaniel.

Young Will's light brown hair did not stay neatly inside its leather tie, as did her husband's, but in many ways, he resembled the elder William. She liked to look at him and after a few minutes of it, he set down his cup and gazed at her.

"Have you missed me so much, or is it only that I am so like my uncle?"

She feared at first she may have offended him, but then his signature grin escaped its bounds and she felt easier. "I have missed you, of course." They ate in silence for a few minutes. "We have had a bit of excitement here as well." She briefly recounted the tale of the strange visitors, deftly sidestepping her part in it.

Young Will's eyes widened, his spoon hesitated in midair. His mouth formed words, but no sound came.

She laughed heartily. "I imagine it was a sight to behold, those grown men running away so swiftly!"

Young Will put down his spoon. Apparently, he was not so amused. He all but stood, poised upon the edge of his stool. "My lady, your husband must come at once – he cannot know the danger you are in."

She caught his eyes with hers. "No, dear nephew, he must not be told. He must do what he can to protect the kingdom, of that I know you are well aware. His presence amongst the troops is vital. Any delay could endanger hundreds of lives."

"Aye, I do know – full well – my lady, but I am quite certain if he knew of the danger he would want to come."

She nodded slowly. "I am certain of it, but he must not. In this I do my part, you see."

He relaxed a bit, took up his spoon again and began to eat. "I am ever amazed at your fortitude, Aunt."

Jael smiled peacefully. "Why should I fear nephew – when God has sent you to protect me?"

Young Will looked at her, his eyes unwavering. "I do not know that your confidence is earned, though I do appreciate the encouragement." Having finished his meal, he sat back and looked at her. "I hear you have a Roman living at Greshne?"

Jael smiled. "He is an amazing fellow. You will like him, I've no doubt."

"My uncle spoke very highly of him. I hear he has done great good already."

"If all he has done is train my poor head to read and write it would be quite a feat."

Young Will laughed. "You are much too modest, fair lady. I am well aware of your accomplishments."

"We are trading compliments, dear sir. How polite we sound."

"It is long since we have been in each other's company. In short order, we will again be comfortable enough to speak frankly. But for now, I am content to have my feathers preened. Now, if you will excuse me, I will inquire whether my Aunt Elizabeth is ready to receive me." He rose carefully from the too small chair and with a parting word for Denys, left the room.

Jael found a quiet corner where she could read her husband's letter in solitude. His words were not comforting, for she knew he hid the truth from her. She folded it and held it to her cheek. She missed him so and held little hope of seeing him before the frost.

Jael stayed on at Wrenook for nearly a fortnight, until she was quite certain that all was well with Elizabeth and the child. Toldar depended upon her to take care of his family in his absence.

"How fares the lady and Miss Elizabeth Rose?" Crispus surprised her by asking as she entered the main door.

"News travels fast. Someone has taken away my pleasure in announcing it."

Crispus smiled brightly. "You must take that up with our Lord, for I only heard it in my meditation."

Jael shook her head. The man was a constant source of astonishment. She accepted Elayna's help with her cloak and then turned back to him. "Will you join me by the fire this even, Crispus?"

"Aye my lady, for I have stories to tell which shall entertain you, I think."

Jael gave him a sideways glance and wondered what he knew. When she was settled in, she made her way to the small parlor where Crispus stood looking into the flames. At the sound of her entry, he turned and smiled. "Ah, there you are. You will be pleased with what I have to tell."

"I do hope so, for otherwise, the meal will be quite dull."

Crispus laughed. "Young Will is to join us, I believe?"

"Yes, but we may begin. He is always behind times."

"He was most inquisitive about the … incident which occurred directly prior to your leaving for Wrenook."

"And I am certain you supplied him with all the details?"

"You know me well. He had heard a slightly different rendering of the story."

She ignored his insinuation. "I do not tell so colorful a tale as you."

"Aye and you do tend to smooth out rough edges."

She broke off a piece of bread and dipped it in the stew. "My telling of it was completely factual."

"It was indeed, I did notice that."

At that moment, the door opened and Young Will entered. He eyed them both curiously, bowed to her ladyship and took his chair at the opposite end of the table. "This seems a pleasant dinner party. Please excuse my tardiness. I was giving orders to the men."

Jael lifted her spoon to him. "You are always forgiven your tardiness, dear nephew. Crispus was just challenging my storytelling abilities."

"Ah yes, I would have to take sides with Crispus. I know full well your habits, so I was particularly interested in the blue cloak. 'Tis strange that the former Queen chose to wear the same color as you so often do." He munched a corner of bread crust. "She was not unlike you in appearance – though I hear she was a bit taller – but then most people are."

Jael sat back and gazed at him. "There is no need for cruelty, nephew." Try as she might, she could not hold a stern countenance. A smile broke loose and it was met by a mischievous twinkle in Young Will's eyes.

"I did not say it was a bad thing. I believe it must have been a Rogan family trait."

"The Rogan men were of middling height. I was told my mother was quite small of stature. That is where I inherited it, I am quite certain, from my mother's side of the family. Grandma Lura was as tall as my father."

"Yes, she was a du Frain, I believe," Young Will said.

Jael had to give him that one.

After a few moments, he continued, "This … ability of yours … this … whatever it is … can you control it? Are you able to disappear at will?"

Jael leveled her gaze at him, gripped the edge of the table and leaned forward to whisper, "Do not speak of it. I will not have it common knowledge." She glared at Crispus, who held up his hand and shook his head as if to say he had no part in any of this.

Young Will seemed undaunted, but he did lower his voice. "I am sorry, Aunt, but you cannot keep it a secret amongst those closest to you. Crispus seems a discerning man and I am quite certain my uncle is aware of your attributes as well."

"He knows."

"Well, you can still answer my questions without giving away too much, can you not? Who knows but we may be able to make use of such a talent. We know not what may come before this war has ended. At the very least, someone should be aware that such a thing exists, should you suddenly … not be found."

Jael sat back and gazed into the fire. She still did not like to speak of her gift. "If such a time should arise, I will be most willing to do whatever I can."

Young Will watched her. "I am sorry, dear lady, for my over-curiosity. You may attribute it to youth or foolishness if you wish." He gave her a boyish grin, which always melted her heart.

He reached his hand towards her. "I hope you will not place your life in jeopardy – that is all."

"She seldom gives thought of her own life," Crispus said, "when the lives of others are at stake. This I have observed since the beginning of our acquaintance."

Chapter 14 – Settling In

𝔜oung Will was looking for Crispus when he entered the library and came face to face with Adrina. Her resemblance to Lady Jael was uncanny. Adrina was a bit taller and wore a rough garment, quite plain in appearance. Her hair – though similar in color to Jael's – hung down her back in a single braid.

He inclined his head. "I beg pardon, my lady. I was looking for Crispus."

Adrina curtseyed. "My lord, you have no need to apologize to me. I am not … I am but a servant to the Lady Jael."

"Ah," he said, "then you must be Adrina. Crispus spoke of you."

She returned to her work, cataloguing a pile of ancient scrolls. "You will not find Crispus about until later, my lord. He teaches, of a morning."

"I see. Well then, perhaps you could assist me?"

"I shall certainly try," she said.

"He spoke of a family history he was preparing."

She smiled and nodded at the table before her. "Oh aye, it is here, spread out upon the worktable. He keeps it thus. He has made a deal of progress of late."

Young Will inched closer and bent to look at it. "I see that he has."

He glanced at her. She blushed and moved away.

Her tone was low and respectful and she kept her eyes on the table before her. "He is quite proud of his work. Perhaps you could return when he is here to tell you of it."

Discerning her discomfort, he said, "You may be sure that I will. Good day, Adrina."

She curtsied again. "My lord."

With difficulty, he drew his eyes away from her. She piqued his curiosity. Who was this lady? For she most certainly was a lady. He knew no servant who spoke so well. Though she was dressed as one, she conducted herself as well as any of the aristocracy.

Intent on speaking to his aunt about her, Young Will climbed the steps to Jael's quarters. She had only recently returned to the castle after a long sojourn at Wrenook, but he seldom found her at home. She was always out visiting the sick or simply wandering about in that strange way of hers. Today was no different. Her room stood open, as did the double door that led out onto a wide porch above the Greshne. Here, tendrils of some flowering vine twined about, forming a dense overhang in the summer months. It dropped down fragrant purple blooms that looked almost like bunches of grapes. He wandered there and leaned upon the stone railing.

Down below, the clear water of the Greshne reflected the vivid blue sky. Out upon the water, a small rowboat scudded – its occupant intent upon something, no doubt a fish on the end of his hook. So caught up in the scene was he, that Will almost did not hear the soft sound from the room behind him. After a moment, another more insistent sound drew his attention. He moved slowly back inside the room, looking about him. It took several seconds for his eyes to adjust to the indoors, so he stood still and in that moment, he heard the sound again. It was almost like a hissing or spitting sound. He had heard it before, but long ago. His heart beat faster as he moved forward, seeking the source.

In the middle of the dressing room floor sat a beautiful painted basket with a brightly colored scarf thrown over the top. It seemed out of place, so he stood in the doorway scrutinizing it a moment. Then he moved nearer and crouched before it, for he could have sworn it moved. He was tempted to back up a bit. He reached out to remove the scarf, but his hand halted in midair at another sound from behind him. He peered over his shoulder just as a large yellow cat crept into the room, no doubt curious at his presence. He relaxed a bit and turned back to the basket.

Before he could make another move, the hissing sound started again and immediately, the cat was on alert. Will moved back and drew his longknife from its sheaf. He stretched it forth and slipped the point of it beneath a corner of the scarf. He tossed it aside. Immediately, a serpent leapt up and seemed almost to hang in the air, undulating to some inner music.

The cat's back arched and it spit at the serpent. The creature puffed out its neck and Young Will's breath caught in his throat. He had only heard of such a creature, had certainly never seen one, but he knew from those tales that this was a deadly serpent. Ever so slowly, he backed away. The yellow cat held the serpent's attention at first until the thing noticed Will's movement and turned its ugly head in his direction. The sheer size of it kept him mesmerized. Just when it would have thrown its entire length at Young Will, the cat pounced. A deadly struggle ensued. Young Will moved quickly to sever the creature's head with his knife, but it was already too late for the cat.

Young Will did not allow it to suffer. He called for Denys, to assist him in cleaning up the grisly mess and then both of them inspected every inch of the room for clues. Someone had entered here and set that vile basket in a place where Jael would have found it. No doubt it was meant for her. Had she been the one to enter first – he shook off the thought and went out to order the men to search the castle and grounds. Then he remembered something, went back out on the porch and stood looking over the lake where the fishing boat he'd seen earlier lay abandoned on the far shore.

He took the steps three at a time, and ran towards the distant shore. He motioned for several of the young warriors to follow him.

When they drew near the boat, he held up a hand. "Search for tracks!"

The boat's occupant had disembarked at a place where the ground was rocky and difficult to read. Young Will called in an experienced tracker, but he found little to go on.

Jael found a chair and sat down hard. She covered her mouth with her hand. Her thoughts flew to the day the yellow cat first appeared. She described her experience to Young Will. He stood for a long time gazing out of the window into the gathering darkness. Jael could not be still. She jumped up and moved about the room, straightening chairs and swiping at imaginary dust.

"We sit here waiting for them to attack." Young Will spoke as if to himself, but Jael heard his words and drew near.

"What are you thinking?"

His eyes flashed with sudden anger. "How can we continue to sit here and wait until they manage to hurt you?"

She touched his arm. "What choice do we have? There are but few warriors left to defend us and they are young and inexperienced. Only you and Brannon have any battle training at all."

"You must allow me to send word, my lady," he spun about to face her. "We must not delay. I am told that winter comes quickly upon the heels of summer here with barely any autumn. We cannot risk the deep of winter when help will be even slower in coming."

She spoke in a calm, firm voice. "But do you not see, nephew? It is already too late. These men were sent on purpose to do me harm. Why?" She gave a quick shake of her head. "It is quite plain to me. My husband is having some success. He has a chance to win this war. If not, they would have no interest in us."

She laid her hand upon his arm and peered into his face. "No, Will, we must look after ourselves. We must tighten our ranks. Where there is weakness, we must build it up. You are able to train these young men to fight. Where they lack skill, give them cunning. You are wise, Young Will, share your knowledge."

He gazed at her for several moments without answering. She could almost see his mind working, tossing about, looking for other alternatives, but they both knew there were none. She would not give in. She would not allow him to send word of their plight.

He took a deep breath and exhaled. "In my heart, I know you are right, but I cannot stand idly by." He shook his head at her. "I will not be taken unawares. We will seek them. No doubt, we will find them, and when we do – " His fist came down hard on the window sill.

Jael flinched. He did not have to finish the sentence. Her heart filled with dread. Why must there always be conflict? Why can we not live in peace?

She took a step nearer and looked up into his face, still darkened by distress. Her heart ached for him. "I will pray for you as you seek God's will," she said.

Chapter 15 – Regal Peasant

King George paced about his quarters, unable to sit still. The rumors had not ceased, the dark army approached. Where was his son? Where were the men of the North? He had sent the alert to Solis and the Southern infantry at Corwinder-by-the-Sea, and the army of Coldthwaite stood at the ready. The fleet was in place, with ten large vessels lining the coast from Coldthwaite to Verani Inlet. If only he had listened to William and built more ships, but with the Magistrate's evil tirade ended, he hadn't seen the need.

Now his armies were strung out across the countryside, depleted as they were by the too recent wars. To calm his fears, he sent his dear wife, Lady Bethalyn, to spend time with their daughter at Wrenook, where he hoped she would be safe. That wise lady had fought his suggestion tooth and nail, unwilling to leave his side at such a time. In the end, he had won and she went away dressed as a peasant.

He smiled at the memory. A fishing vessel would carry her as far upriver as was feasible and under cover of darkness they would continue on to Duflec, where he hoped she may join up with either Toldar or William for safe travel through the Touris. It was a most difficult journey, but he knew she would be all right. She was strong and as brave as any among his warriors.

The sight of his regal mother-in-law rendered Toldar speechless. She had been driven there in a donkey cart of all things. He bowed, then looked at her with wondering eyes.

"Do not glare at me so," she said. "I am fully aware of how it looks, but I have been assured that it was quite necessary."

"The situation must be grave indeed," he said, barely able to hold his countenance.

The Queen touched her brow with a handkerchief. "You may laugh if you wish. My husband did, and yes, the situation is grave. Word has come that the dark army approaches the coast. I go therefore, for an extended visit to my daughter at Wrenook."

Toldar's humor faded. "There is no guarantee of your safety there, Mother. We can hardly spare men to escort you."

"I do not ask for such comfort." She waved a hand toward a small band of men. "I have my escort."

Toldar considered what was best to do. "William is nearby, let me at least send word to him."

"You may if it pleases you. I was told I may find safety here for a short respite."

He nodded. "It is indeed a safe region, my lady. Please, allow me to make you comfortable in my quarters."

"I would not take a warrior's place. You have need of comfort."

He blew out a quick breath. "You may not describe it so after a night upon what passes as a bed here, my lady. You will be warm and dry at the least."

Toldar sent a messenger to William, who lost no time in joining Toldar at Duflec, a fortress at the base of the Touris. The natives of that settlement dug deep into the mountainside, connecting into an underground network of caves. This had proved to be their salvation many times in their long history.

Upon entering Toldar's temporary lodging, William asked, "What is this? Why is she here?"

"I have a letter here from your father. Coldthwaite is under threat of attack. He has readied the armies of Corwinder as well and the fleet is prepared."

William's eyes narrowed. "How is it that we are just now hearing of this?"

"I do not know, brother."

William sent for the Captain of the Guard who had accompanied Lady Bethalyn.

"No notice was given save this," Lowen pointed to the letter in

William's hand. "Less chance of a message going astray, so said the King. Never in all me time in his service have I seen him so fretful, my lord."

After several moments of complete silence, William turned and strode from the room, with Toldar close on his heels.

Lady Bethalyn reclined upon the rough couch in Toldar's quarters. "He was quite right. It is not in any way comfortable."

"My lady?" The maid peered at her.

"I was just complaining of the lumps in this bed!"

"Oh aye, my lady, I can see 'tis rather lumpy. Perhaps I could work them out for ye?"

"Oh no, do not trouble yourself. If my son-in-law can bear it, I should be glad of it."

At that moment, Toldar's voice boomed. "Did I not warn you, Mother?"

She looked up and smiled when she saw William with him.

He knelt beside her and kissed her cheek. "Mother, how good it is to see you looking so well."

"Do not tease me son. I know how I look."

"I do not tease Mother; you have good color in your cheeks."

"Probably a fever, then." She gave a dismissive wave of her hand. "It is a joy to see you also. I have missed my children dreadfully."

"I do not doubt it, but what dire circumstances have brought you here? How was my father when you left him?"

"Oh dear, he was not himself and I am most anxious for him. You will go to him, will you not?"

"If it is true the dark army advances there, I will go at once." His brow furrowed. "I have seen no sign of it, however." He glanced at Toldar. "We think there may be duplicity involved. We will certainly seek out the truth."

Her hand caressed his cheek. "Do not delay too long, son."

"On that you may depend, Mother. I will not rest until I know the truth."

Crispus picked up a scroll that lay on a stool nearby and studied it again. What could it mean? He looked out the window toward the West, where Wrenook sat in peaceful splendor, like a crown upon a fine golden head. Autumn came quickly to the northern reaches, followed closely by the first snowfall, usually before the leaves had fully gone from the trees.

Lady Jael and her nephew were at Wrenook, for any day now, they expected an important visitor. For some strange reason beyond all comprehension, the Queen was coming to Cragmorton. The thought troubled Crispus, because of the visitor who had just left the castle. He ordered a servant to saddle his pony and set out for Wrenook.

At once Jael recognized the seal as that of her father-in-law, King George Horatio.

Crispus pressed his palms together. "Aye, you see what it is, but look at the contents of it, my lady. Do you recognize it?"

Oddly enough she did, though she could not decipher its meaning. She raised her eyes to Crispus.

His head bobbed up and down. "I believe it is the ancient tongue my lady, in written form."

Jael shook her head slowly, unable to comprehend it. "But how do you know this? You do not know that tongue, it is forbidden."

His eyes shone like round ebony stones. "Yes, it is forbidden, yet the King himself has given it his signature and seal."

"How came you to have this, Crispus? From whence does it come? And how do you know what it is? Neither of us has ever seen these letters …"

His chin came up. "Ah, but we have my lady – both of us – remember where you found me?"

She frowned. "What saw you there?"

"For many days ere your arrival, I dwelt among the ruins of the Haven. I found a door which led beneath the cottage." At Jael's swift intake of breath, he paused. When she did not speak, he continued. "I believe you forgave me my trespass at the time." She waved him on, eager to learn the rest. "Above the door, carved into the stone, were some of the same forms –"

Her hand shot out. "Let me see that." She carefully unrolled it and examined the beautiful drawings that formed the writing. Altogether, it was done with great skill. Here and there, a letter matched something in her memory. She stood and crossed to a writing desk in the corner. After gathering a scrap of parchment, a quill, and some ink, she returned to the table and sat. She thought for a moment and began to draw.

"Is this what you saw?" She held the parchment out to him. Her figures were rough and ragged, but drawn as well as she remembered.

His dark eyebrows knit together. "I believe it is … yes, quite similar. Do you know their meaning?"

Jael sat still and closed her eyes, searching out the exact words. She imagined her father, standing beside her, running his finger along the carvings. "Papa," she had asked, "what mean these drawings?" He had answered, "*Se lunior se spare … quon se din a domior … aberono.*" She repeated the words aloud, but softly, flooded with melancholy memories.

Crispus jumped up. "Write them down, my lady."

Jael shook her head. "Wait … there is more … " She concentrated harder, saw her father smile and kneel beside her. "*Se abo se spare … quon se din a domior … veni.*" It was done. The picture in her mind vanished. She took up the pen and carefully wrote out the two sayings. "I do not see how this can help. I am not certain of the correct spelling."

"It matters not." He looked at the words and then at the forms. "Oh aye, my lady, see?" He pointed at a set of drawings. "The forms here compare to what is written in the letter." His eyes sparkled. "It is like a game for me. By your leave, I will work on it."

Jael stood to face him. "But this letter is not meant for us. Wait – you did not say from whence it came."

Crispus sat down beside the fire. He rerolled the parchment and held it on his lap. "A lone traveler came whilst you were away. He had the speech of the Milos – island dwellers far south of here. I was surprised to see him and even more so when he spoke the Crag dialect. He was a learned man, it seems. He would not give his name, only that the lady should receive this." He nodded at the scroll.

Jael handed him the scrap on which she had written the words, and he looked at it.

"Let me see if I remember these words correctly. Look; stand … count it all well … ah …"

She eyed him curiously. He had picked up a bit of the language. She corrected his translation. "Watch; wait … when it is all well … open."

He jotted down the translation, nodding his head as he repeated the words. Then he began again, "Hear … ah no … listen. Es … ah … wait … wait … when it is all well … tr … travel." He frowned and shook his head, trying to unravel its meaning.

"Travel," she said, "go or proceed, this is what it means. Listen, wait …

when it is all well; proceed. Papa called it a rule of conduct. It was a warning regarding the disappearing trail. When you were inside, you could not always see or even hear what was outside. Therefore, you must be careful, lest you be … captured." Like Papa.

"As he was," Crispus said.

Jael gazed into his eyes. She must be careful, for he was adept at discerning her thoughts.

When Crispus returned to Cragmorton, Jael went to her room at Wrenook but not to rest, for her mind was much too active.

A native of Milos had delivered a message written in the forbidden tongue, signed and sealed by King George. What could this possibly mean? She remembered the man so long ago, who said he had sailed over the Great Sea. Milosee was the name he'd given. Milosee … and he had spoken many tongues.

The fire died back to a single jagged tongue of many hues. She stared at it in wonder. This Milosee would not know that she could not read the language. He only knew she spoke it fluently. Whatever was in that message was important and sensitive. And it was meant for her.

Jael was out early the next morning in response to an invitation from Young Will. She found him in the stables, with their horses saddled and ready to ride. She gazed into his eyes. His expression was unreadable. Odd. He was usually so open with her.

"I thought you may like to ride out with me to meet my Grandmother," he said.

She narrowed her eyes at him. It was something she could not quite define, like a poorly disguised lie. A crooked smile, a slight spark of mischief in his eyes.

"I will, if you insist," she said. He cupped his hands for her foot.

She rode behind him in silence. Since he seemed to have nothing to say, she turned her attention to the scenery. Autumn, short but vibrant. Here and there, golden leaves danced upon gray stems, and it was so quiet one could almost believe that all was at peace. Jael looked up at the white cliffs of the pass towering above them. The horses' hoofbeats echoed along the barren trail.

"Within a few short weeks these great cliffs will bear a heavy burden of snow. Frigid winds will whistle through these walls, carving intricate patterns in the ice," she said to Young Will.

"I look forward to it." The look on his face told her otherwise.

In near darkness they descended the close trail, breaking out on the western side in sun so bright they had to stop and turn away for a few moments.

They rode for some time in almost complete silence. Jael watched the young man's back and wondered what could be going on in that head of his? Is it only that he did not want to face his grandmother alone after having fled the country to escape her matchmaking? She smiled. Surely Lady Bethalyn will no longer pursue such a liaison. She did have that stubborn streak, though.

Jael was startled out of her musings by Will's drawing up beside her.

"We have some ways yet to go. Perhaps we had better rest our horses here."

Jael looked around. She had been so caught up in her thoughts she hadn't noticed the leveling out of the trail. A rugged mountain stream cut through a low valley just ahead. They rode forward.

Will tied the horses to a Whispering Yew and then walked to a nearby boulder and sat down upon it. Jael knelt near the water's edge and washed the trail dirt from her hands and face. A jingle of bridle and echo of voices at a distance caught her ear and she turned her head. Downstream it was and beyond a fall of rocks. She turned to Will. "Riders approach."

He stood up and moved nearer to her. "How soon?"

"Within a two-hour, I believe. They are some distance yet."

"We'd best get on then. I thought to meet at the turning."

Jael's memories of this trail were hazy. She could not picture the turning in her mind. She allowed him to lift her into the saddle and they set out again, but at a quicker pace. Now he had spurred her curiosity as well. Why was he being so vague? Why did he speak so little? He was not usually so reticent. She moved nearer and lifted her voice. "You do not dread your Grandmother's visit, surely?"

He gave her a look of surprise. "Nay, I do not. Do I give that impression?"

She sharpened her eyes at him. "You are somewhat more quiet than usual is all." She smiled. "It is not your ... habit."

"I am not usually quiet? Is that what you are saying?" He chuckled softly and shook his head. "I am thoughtful only, Lady. I bear no ill will against my grandmother. She means well."

"Aye she does. You do not think it strange then, that she visits at this time?"

He cast a glance at her. "I do not like the connotations of such a visit. I am concerned that my grandfather fears for her safety in such a place as Coldthwaite, which has stood unchallenged for many years. Such a thought shakes me to the core of my being."

"This alone would be good reason for reticence. I understand it well." She shifted her weight and tightened her grip on the reins. "I never thought to see the Haven challenged. Yet it was destroyed – as was my venerable father."

Young Will gazed at the horizon. "We are all at risk dear Aunt. There is no safe place on earth as long as our ultimate enemy is allowed to rule."

"He does not rule our hearts at least. We can still stand against him."

𝔜oung Will smiled. If all went according to plan, she would soon be very happy indeed. He spurred his horse forward and Sandelstar followed along behind. They had been traveling now for nearly five hours and must soon come up on a campsite.

Jael sang softly as they rode.

Sing to 'Vah, ye sons of the mighty,
Sing to 'Vah honour and strength.
Sing to 'Vah, praise ye His name ...

As they rounded the next bend, the stream they had been following widened and the narrow trail opened up into a smallish valley. At the far end, an encampment upon the stream's edge caught Jael's attention. She pulled up and sat still a moment.

Young Will returned to her. "What is it, Aunt?"

"It looks to be a caravan, at the far end. It is early yet to stop for the day."

"Who knows but they may have trouble. I will ride ahead and find out."

She hung back a bit, but did not allow too much distance between them. After a brief consultation with one of the men at the campsite, he returned.

Jael waited for him in the shadow of a sycamore tree near the water's edge.

He jumped down from his horse and strode to her side. "You need not fear, Aunt. It is an advance party of the Queen's servants. They prepare for her imminent arrival. She wishes to stop here and arrive somewhat rested and refreshed on the morrow."

Jael frowned. "When she could make Wrenook by nightfall? Shall we ride on ahead then?"

"I think not. We will wait here and surprise my grandmother."

"She'll be surprised, all right."

𝔍𝔯𝔬𝔪 his post atop the lookout point, Young Will was the first to sight the caravan. His jaw dropped at the sight of the Queen riding upon a donkey. He had expected a palanquin at the least. He smiled at the sight of her, dressed in peasant costume. She still managed to look regal, though dressed so humbly.

But it was not the Queen that he searched for as he waited. Out ahead of the main party he saw him, threading his way through the rocks and choosing the easiest ascent into the valley. Then he would return and lead his mother onward.

He spurred his horse forward to take his uncle's place.

William looked up at his approach and called, "Young Will! Again we meet along this trail."

Young Will beamed. "But this time I do not come empty-handed."

William's face lit up. "She has come?"

"Aye, she has and did not question me. She has no idea."

"Do not be so sure of that. She may be listening, even now." They laughed together and then parted.

𝔜𝔬𝔲𝔫𝔤 Will advanced to Lady Bethalyn. At the look on her face, he bit back a smile. He inclined his head. "I trust you had a good journey Grandmother?"

She frowned. "You take my son's place? He rides on then?"

"Only a short distance now, Grandmother. Lady Jael awaits him at the campsite."

She gazed into the distance, beyond Young Will. "You have brought her then."

"Aye Grandmother, she came with me to attend you."

"To attend me? To meet with her husband, I would rather think."

Young Will grinned. "She did not know he would be here."

Lady Bethalyn gave him a look of disbelief. "I have never known her ladyship to be taken in complete surprise." She spurred her mount forward and Young Will moved along beside her.

She turned to gaze at him. "How does Elizabeth fare?"

Jael found a resting place in the shadow of a great boulder, from whence she could watch the road earlier traversed by her nephew. The noise of servants at work in the camp receded as she concentrated on sounds more distant. A few minutes had made a slow passing when she heard an approaching rider. She looked up expecting to see her nephew and almost thought it was he, so nearly did the two resemble one another. Her heart paused its beating and the breath caught in her throat as Lodan's steps quickened where the road leveled out to cross the stream. The sound of water splashing beneath his hooves filled her ears.

A moment only and she was in his arms. Her eyes awash with tears, she leaned back to look at him. His face had become so weather beaten and brown, but the eyes were the same as he gazed at her.

"What a wonderful surprise!"

He grinned. "You did not suspect? I am a bit disappointed. I thought at least you would have discerned it."

"As I told you a long time ago, I cannot read minds, my lord."

"Sometimes a good thing."

She raised an eyebrow at him. "And have you thoughts to hide then?"

He shook his head. "Not from you my love – never from you."

The bustle in the camp increased as the other travelers crested the trail's head. Young Will jumped down. Jael shook her head at him and smiled.

"Help me down from this beast," Lady Bethalyn said. William stepped up to assist her. Jael bowed her head. "I hope you had a good journey, my lady."

Lady Bethalyn gazed at Jael and gave a heavy sigh. "I am glad to see you looking so well, Lady Jael."

"Do not address each other so formally," William said. "We are still at risk."

Jael nodded her understanding.

Lady Bethalyn set off for her tent. "You will all join me later for the evening meal, I hope?"

William and Young Will exchanged smiles.

"Was that an invitation or an order?" Jael asked.

There was no fancy food, which surprised Jael, but a substantial stew was ladled into rough bowls and presented to each one along with a loaf of flatbread.

"I compliment your cook, Grandmother," Young Will said. "He has done much with little."

"I have gained an appreciation for trail food," Lady Bethalyn said.

Jael found it difficult to control her countenance.

Lady Bethalyn did not seem to notice. "I must say I am a bit disappointed that Elizabeth did not accompany you."

"She is hardly ready for a long ride, Mother," William said.

Jael tore her eyes away from his face to address her mother-in-law. "You will be happy, I think, with the child. She is quite lovely."

Lady Bethalyn gave her a smug smile. "Our girls do tend to be quite fine in appearance. Young Will's mother was quite a beauty."

Young Will set his cup aside. "I wish someone had taken her portrait. I have only the rude drawing done at her coming of age."

Lady Bethalyn nodded. "It is too bad we did not think of it." She gazed rather pointedly at Jael. "You assume you have so much time and then it is suddenly taken away."

Jael was not certain of her meaning, but she wished for a change of subject, which William soon provided.

"You are coming to Wrenook at a very good time, Mother. The roses will be blooming yet."

"I have heard so much of them, they had better be quite fine."

"You will not be disappointed," Jael said, "and the air all about Wrenook is scented by their aroma. Lady Blessingstock gave me a cutting, but it does not do so well at Cragmorton."

Lady Bethalyn handed her bowl to the servant. "Perhaps it is the lake. I've found that great water near at hand changes the air so."

"You may have hit upon the answer; however, the Wistra does well."

Lady Bethalyn glanced up. "The Wistra? You have Wistra at Cragmorton?"

"Aye," William said. "It is said to have been planted by John Twain and has quite taken over the porch outside our living quarters."

"Does it bloom well?"

"Aye," Jael said, "and it is highly scented as well."

"I suppose it is too late in the year to see it. I have only heard tales of the Wistra."

"It is not too late," Jael said. "It blooms still. Our seasons are behind times, our winters are overlong."

Lady Bethalyn's brow furrowed. "I do not like that thought."

William smiled at his mother. "It is not so very bad, Mother. You have never seen so beautiful a place in winter."

Young Will groaned. "It is all I have heard. I rather think it will be confining."

"Not so," William said. "The natives are fond of the cold. They spend many hours in it." He waved his hand in front of his face. "Their skin grows brown of a winter, from the sun's reflection off the surface of the snow."

"There's a sight to look forward to," Young Will said with a wry tone to his voice.

Jael chuckled. "We are so near the sun."

"If that were so," Lady Bethalyn said, "the snow would stand no chance in it."

William held up his cup for more tea. "Oh it is fully winter and quite cold, but the sun does seem warm in comparison. Should you step into the shadows, you would know the difference soon enough."

Lady Bethalyn crossed her arms in front of her as though she already felt the cold. "How does one manage to keep warm?"

"In the wearing of many furs," Jael said.

William agreed. "And the burning of many trees."

Jael stepped out of Lady Bethalyn's tent and waited for her husband. A full moon bathed the small canyon in its ethereal light. Young Will had joined his friends at the campfire, where he would sleep. It seemed William had something different in mind.

"This is one of my favorite places in all the Touris," he whispered to Jael. They stood at the base of a fall of water not far from the campsite. The water cascaded from such a distance, she could barely make out its beginning, yet it was not much wider than two men standing side by side.

The noise it created was thrilling – reminiscent of her home in Verani Haven. Here they made their bed for the night, beneath a blanket of stars.

Jael could not imagine a more perfect moment than this. She snuggled into the curve of her husband's body as he slept, so close she could hear his heart beating. In this moment – this perfect moment – she longed to remain, but she knew twas not to be.

The North Star was still high in the sky when William rose to prepare for the day's journey. As he drew on his boots, he watched Jael braid her platinum hair. He memorized her every move and savored their last few moments. Their eyes met when she smiled up at him. He held out his hand to her.

They walked together in silence, each sensing the other's feelings. A few minutes only would pass and their time together would end. He would return to the front, she would retreat to Cragmorton.

"I thought it would become easier," she said, "with so much practice. Instead it becomes more burdensome. Indeed, I seem to die a little inside with every parting."

He drew her to him and kissed her softly one last time before they came within view of the camp. "Do not speak so, my lady, though I am honored by the deep sorrow of your heart. 'Tis proof of your devotion."

"Never doubt it, my lord husband."

When William and his men left for Duflec where the main body of the warriors awaited them, Jael put on a brave front. Her mother-in-law watched from a distance. You married a warrior, her eyes seemed to say.

Sandelstar touched her arm with his nose and she turned to lean against his side. He always seemed to sense her moods. Young Will strode forward to lift her into the saddle. Already William and his men were gone from their sight.

Chapter 16 – Crossings

Jael, Lady Bethalyn and Young Will drew up their mounts and took in the view.

"So this is the fair vale of Cragmorton." Lady Bethalyn sighed. "It is worth the journey, I suppose. That house upon yon hill is Wrenook, I hope?"

"Aye Grandmother," Young Will said, "it is, and your family awaits you there."

"Well, lead on then. I should not like to keep them waiting beyond the dark. It comes quickly here."

The last mile seemed but a short distance to Jael and Young Will. However for Lady Bethalyn, it was far too long and she expressed her displeasure more than once. "I am short of patience," she said. "My journey has lasted many weeks and I do not know how long it will be until I may return."

Jael glanced at her in surprise. She rarely spoke so. She must miss her home and her husband horribly, for they were seldom parted these days. They were not young as when he had run about the countryside fighting wars. The new baby would be just the thing. Lady Bethalyn's heart would be lighter then.

Crispus came to Wrenook the next afternoon. Lady Bethalyn was resting in her room. Jael related her apologies.

He shook his head and waved away her apologies. "Fine, fine." He seemed barely able to contain his excitement. Though he made the effort to be polite, it was obvious he was quite preoccupied.

He bowed to Lady Elizabeth, made over the baby a bit, took Nathaniel to sit upon his knee, which was his usual routine. When finally they were able to speak in private, he was effusive.

"It holds some similarities to Latin, which is my native tongue," he said. Jael smiled her indulgence as he continued. "When first you taught me a few words, I thought it must be so, but when I saw it written, it is different. These are more like hieroglyphs." At her frown, he explained, "Picture writing; an ancient form of script."

Impressive. "Apparently you have worked very hard. Have you deciphered any of it?"

"I believe so, but I will let you decide."

Jael frowned at the jumbled notes.

"To the Lady descended of Rogan," she read aloud. "A warning I do give." She glanced up at Crispus. He nodded and urged her on, then began to pace back and forth.

"News has gone out of your … place. A prize is offered. Your gifts are known. The center of the crown for the prize."

Crispus rushed forward. "What do you think of it?"

Her hand shook as the words sank in. "'News has gone out of your place,' I think this must mean, whereabouts. 'News has gone out of your whereabouts' – yes, that makes more sense. 'The center of the crown for the prize,' I think must be – 'the heart of the crown … for the prize.'" She looked at him wide-eyed. "It is most disturbing."

Crispus frowned and rubbed his chin. "The heart of the crown for the prize – this is quite plain, my lady – you are the beloved of the heir to the crown. If the enemy has you, my lady, he has the prize."

Jael sank into the nearest chair, feeling as though all the blood had drained from her. Crispus sat down across from her.

"You must not fear, my lady. We have this warning in time."

She bit her lip and swiped at a tear. "I am pursued, Crispus – again."

He leaned forward, his elbows on his knees. "Aye, but this time, my lady, you are not alone."

Jael gazed at him for several long moments, her mind working over the words of the message. She drew in a sharp breath and stood so quickly the chair clattered to the floor.

Crispus stared up at her. "My lady?"

"The heart of the crown – we are *all* here, Crispus." She knelt in front of him and looked up into his face. "All three of us."

"Now I understand the degree of foreboding I've experienced of late." He rose, holding the scroll in his hands. "Precautions are in order, my lady. I must take this to Brannon and Young Will at once."

"I would be present in that meeting, Crispus."

"Of course, I will just copy this out with more clarity."

Jael returned to her room to gather her thoughts. When she was settled, she went into the drawing room and sat down with the two women of the house of du Frain. "I have something to tell you," she said.

As she told them of the scroll and its message, Lady Bethalyn was quiet.

Elizabeth clapped her hands over her face and moaned. "What will we do? Where will we go?"

Jael spoke softly, belying the panic she felt. "This is as safe a place as any. The last time they came, they went directly to the castle gates. That is where they will expect us to be."

"The last time," Lady Bethalyn said, rising from her seat. "Are you saying they have been here before?"

Jael kept her voice and countenance calm. "A brief visit only. They were turned away at Cragmorton's gate and they … ah … escaped, all but one."

Lady Bethalyn glared at Jael. "Why is it that I have heard nothing of this? I should think my son must have mentioned it. Unless, he did not know?"

Jael lifted her eyes to Lady Bethalyn's. "I would not allow him to be told, Your Highness. He is burdened enough. We must deal with these problems on our own."

"It is you who must deal with it." Elizabeth turned to her mother. "She has done marvelously, Mother. It is wrong of you to challenge her leadership."

Lady Bethalyn sat back in her chair and folded her hands. "I do not challenge her. I am only alarmed. We must think of the children."

"We have thought of little else, Mother, and I think Jael is right. We are much safer here at Wrenook. Our tower provides a thorough view of all the surrounds. Guards are stationed there around the clock. It is they who gave the warning to Cragmorton the last time."

After a few more minutes, Lady Bethalyn retired to her room in a nervous state.

"I am sorry," Elizabeth told Jael. "She does not mean to be so overbearing. She will pace about and gather her thoughts and her strength. She often reacts badly in the beginning, only to calm down considerably after a time of meditation and prayer. You will see."

Jael clenched her hands so tight, her knuckles paled. "It is right that she should worry. Such a thing as this has never occurred since she has reigned as Queen."

Elizabeth leaned forward and laid her hands on Jael's. "Aye, dear friend, it has not. Though the Magistrate wreaked havoc all about us, he never dared come nigh to Coldthwaite."

Dark fingers of dread clawed at Jael's throat, but she fought their fearful attack. If they were to survive this, she must keep her faith intact. Gazing into the fire, she began to sing the words of a psalm learned from Crispus.

Whither do I go from Thy Spirit?
And whither from Thy face do I flee?
If I ascend the heavens, there Thou art,
And spread out a couch in Sheol,
I find Thee!
I take the wings of morning,
I dwell in the uttermost part of the sea,
There also Thy hand leads me,
And Thy right hand holds me.

Chapter 17 – Passages

Benabi stood on the bank of the Ishcairne River, still as a statue. He had not been seen. Din Glun's men passed by without a challenge.

He was familiar with the men, the first party sent to capture William's lady. So they had not rejoined the mob, but stayed to the North. No doubt they knew what fate awaited them should they return, having failed in their mission. Benabi had no doubt, the next group would not give up so easily. This was why he had taken such a great risk. He sincerely hoped the man Crispus was trustworthy.

Now he had a decision to make. Should he return at all? Things had advanced to such a point, perhaps it would be best to send for reinforcements. He knelt beside the river, in the shelter of some willow trees, and inquired of the Lord. His only concern was for Rondar, left on his own among the enemy, but Benabi knew him to be a wise man used to hardship. Rondar would know to hold his tongue.

The voice of the waters filled his ears as he cast his eyes heavenward and spoke words of praise in his native tongue. Sometime later, he returned to his horse. His path would take a southern turn.

Jael had barely spoken with Brannon since that first altercation. She had taken Crispus' advice to accept his leadership for the sake of the locals. Brannon had proven himself loyal and trustworthy. But this didn't mean she had to agree with every decision he made.

"I think ye must stay at Wrenook my lady," he said after hearing the story from Crispus.

She bristled at his tone. "I would prefer to stay here, sir. The fortifications are – "

"As ye full know my lady," he said, " my men are young and untried. They are not skillful as them to which ye are used in Corwinder."

Jael did not say what ran so prevalent in her mind, that Brannon's men would ever be young and untried, did they never fight a battle. She drew herself up to her full height and looked him in the eye.

"But the Lady of Wrenook and her children, sir ... my presence would only endanger their lives."

Unmoved, Brannon said. "Ye have asked my opinion and I have given it. I think we must move ye to Wrenook."

Jael cast a glance at Young Will who stood near the window, his arms folded over his chest. His face held an amused expression as she butted heads with Brannon. His eyes met hers and he stepped forward. She gave Brannon a smug smile, assured of Young Will's support.

"If you need a tiebreaker, I would like to cast my vote." He cocked his head at Jael. "I believe you must go, my lady." When she opened her mouth to object, he held up his hand to stop her. "Wrenook is far more qualified than you know. I hear it has a secret room."

Jael elevated one eyebrow. "A secret room?"

He leaned near and spoke in a low voice. "Not so secret and protected as the disappearing trail, but quite secure, so I am told."

Jael gazed into his eyes. "You would trust your young cousins and your grandmother to this security?"

Brannon stepped closer and addressed Young Will. "It is quite safe, sir. I will have my men inspect it, if ye wish, but it is kept by those of Wrenook. It has proved to be invaluable over time."

Crispus stepped forward. "You saw what occurred last time, Lady Jael. Those men rode past Wrenook, they had no interest in it. They made straight for Cragmorton Castle."

Jael gazed through the open window at the stalwart peaks on the horizon. "By now they may know that I have been often at Wrenook. Have they spies about, they may not be so easily swayed."

"They will most certainly be on their guard, after that last incident," Brannon said, "but I still think ye'd be best off at Wrenook."

"It would not injure our cause," Crispus said, "to have someone in residence here, someone ... ah ... who resembles the lady." All eyes turned to Crispus. "In stature, at least."

Jael narrowed her eyes at him. Had he just made a crack at her height? Rogue! What mischief does he contemplate? She could guess who it was that he had in mind.

Young Will nodded his head slowly, as though he agreed with Crispus.

"Aye, you know the lady will come and will be honored to serve you."

Jael set her fists upon her hips. "And her so recently returned to her rightful home?" She glared from one to the other. "No doubt the two of you will be most happy to have her nearby."

Neither Crispus nor Young Will made a reply. Brannon scowled at everyone.

Jael sighed in resignation. "Her life would be in danger as well, you know."

Crispus was the first to speak. "Aye, but less would be at stake, milady."

Jael was puzzled by their expressions. "So you would be willing to make such a sacrifice?"

Young Will stepped forward. "We must first see if she is willing, but I believe she will be."

Brannon bowed to Jael. "If I may, my lady, will ye be going?"

Jael turned and faced the fire and by its warmth and light, made her decision. They must not chance capture. She had no wish to be used as a pawn in a cruel game to win the empire away from her beloved and knew the other ladies would feel the same. She remembered the fate of her own mother and trembled. Turning back again, she nodded. "I will go."

Brannon gave her a curt nod. "There's a storm growing on the horizon," he said to Young Will. "If ye agree, we may use its cover to move her." Young Will nodded and sent one last glance at Jael before he followed Brannon from the room.

Brannon paused in front of Crispus. "Ye will see to the other?" Crispus nodded his assent.

Jael turned back to the fire and whispered, "Unto Thee, O Jehovah, my soul I lift up. My God, in Thee I have trusted, Let me not be ashamed, Let not mine enemies exult over me."

Crispus came to stand by her. "They will not my lady, of that I am most certain."

Jael gazed at him through misty eyes, but made no reply.

The five-mile journey between Cragmorton and Wrenook seemed longer than ever before as they kept to the meadows away from the road. The wind whipped furiously and found its way into every opening in Jael's garments.

Already there was a definite chill in the air. A full moon climbed and occasionally cleared the cloud bank. Always, they kept their eyes on the twinkling lantern at Wrenook, lest they lose their way in the blowing rain. She arrived worn and hardly caring whether she removed her outer clothing before falling into whatever bed presented itself.

Elizabeth did not like the look in Lady Jael's eyes. It was evident that she had pushed herself beyond all limits. "You are unwell, sister."

Jael opened her eyes a bit to peer at Elizabeth in the glow of the candle. "Nay, only weary beyond measure. The wind saps every bit of strength from one's bones. I will fare better after a good night's rest." She yawned. "We have much to discuss on the morrow, but tonight I must have rest."

"I will leave you to it then. You know where to find me if you need me."

After leaving Jael's bedside, Elizabeth sent Hilda to make her more comfortable. "So weary was she, she'd not even the strength to free herself from her robes."

Chapter 18 – Decoys and Comrades

Young Will was pleased when Adrina did not hesitate to stand in for Lady Jael, even when she knew the danger. Early every morning, she would walk out upon the porch overlooking the lake. She always wore a heavy blue cloak, its hood pushed back to reveal her golden hair. From a distance, anyone would think that Lady Jael walked there still.

The likeness amazed Young Will. He came often to speak with Crispus, bringing news of Wrenook.

"'Tis uncanny," he said after one such visit.

"It is indeed," Crispus said. "One would think they were sisters."

Young Will stared at Crispus. "You do not think – "

Crispus cocked his head and smoothed out a scroll. "I have been searching through the royal library, my lord, but … still it remains a mystery."

"There is no book of registry?"

"There is one, yes. Miss Grumfeld does not have an exact date, so it is not easy to prove, but only one girl child was registered during that season. She was stillborn, however and – " He paused.

Young Will took a step nearer. "And?"

Crispus looked back at the younger man and shrugged. "That one was born to the royal family, my lord."

"Are you certain she was stillborn?"

"The registry says it is so," Crispus said.

Young Will grabbed a stool and sat down opposite Crispus. "Tell me all that you know of it."

Lady Bethalyn settled in to Wrenook much quicker than Jael or even

Elizabeth would have expected. The only time she ever complained was when the icy winds began to blow.

She rubbed her shoulders with gloved hands. "How quickly the ice comes upon the languid days of autumn. There is no lingering of summer here. Are there no inner rooms without window holes in them? These shutters hardly keep out the air."

Elizabeth did not even look up from her embroidery. "It is a frigid climate, Mother."

Jael turned her work over, tied off a thread and snipped the ends. Then she held it up to the candle light to check it. "Once the ice fills the cracks in the shutters, it is much warmer."

Elizabeth barely suppressed laughter, but her mother only frowned and turned away. Jael set aside her embroidery, crossed to the fire, and threw on another log.

Lady Bethalyn blew her nose and tucked the handkerchief into her sleeve. "Whatever possessed them to build such monstrous halls? You must have immense fires to warm them."

"I have often wondered the same thing." Jael said. She laid her work aside again and gave her full attention to Lady Bethalyn. "The large windows provide wonderful breezes in the warmth of summer when we are so near the sun's heat, but in winter, they are covered only by rickety shutters which allow snow showers within. Someday, someone will no doubt invent a better cover for them."

At Rose's soft cry, Elizabeth bent forward to pick her up. "Until then we shall just have to make do. I would not like to cover them over completely. To be shut in here without benefit of light – one would hardly know whether it was day or night. Here, Mother, take Rose for a bit, she will warm you. She is almost as effective as a warming pan." Elizabeth handed the baby to her mother.

"I will take her, thank you." Lady Bethalyn touched the baby's cheek and peered at Elizabeth. "She is not over warm, is she?"

"No, Mother, it is not a feverish warmth. While you have her, perhaps I will take a walk. I am weary of sitting still."

Lady Bethalyn nodded her agreement. "You go along with her, Lady Jael. She is troubled of late. You know her habits."

Jael did go, though her own state of mind was not much better.

"Always in the past," Elizabeth said, as they strolled arm-in-arm down the long corridor, "I have been able to withstand, but another winter arrives to divide us from those we love most. No word comes and my heart begins to fail me – and now this strange threat hangs over us – oh how I long for dear Pastor Stephen to calm me with his words of hope."

"We shall have Crispus on the morrow," Jael said. "He will play and sing and speak as much as you like."

Elizabeth nodded. "Aye, he is good, but I do miss Pastor Stephen and his lady wife. They were such a comfort to me." They walked in silence for several moments before Elizabeth spoke again. "You know my ways, dear Jael. My mind runs to worry. How I do wish I had your steadfastness. You are at all times so peaceful."

"You should not assume that I don't have the same feelings as you. It is only that I don't speak of them."

"Yes, I have always been told that quietness is better, but I cannot seem to keep my thoughts from rattling away upon my tongue."

Jael chuckled softly at her friend's candid confession. As they neared the stairwell, a door closing below drew their attention. They moved to the landing and waited until Young Will made his entrance.

"How fares Greshne, dear nephew?" Jael asked.

He came to bow before them and offered an arm to both. "All is quiet for now. Adrina sends word that your wise friend has sent another batch of children forth, whatever that means."

Jael threw her head back and laughed. "My wise friend is an owl, dear Will, who preceded me as mistress of Cragmorton. She was allowed to stay and has hatched several families in the interim."

"Owls are a sign of good fortune you know," Elizabeth said.

"This one certainly is."

Young Will shook his head and smiled. "Only a Rogan could befriend such a creature. I have oft heard tales of their communications with animals."

"Fables, dear Will," Jael said. "Though the creatures do seem to respond favorably to kindness and like to hear the ancient tongue spoken in a low voice. It seems to soothe them."

"Ah you see, 'tis more than fable. 'Tis true I think, and another secret you will lend no truth to."

"What secrets?" Elizabeth asked. She'd seemed distracted and Jael was surprised to find she had been listening.

Young Will caught Jael's eye, but made no immediate reply. Elizabeth soon forgot all about it and no response was needed.

By the time they returned to the door of Elizabeth's room, they found Lady Bethalyn and Aunt Blessingstock within, deep in discussion of former child-rearing practices. Jael and Elizabeth looked at one another, their eyebrows arched. Young Will made the excuse that he had other business and left them to another evening of incredible boredom. This life was not what Jael preferred. She had much rather be on her own again, at Cragmorton.

𝔜oung Will too, wished to be away. He soon found the tranquility of Wrenook a bit more than he could bear. Cragmorton and its unskilled warriors beckoned. He went there and after a prolonged conference with Brannon, he began to train the warriors. Most of them had begun under his uncle's skillful tutelage, but that had not lasted quite long enough. Will had them out practicing daily, riding and running about. They forded the river and manned rowboats on the Greshne until it froze over.

After their first target practice, Young Will took Brannon aside. "I am … ah … a bit disappointed in their archery skills."

Brannon smiled. "I am afraid most of these is farmers and shepherds, sir. They has no learned skills."

"They shall gain it and quickly then, for we cannot know when we will be challenged. Therefore, we must be ready. We have the royal ladies to guard."

Though Brannon seemed a good sort of man and quite trustworthy, he did not get in a hurry about sharpening skills. He seemed to think they had plenty of time. Young Will became impatient with this attitude which was so prevalent in the Cragmorton people.

Crispus joined him in the evening for dinner on a regular basis. They found much in common, since Crispus had also encountered these attitudes in the education of the young.

"I have tried to set down paths of learning but each step forward seems to be followed by two steps backward. Since the near annihilation of the nobility in these parts, education is at an all-time low. I thought perhaps they might look to better themselves."

"The opportunities are ripe," Young Will said. "A man of little or no fortune could raise himself to landowner simply by serving well among the warriors. A little learning thrown in would elevate his spirit as well." Denys refilled his cup with hot tea.

"And since you have alluded to spiritual matters, they do not attend services as they ought. They are always busy or resting from their business."

Young Will leaned forward. "Perhaps we may work together then. How could we combine our lessons?"

Crispus' countenance brightened. "I do see benefit there. Hard winter is coming on when training may fill their days. The great hall stands deserted. Let us transform it into a schoolroom, shall we?"

They spent the remainder of the evening laying out plans for their new enterprise. "I will take these plans to Brannon," Young Will said, "for he is the Captain of the Guard, appointed by my uncle. In truth, he should be the one to give final orders." Crispus made a sound very like a snort and Young Will drew his head back to gape at him.

Crispus smiled as he told Young Will of the enmity between Lady Jael and Brannon. "He is set in his ways, and has no great love for the royal family. I only hope he will not delay too long."

𝔜oung Will took up residence near the hall and began the seriousness of training. From time to time, he would catch sight of Adrina, but seldom had the chance to speak with her. He found in her a quick mind and wit that came near that of the women in his own family. One day, to get a brief respite from the brutal north wind, he visited the library.

Crispus was there too, buried in some ancient text. "'Tis a hobby of mine to rewrite these ancient manuscripts. The less they are used, the longer they will last."

"It seems a boring pastime," Young Will said with a quick glance at Adrina. "But you do seem to glean interesting tidbits to share with the men." He forced himself to concentrate on Crispus, and keep his eyes trained on the table before him.

"You noticed?" Crispus said. He laid his quill down and blew on the finely crafted letters. He lifted his eyes to Young Will. "I find their minds open at once to a mention of their proud ancestry."

Adrina stood nearby, and looked as though she wondered whether to find another corner in which to work. Young Will gave her a sideways grin. "I have not seen you out of late. I must admit, it gives me a start every time I see you walking about in that blue cloak."

She inclined her head. "I am so sorry to cause you any discomfort, sir."

"Oh no, twas a surprise of the pleasant sort, lady."

Crispus cleared his throat and interrupted their quiet repartee. "Here is a passage well versed, young sir. I believe I must use it tomorrow. 'To defend one's home is to honor it. True love of home and country results in said honor.'"

"I like that, though I do not know that the men will understand it. Who writes?" Young Will noticed Crispus' eyes were on Adrina as he spoke.

Crispus frowned at the script before him. "It was copied into text by a scribe of King John's. The scribe's name was … apparently, Demetrius. That's interesting. The name … is Roman."

Young Will slapped his knee. "Hah! Most likely a slave, then."

Crispus eyed him, arching his brows. "Aye, most likely."

The two men were alone in the library the next evening, searching through a stack of scrolls when something fell out at their feet. Young Will bent to retrieve it. He rolled it between his thumb and forefinger.

"A miniature scroll." He spread it open upon the table and stood looking down at it. "Here is a note you may have missed."

"It is a different hand," Crispus said, brow furrowed in concentration.

Young Will leaned on his elbows and pointed at something. "A smallish symbol upon the bottom is pressed in wax – a seal I have not seen."

Crispus got up and crossed the room to a shelf where more recent letters lay. "I believe I have seen this before." After several moments of searching, he picked one up and opened it. "Aye, here it is. See if you think it may be similar."

"Grumfeld," Young Will read. "But this is older, see?" He pointed to the seal found on the first document.

"Aye and worn as if it were handled much."

"Or perhaps kept upon one's person for a time."

Crispus gazed at Young Will. "What are you thinking?"

Young Will pursed his lips as he reasoned. "This was placed here some time ago, by one who wished it to be found at some future date."

"You don't think it was more recent?"

Young Will shook his head. "There is too much dust."

Crispus nodded slowly. "H. Grumfeld would most likely be – "

"Hedda, for she could write, that we know. She it was who – " He looked at Crispus, who jumped up and crossed to the table where he kept the family register. He opened it and pointed to the last entry, glanced up at Young Will, who peered over his shoulder.

"It is the same hand?"

Crispus nodded. "I believe it is."

Young Will concentrated on a lamp burning across the room, as he listened to Crispus reading the note.

"L. C. dF. Lives still. I kept my vow to HRH. No word was ever spoken. Herein I will write it lest it be lost upon my death. A remnant remains, though it be only the one. Very fair is she and I have raised her as my own. I hope that with God's help, she will find her way home. This is my most earnest prayer – H. Grumfeld."

Crispus laid the letter carefully down, placed his hands on the table in front of him and looked at Young Will.

"In my mind, 'tis positive proof," Young Will said.

Crispus smiled. "If one needs proof."

Young Will grinned back at Crispus, all the while forming a mental plan to escape and be the first to tell Adrina.

Rondar heard Din Glun speak of the great King of this vast empire and how he dwelt in a castle atop a high cliff to the north of the Verani. He gestured toward the basin, its water smooth in the still of evening, where all along the shores, fishing vessels sat at anchor. Rondar's stomach felt queasy. He must find a way to get word to the southern forces at Corwinder.

Din Glun and his army had managed to push through to the coastal regions. They were situated near the southernmost point of the Verani Basin. Thus far, they were undetected, but they were on the opposite side of that great body of water. They moved in the deep of night. As many vessels as they could confiscate were put to work ferrying men, animals and supplies across the wide expanse of water. Rondar was put to work on one of the vessels, so would be one of the last men out.

It took much longer than had been anticipated. By daybreak, only about half of Din Glun's army stood on the North side of the Basin. He sent them on to a remote valley where they would bivouac until their full force was realized. When morning came and the area fishermen saw what was taking place, they scattered. Rondar hoped they carried the news with them.

Sometime during that second night as the remaining forces were being ferried across the Basin, one of the larger boats lost a passenger. Rondar was certain he would not be missed for some time. In a quiet cove along the eastern bank, far upriver from the docks, he rose up from the waters and made his way stealthily along the shore to the nearby forest. After that short interval, no other sound was heard until a loon cried alerting its cronies that daybreak had come.

William's spies returned with the news; the main portion of Din Glun's army had gone. They'd moved many times in the past year, breaking off and regrouping in a new place, scattered widely and well, leaving little trace behind. At William's command, the neighboring towns and villages were all evacuated, every available man was armed. Many of the women and children made their way into the sanctuary of Duflec where the caves beneath the surface provided shelter and security.

William sat upon his horse, looking out over the valley below. Night had fallen and campfires dotted the landscape. Only a few enemy troops remained, though a great lot of tents and rubbish still stood there.

"What now brother?" Toldar drew up his horse next to William's.

William glanced over his shoulder then back at the scene before him. "We go to Corwinder."

Toldar gripped the reins as his mount tossed his head and snorted. "You think they have pushed so far?"

William struggled with his emotions. He could no longer deny the truth. "I have little doubt we must ride swiftly to deliver aid to my father's forces."

"Why not sail the Verani, as in the past? We would save much time."

William looked out over the surrounding countryside. He could not explain the gnawing feeling he had inside. "We must travel overland. There is danger along the Verani."

Toldar nodded. "I will give orders to the men."

Long after Toldar had gone, William sat watching the stars sparkle overhead. Far away, in the northern reaches, he knew Jael watched too. There, the winter snows would have begun to fall. He imagined her, lending strength to his sister and mother. Her face came before him so vividly he almost reached out to touch her. Her voice whispered to him on the night wind. His heart constricted painfully. "Does it ever get any easier?" he asked. No one answered, for no one was about. He bowed his head and prayed.

In the dead of night, Jael awoke to the sound of crying. She sat up in bed – her heart raced wildly – for it seemed almost as if the cry had come from her. She draped a shawl over her shoulders, crept from the room and drew near to Elizabeth's quarters, for she assumed it must be Rose crying. As she passed the landing, a movement in the moonlight arrested her. Heart lurching, she retreated behind the corner of the wall and waited there, listening and watching.

A footstep sounded nearby. Jael turned to look and came face to face with Young Will, who seemed agitated.

"My lady, go at once to Aunt Elizabeth and the children. You must all get to the stronghold. I go to my grandmother."

"What is it?"

He gripped her shoulders. "There is no time, just go." He ran swiftly and silently away, keeping to the shadows.

Elizabeth was notoriously difficult to wake at times and this cold night was one of those. At Jael's bidding, the nurse who slept nearby, ran to help prepare the stronghold. Jael took the sleeping Nathaniel up in her arms and then stopped again at Elizabeth's bed. "Come, Elizabeth, we must hurry. We must get below at once."

Elizabeth moaned and stretched out her arm. "I am sleeping dear, please do not wake me."

At a sound from without, Jael laid Nathaniel beside his mother and ran out into the corridor. She could hear voices plainly now. There were men below stairs and the words they spoke were unfamiliar to her. Without a moment's delay, she ran back to Elizabeth's quarters and closed the door behind her. Elizabeth, awake now and holding Rose, jumped at Jael's forceful entry. Jael waved her hands in a shooing motion.

"Get up, we have to go." She tossed Elizabeth's cloak at her. "There is no time for explanation." She took a quick survey of the room and went to throw open the shutters. This proved difficult, but somehow she felt it was important. Perhaps those men would think they had escaped through the window. She took Nathaniel in her arms and sped past Elizabeth into the next room.

Elizabeth ran to and fro. She grabbed her shawl and blanket. "The stronghold – we must get to the stronghold."

Jael called softly, "There is no time, we cannot now go that way." She peeked through the doorway. "You must come with me."

Elizabeth followed, but not without objections. "This is my dressing room, there is no way out of there – we have to get out – " Her voice broke.

Jael stood directly in front of her and looked into her fear-filled eyes. "Calm yourself Elizabeth, for the sake of the children. You have to trust me."

The sounds outside the rooms told Jael the men were near at hand and apparently destroying everything in their path. At any moment, they would burst through that door. Jael scanned the small interior room and then turned to Elizabeth. "Go to the back corner and kneel down."

"What? We cannot hide here. They will find us. Oh Jael!"

Jael held her gaze and spoke steadily, but with as much courage as she could muster. "Trust me, Elizabeth. We have only one hope of escape. You must be calm." She looked at Nathaniel, who was now wide-awake with his lower lip trembling. "You are scaring Nathaniel."

Elizabeth knelt, holding her sleeping baby close to her breast. Jael set Nathaniel down beside his mother and knelt before him. She caressed his cheek with her hand and spoke softly, looking into his eyes. "Be at peace, Nathaniel, make no sound." He looked up at her, eyes trusting and laid his head against his mother's side. Elizabeth encircled his small body with her arm. Her panic-filled eyes met those of her sister-in-law.

As the noises increased on the other side of the door, Jael mouthed the word, "Pray."

Elizabeth squeezed her eyes tightly shut as her lips began to form silent words.

Jael stood and glanced about. *What can I do? How will we escape?* After a moment's hesitation, she turned her back to Elizabeth. She spread the skirt of her nightdress to cover them. She placed one hand on the wall to their left and the other on the wall to their right. She drew in a deep breath to calm herself and glanced upwards.

She had no idea whether this would work, but knew that she must try. There was, at present, no alternative. She began to pray and then to praise

God, centering her heart and mind on him. The three in her shelter made no sound; all other sound retreated as Jael communed with God. The dark walls of the little dressing room seemed to fade from view as her soul filled with brightness. She knew then that they were safe – even when the door was thrown brutally open – and men with torches ran in upon them, turning over furniture and smashing everything in reach.

Their unfamiliar words sounded ugly and filled with curses, but they could not find anyone within. Jael had never been so challenged. In the past, she'd had difficulty remaining in her meditative state, but this time, though the room stank of their presence, she was unmoved. She remained within the calm circle of the presence of God, singing praises in the ancient tongue, yet fully awake and aware.

Suddenly a hand of one of the intruders went up and all grew quiet. Until that moment, she had not considered that they could hear her. She stood completely still and did not even breathe. The apparent leader stepped forward – almost on top of her – and scowled at what he perceived as the dark stony surface of the wall. After what seemed an eternity of incredible silence in which the brutish stranger scrutinized the wall, he turned and strode from the room, his entourage close upon his heels. She heard them moving throughout the house and prayed that everyone else had been able to escape to the secret stair.

At the sounds of their departure, Jael climbed on a trunk and peeked through a crack in the shutter. Outside, a fresh snowfall reflected moonlight. Stars sparkled overhead, as if there was no evil in the world. Out upon the road, the ugly mob cast about, searching for signs of escape from Wrenook. She turned to Elizabeth who moved carefully, not to disturb her children. They found Nathaniel curled up, fast asleep.

"How odd," Elizabeth said. She covered him with her shawl and moved to stand near her sister-in-law. "Have they gone?"

"They are waiting for something."

Elizabeth stared at her. "You understand them?"

"Nay, their language is brutish and difficult. I have not heard it spoken before." Soon the men were joined by several others riding in from Cragmorton, and after a short conference and much pointing at tracks in the snow, they rode off toward the pass. When she had seen them ride away, Jael climbed down from the trunk to face Elizabeth.

Elizabeth shuddered. "I do not understand what has happened, Jael."

Jael laid her hand upon Elizabeth's arm and spoke calmly, but with authority. "Let us get the children into bed, Elizabeth. I will assist you and then I will go and give news of their departure to the others."

"But – how did they not see us? I do not understand what has happened."

"God protected us from them, Elizabeth. We prayed and He shielded us." Jael bent to take up the sleeping Nathaniel. She looked over her shoulder at Elizabeth. "It was not our time."

She could tell Elizabeth was not satisfied, but she dutifully tended her children. Jael lit a candle and they stood in silent horror to behold the destruction of Elizabeth's quarters.

Jael took her hand and spoke softly to her. "Do not trouble yourself, only look after the little ones. I will go now and alert the servants. I will send someone to you at once. They will take care of everything."

Jael hurried to the secret stair and pulled a hidden string. A small wooden slat attached to the string whispered a soft noise inside the room and notified those within that all was clear. Almost immediately, Darien stepped out.

"All is well for now," Jael said.

"We feared the worst, my lady, when ye did not appear."

Jael assured him that they were all fine.

"And Doro ... was he with ye also?"

Jael shook her head. "I have not seen Doro."

Darien opened the door and called to the others. Slowly the servants emerged, the last of which led Lady Blessingstock and Lady Bethalyn, who demanded to know what had happened to her daughter. Jael assured them the children and Lady Elizabeth were safe and sent servants to their aid. Everyone began immediately to take stock of the damage, except for the cook, who went below to make tea at Lady Blessingstock's orders.

"Is everyone safe here?" Young Will asked Jael upon his return.

"We have lost only one, Old Doro, a groom. He apparently made a brave stand, giving everyone time to escape."

Young Will shook his head sadly and turned troubled eyes to her face. "They have taken Adrina."

Jael drew in a quick breath and grasped at her shawl. "Oh no."

"It is as you feared, my lady. They have taken her, believing she was you. I am leaving at once."

"You do not go alone?" She bit her lip to stop its trembling.

"A few of the young men will ride with me. It was all I could do to talk Crispus out of going also. I must away quickly." He dropped a kiss upon her hand. "Take care, Aunt. This may not be over."

It was not over. Something was quite wrong. Jael watched all the while that the men made ready for their departure. Something moved within her and she could not stand idly by. As she waited in her room she was overcome by the anguish of it. She gave herself over to the troubling vision, and a moment later, she stood watching as those young men rode into a bloody ambush. They were beaten down and the snowy ground was littered with their bodies. When she came to herself, she could hardly breathe for the strength of the vision. After only a moment's hesitation, she ran from the room and down the stairs.

In the wee hours of the morning, a storm blew in. Snow covered the prints left behind overnight. Already, the heavy snows of the past few days formed high drifts on either side of the narrow pass out of Cragmorton. It was to this very place that Jael came, just behind the men. She stood and watched in horror as they rode out of sight. She was too late. She fought her way through the snow and stood for a moment, watching. She knew not where they went from here, so she could not go to them. She needed her horse.

Jael concentrated then on the stables at Wrenook and soon found herself there, standing in the shadows. It was very early, and no one was about. Sandlestar nickered, sensing her there. She found a suitable saddle, not her own sidesaddle, for she was dressed as a man. One last thing was wanting. She ran inside, gathered what herbs she may need and then took a moment to scribble a quick note.

Chapter 20 – On the Road Again

Hours passed for Jael, with no sign of Young Will and his warriors. She was unfamiliar with the terrain and feared lest she become lost in the wilderness. When the snow ceased for a time, she found a high perch and stood upon it, looking all around and listening for the sounds of their journey.

A movement to the West caught her attention. A solitary rider moved along a narrow ledge, then another followed and another. Small horses – and the men wore thick fur caps. She had found the abductors. She hastened down from the heights and mounted Sandelstar. It was some time before she located the place where the riders had been. She dismounted and stood looking out over the snowy landscape, wondering how best to continue. Intent on the scene before her, she abandoned the reins and inched forward.

Fear pressed in upon her as she searched. She had been foolish and naive to believe she could do this. She pressed her palms against her cheeks as tears stung her eyes. A sudden gust of snow laden air beat against her face and she pulled her hood up. Courage, Jael. *You've been in worse situations.* Panic sent shivers up and down her spine. "Oh God, please help me find Young Will!"

She drew in a jagged breath of frozen air. She must get back to her horse. She turned about and jerked so hard, she nearly lost her footing on the narrow icy trail. She was face to face with Young Will, Sandelstar's reins in his hand. He did not look happy.

"Imagine my surprise in finding Sandelstar upon this remote trail," he said. "I thought at first he had been stolen by yon band of renegades." He stepped nearer, steel grey eyes boring into hers. "I would not have thought it possible to come up on the Lady of the Haven … unawares."

Jael returned his gaze, unflinching. "Another time you would not." She stepped nearer, her eyes never leaving his face. "I am so glad to see you unharmed, dear Will. I had such a frightful vision ... " Her voice trailed off.

Young Will's face turned ashen. "Not unfounded, Aunt. I have lost all but three of the brave young warriors who followed me. The rest have returned to assure the safety of the vale."

She drew in a quick breath. "You go on alone then?"

His eyes held hers, his jaw set. Slowly, he shook his head. "Not alone, for you are with me."

Motionless, she watched him. "You will not force me to return?"

"No, my lady, if we are to rescue our friend, I think we may have need of your skill." He held out Sandelstar's reins and she took them from him.

"You have seen her?"

"Aye," he said, "she is with them. They will not harm her. They think she is a sorceress." A crooked smile curved his lips briefly. "They think she is you."

She frowned. "I am not a sorceress."

"Of that, I am well aware, dear Aunt." He assisted her to mount and then led her horse to the place where his own was tethered. Once astride his horse, he asked her, "How did you plan to go on?"

"I would have followed that way." She pointed to the ledge where the men had gone.

"There is a nearer way, I have found it."

"Lead on then, nephew. I will follow."

He urged his horse ahead of her and as he passed by said, "You are no tracker, lady. You would have been lost already, except for the grace of God which keeps you."

She saw the smile upon his face, so gave no answer. He was teasing her again, she knew. "You are quite right, I am no tracker. I am ever amazed at how God gives attendance to our needs."

Snow continued to fall throughout the day as Jael followed closely behind Young Will. So far they had managed to stay within a few hours of the abductors.

"I know where they are headed," he said. "If we lose their trail, we should be able to catch them the other side of Inglethwaite."

"That is a long journey."

"Aye, it is and longer still, do we not come upon them there."

She knew he hoped to catch them before they connected with more of their men. In this party, there were only nine men. Two against nine was not so bad. All along the trail, Jael tried to think of ways that they could accomplish the rescue. In all of those ways, she and Will would be open to retaliation. They must plan carefully. A backup plan would not be a bad thing.

$\approx$

Hilda brought Jael's note to Elizabeth with her morning tea. Elizabeth read the hastily written missive and dropped her head in her hands. "Oh Jael, what have you done now?" She gazed into the steaming tea and pressed her lips together. She must not say anything of this to Mother.

As they sat together later in the morning embroidering coverlets, Elizabeth told her mother that Jael was called away on business. She neglected to say where.

"She seems to have adjusted well to her station," was all her mother said.

Elizabeth smiled her relief. "As mistress of Cragmorton, she is kept quite busy."

Lady Bethalyn tugged at a stubborn knot. "She still pursues this business of healer as well?"

"Of course she does, Mother. Lady Jael considers it her calling. When someone needs help, she delivers it." She lifted her eyes to her mother's face. "It is not so very different from our efforts of giving aid to the poor."

Lady Bethalyn frowned as she snipped a loose thread. "Sending food or clothing … other necessities of life … that is genteel work."

"Doing good is genteel work, Mother, whatever form it takes."

"Ah, well I can see where this is going." Lady Bethalyn sighed. "I have not the energy to argue the point. I am so tired." She paused to scan her daughter's face. "Do you not feel the same? I fear you must." She held her hands closer to the flame. "I do hope those awful men have gone away for good."

"No doubt they will have. Snow has been falling steadily. According to Young Will, they would not like to be trapped here for the winter."

At the mention of Young Will's name, Lady Bethalyn's expression clouded. "Has there been word of him since you awoke?"

Elizabeth shook her head. "Alas, there has not."

"I am concerned for him. He did not like to go, I think."

"Perhaps not. You know he won't return until he has made sure of our safety, for that is why he was sent here."

Lady Bethalyn laid her well-toasted hands upon her cheeks. Her eyes revealed her weariness. "Yes, if only our husbands knew of our danger. I am certain they would have sent more than Young Will to assure our safety."

Elizabeth's fingers paused in their work. "How could they anticipate such a thing?"

Lady Bethalyn seemed not to notice her daughter's irritation. She spoke quietly, her gaze on the fire. "I cannot help thinking there is more to this than meets the eye." She rose from her chair and waited while her maid straightened her skirt and draped a fur cloak over her shoulders. "I will return to my room. Should you hear anything further, please send for me. I am most anxious."

Alone in the parlor, Elizabeth drew out the note and looked at it again. "Dear Jael," she whispered. "Please be safe. How will we all go on without you?"

Chapter 21 – Mighty Army

As King George Horatio's eyes scanned the fair city of Coldthwaite, a tremor passed through him. *The safety of this great city falls expressly upon me.*

He had done all he could to ensure that safety. Now they would wait. A commotion in the courtyard below signaled the arrival of a runner. He waited, none too patiently, for the message. The door swung open and a young corporal stood in his presence, head bowed. Eldred entered the room behind the young man.

The king stepped forward. "What word?"

The corporal raised his head and addressed the king. "A message from Captain of the Guard, Your Majesty: the enemy forces have been sighted below Corwinder. Three days – four at most – will bring them to Coldthwaite."

Eldred stepped forward and dismissed the young corporal. He turned to face the king. "Word has gone forth a second time to Prince William's army. That runner has not yet returned."

King George squeezed his eyes shut. "Would that I was young and fit, I would ride out and see the situation for myself. How it chafes me to be stuck here and all but helpless." He rubbed his brow and was surprised to find such dampness there. His head hurt him of late, and he knew it was anxiety. It seemed to tighten its grip upon him daily. He could not sleep but blamed that upon the absence of his wife. Until she was gone, he had not realized how much he depended on her.

Eldred cleared his throat. "Shall I order tea, sir?"

King George sat down heavily in the nearest chair. "Not yet, Eldred. I am only tired, I think."

"Yes, Your Majesty." Behind him, the door opened again. Eldred turned to find a young page standing in the doorway.

"Beg pardon, Your Highness, but Master Worther has come."

Eldred bowed. "By your leave, sir?"

"Show him to my sitting room," King George said. "I shall be there shortly."

The young page bowed and left the room, followed by Eldred. King George rose and crossed to the window. From there, he surveyed his kingdom, eyes straining for the sight of reinforcements, but none could be seen. He sighed and turned to walk slowly through an inner corridor to his private quarters.

𝔊𝔢𝔬𝔯𝔤𝔢 Horatio and Abraham Worther had been comrades since the days of their youth. Abraham had followed in his father's footsteps, had become a gifted weaver of tapestries and an excellent historian. Prince George, after distinguishing himself on the battlefield, took his father's place as regent. Through it all, they had remained fast friends.

"Abraham, my good friend, how good of you to come. I have need of fellowship of some sort or other. I hope you have a diverting story or two to tell."

Abraham smiled. "I have more than that Your Highness. I bring my latest creation, the gift you ordered for Lady Jael. I finished it just before dawn this very day. I knew you would want to be the first to see it."

King George sighed and lifted a guilt-laden gaze to Abraham. "Even at this moment, as war threatens our fair city, I am looking for diversions. What does that say about me, Abraham? What an old fool I am at times."

Abraham's countenance fell. "My friend, it is never foolish to desire peace, especially in one's elder years. As for this war, I have faith that our God will not forsake us." He gripped his friend's forearm and met his gaze.

King George drew in a jagged breath and released it with a huff. "It is good to hear you say so, in the least." He rubbed his brow again and lowered his head. "He seems long in coming is all."

"God is never late, dear friend. It is just that His timing is different from ours." He waved a hand in the direction of the royal gallery. "Come, look upon the fruit of my labor and tell me what you think."

King George frowned. "I spoke of William, but your comforting words are welcome all the same. Let us go and see this masterpiece of yours."

The tapestry had been rolled out upon the floor of a long gallery, where light flowed in from many large open windows. King George walked around the perimeter of the tapestry. He bent to get a better look. "Oh my friend, you have outdone every other effort here. I have not seen so great a work."

Abraham beamed. "I knew you would like it. I hate to see it go so far away. I would like to look at it from time to time, just to assure myself that I really did accomplish it."

King George straightened and looked at his friend. "You may not have to send it to Cragmorton after all. We will wait upon the end of this war and see what the outcome will be."

Abraham's brow furrowed and his lips parted, but he said nothing.

King George saw the concern in his friend's eyes and made an effort to smile. "Lady Jael will love this – " he began to say, but his voice broke and he could not continue. For the first time in his life, his hope wavered.

Abraham stepped around the tapestry, knelt near the topmost corner and there laid his hand upon a pair of doves he had fashioned. "See here, friend," he said. "They perch upon the parapet of this very castle."

King George followed the direction of Abraham's hand. "I see what you are trying to say, Master Abraham. I know." He shook his head. "I do know."

The gates at Corwinder-by-the-Sea were thrown open as William and Toldar drew near. Only a few of their warriors accompanied them. Most waited outside with Courin at their lead.

"What news have you of Coldthwaite?" William asked. He did not delay, once he had dismounted, but made straight for headquarters.

Commander Solis wiped his brow with the back of his forearm and frowned. "We have not heard from there in several days, my lord, since receiving a call to arms. We were set to leave at once when we were brutally and most unexpectedly attacked. At your approach, they scattered to the four winds. It seems for every one we kill, they receive two more in his stead."

"'Tisn't true," Toldar said, "'tis only a deception."

Solis turned to look at him. "They run from ye at least, but I would not trust to their remaining hidden."

William held up his hand. "Let us go inside, Solis. We have little time and pressing matters to discuss."

Once inside, William addressed Solis and his officers. "We will not pursue those who troubled you."

Solis made to object, but William silenced him with an uplifted hand. "I believe it is their plan to distract us with these small skirmishes. This much I have learned. They keep us from the main objective, which is a full force attack upon Coldthwaite. We go at once, by the northern route. We go under cover of darkness." He turned to Solis. "Am I to understand that Corwinder is abandoned, other than your forces?"

"Aye sir, 'twas evacuated yesternight."

The captain of Din Glun's battalion scowled at the scene that greeted him as the sun's light broke over the neighboring hills. The great gates of Corwinder stood ajar and there was no sound within. No bodies were left upon the ground, save those of Din Glun's men, and they were lined up respectfully near the outer wall. No wounded lay within. He distrusted this strange turn of events, hesitated to cross the plain and enter the gates, for fear of ambush. For nearly an hour he waited. Then he sent spies ahead to scout out the interior, who soon returned to give the news.

"The city is abandoned. They have run away in the night. Whatever army arrived yesterday no doubt frightened them away."

They found a broad trail where the tracks of many horses led away north and then scattered, much like their own had done on many occasions.

The captain brandished his sword and held it high. "Methinks we may call this a win!" The men shouted and held their swords aloft. Then the captain mounted his horse and turned about, searching the horizon. He gave the signal and headed southwest, toward the coast.

Din Glun sat on a high outcropping of granite, overlooking the tidal basin below Corwinder. From all corners of the countryside, his army poured forth. In a day or two they would begin their forward journey along the coast to Coldthwaite, marching in great force. There, he intended to conquer the mighty seat of government. Already certain of victory, he looked about with a proprietary air.

On the eve of their leave taking, Din Glun called all of his leaders together. To each of them, he issued identical armor formed and fashioned by his artisans. They would all look just like him. No one among the general population of warriors would know who was the real Din Glun. He would seem to be in many places at once, confusing the enemy. He had learned this ruse among the savages of the Far East.

Any day now, he expected his emissaries to arrive from the North with one or perhaps all three royal ladies in tow. He especially hoped to get his hands on that sorceress they called the Lady of the Haven. He had heard many stories of her strength and power. He clenched his fists and gritted his teeth. Having her in his clutches would assure his victory.

Adrina was more tired than she had ever been in her life. She was freezing and her wrists ached from the bindings. Every evening, they pushed her down on the cold damp ground and twisted one arm behind her, fastened it to one of her ankles and loosened the binding on the other hand so she could feed herself.

The food was no better than swill, but she ate to keep her strength up in case Young Will was able to free her. She would not want to be too weak to travel. But every twelve-hour that passed lessened her strength and her hope.

In the beginning of her ordeal she had been able to give praise to God that she was chosen to suffer for such a good cause, but her resolve weakened with time. They were brutal and unkind to be sure. Also the weather turned against them, pelting them with icy winds and heavy falls of snow.

She could not understand the words of the men who held her, but she certainly understood their intent. The big one approached her more than once, bared his ugly yellow teeth at her and pressed the sharp blade of his knife into the tender skin of her throat. He tossed words over his shoulder at the man who seemed to be in charge.

Whatever the meaning of his words, they seemed to challenge the other man, who advanced upon him and gestured wildly while speaking in a low, clipped tone.

Her would-be attacker withdrew his knife and the two stood nose-to-nose in verbal combat. Adrina dropped her head back and closed her eyes. *Kill me then, relieve my misery.*

𝔍𝔱 was not long in such harsh weather until Jael began to wish she had worn more clothes. Already, she was using her sleeping furs as extra cloaks, tied at the waist with a strip of rawhide. On the second night of their journey, they found shelter in a small cave. Wood here was scarce and as a result, the meagre fire provided little warmth.

They huddled close together out of necessity. Young Will was unusually quiet. Jael drew her knees up beneath her chin and wrapped her arms about them. She rested her chin on her knees and gazed into the miserly flame. Young Will's back and head rested against a rock. Through half-closed eyes, he watched the entrance to the cave, now a black hole.

"How long have you loved her?" Jael asked. She could tell her words surprised him. He lifted his head and turned slowly to gaze at her.

"Of whom do you speak, my lady?"

She smiled and raised her eyes to his. "You know full well."

He turned his head away, watching the darkness.

Jael sensed his longing and his hesitation. A close bond existed between them, but some subjects were considered improper.

She touched his forearm. "We are comrades, no? Am I not masculine enough in appearance to listen to your heart?"

Young Will chuckled. "You are in no way masculine in appearance my lady, save that silly costume you wear."

She pushed gently at his arm and laughed softly. "You cannot pretend innocence with me. I know you too well." She cocked her head. "Though I had thought it settled between Crispus and the lady."

Young Will met her eyes. "He was refused."

It was Jael's turn to look surprised. "He was refused? Then he did love her?"

"He thought he did, though now he thinks it otherwise."

"He saw the way she looked at you, no doubt."

This brought a definite smile to his stern face. "How is it that you know so much?"

"She would be a simpleton if she did not fall in love with you."

Again he turned to the darkness. "It may all come to nothing, I fear."

"Do not say it. We must not allow that to happen. She is the last of that great family and her life must be preserved at all costs."

He turned now to look at her straight on. "You know about that?"

"Aye, it is plain to see."

"She denies the possibility. She is content to be Adrina Grumfeld, daughter of Hedda Grumfeld."

"Her humility is commendable."

"She is not unlike her cousin in that quality."

Jael gave him a sideways glance. "Flatterer. Well, how shall we proceed then? Have you given it any thought?"

"I have thought of nothing else." He exhaled loudly and pushed another stick into the flames. "Short of trailing them closely and knocking off one at a time, I have no other plan."

"That is too dangerous, I fear. I cannot have you injured or worse. How would I go on? We must try to think of a better plan."

"You don't have any poison on you, do you? You could sneak into their camp and poison their food." He gave her a wry smile, but she felt he was only half-kidding. Would he be amenable to her taking such a risk?

"They feed Adrina as well," she said, but her mind was processing the suggestion. She leaned over, reaching for her saddlebags. "It may work, however. I do have … endergazen … " She drew out a small cloth bag and held it up to him.

"What does it do?"

"It is a powerful sedative. Too much can cause permanent sleep, but among so many, I think I have just enough to give them a very restful time of it."

"How long would it give us?"

She held up the bag and weighed it in the palm of her hand. "Hmm … maybe as long as six or eight hours."

"What about Adrina?"

"I could warn her not to eat, or … she would sleep also."

He looked askance at her. "It would not harm her?"

"It did not harm you after your injury," she answered with a smile.

He frowned at her and stretched his leg out. "So we have a plan? How then will we accomplish it?"

"I can enter their camp and add it to their stewpot."

He smiled. "They will not see you."

She nodded. "They will not see me."

Will laid his head back again and sighed. Jael, feeling hopeful for the first time since she left the vale, moved a little closer to him for warmth and leaned her head against his arm. He smiled and turned his eyes to the circle of darkness at the mouth of the cave and waited for sunrise.

As the sun cast its shallow warmth upon the late November landscape, William and his army rode hard across the plain. Scouts delivered word that the enemy camp had broken and the massive infantry was on the move. William could only think of his father. He could imagine him, standing upon the ramparts of the castle, wondering how he would get out of this one.

As they drew near the borders of Coldthwaite, William called a halt to their advance. If they did not rest, they would not have a chance of prevailing against so great a number of men. The latest intelligence placed Din Glun's army nearly two days southeast of Coldthwaite.

"We will rest this night," he told his officers. "Give orders to your men. We will head directly west at dawn."

That night, he wrote a lengthy letter to his lady and spent the rest of the time in quiet meditation. He must hear from the Lord. Near dawn, he was face down upon the ground, crying out to God. He heard nothing, but felt a presence so near him that the hair rose up on his forearms. He raised his head and lifted his eyes. She sat next to him, her knees drawn up beneath her chin. She was smiling down at him. "You are not really here," he whispered. "At least you'd better not be. It is far too dangerous and you are far too distracting."

She gave no answer, but continued to smile at him, her eyes aglow. He knew then that she was not really there, but far away and thinking of him. He smiled and would have lowered his head again, had she not spoken.

"Do not be deceived, my love. The enemy will try to persuade you that he has captured me. He has not. I assure you – I am quite safe and very soon you will see me. The Lord bless you and keep you." Her hand moved towards him. He lifted his arm and reached out to her, but the vision faded and he heard a sound not unlike that of a dove in flight. He groaned softly and dropped his head into his arms. Could this be true? Could she really be on her way to him? How he longed for her, but he could not think of that now. He stood up and drew in a deep breath, stepped outside and looked around. All about him, the men were stirring and making final preparations. He centered his mind on the task at hand. Dawn was imminent.

Jael's eyes popped open. She gazed about, to get her bearings. She had dreamt of William and it had seemed so real. She had spoken to him and warned him of Din Glun's attempt to capture her. The words were still on the tip of her tongue, "The Lord bless you and keep you."

Young Will was already saddling the horses, so she made reparations to her appearance and gathered her things. After scattering the dying embers of the fire, she crossed to Sandelstar and packed up her belongings. Young Will made a few last minute adjustments and then helped her to mount.

"If we catch them today and rescue Adrina, we can leave our horses at Duflec and go by way of the river. It will be much faster."

"You do not intend to return to Cragmorton then?"

He looked up at her. "That was never my intention. By now, the pass will be closed if Brannon followed my suggestion."

Jael nodded, understanding his intent. An early blizzard would make the situation conducive to an avalanche. It would be easy to accomplish and would effectively close the pass until spring. The men had discussed it several times. The only other way in or out of the valley was the river above the Greshne. It would be impassable now as well, for it was treacherous and steep even in good weather.

Chapter 22 – Stand Therefore

The sound of childish laughter echoed once more in Cragmorton. Crispus smiled as he made his way through the new fallen snow. Overhead, a brilliant sky stretched out from mountain peak to mountain peak and his heart filled with thankfulness to God. He sensed a deep and abiding peace. He saddled his pony and made his way slowly out and down through the gates of the city. He would ride out to Wrenook, to bring his weekly message to the ladies there. As he rode, his thoughts were of Lady Jael, Young Will and Adrina. He spoke another prayer over them, knowing that their path would not be an easy one.

Wrenook was quiet. Lady Bethalyn's eyes were dark and troubled. Lady Elizabeth was jittery and looked to be on the verge of tears. He sat down with them and took up the lyre and sang a psalm. Then he read from a letter of Paul to the Christians at Ephesus. He strove to impart the inner peace he felt, but it was not working. He stopped reading mid-verse and looked from one to the other.

Lady Bethalyn's distracted gaze rested upon the fire roaring on the great hearth. He was startled when she addressed him. "Speak truthfully, Crispus, if you please. Tell me what you have discerned." It had not taken long for her to know the gift Crispus possessed.

Lady Elizabeth took out a handkerchief and dabbed at her eyes. Just then, the door opened. A servant entered and helped Lady Blessingstock to a chair near the fire. Once settled, the elderly lady smiled. "I am sorry to be late. It seems to take longer and longer to get me ready. Do go on."

Crispus nodded. "Lady Blessingstock, it is good to see you looking so well."

"Please, Crispus," Lady Elizabeth whispered. "If you have a word of encouragement for us, it will be greatly appreciated, by one and all."

Lady Blessingstock sat forward and asked in a rather loud voice,

"Where is Lady Jael? Did she not come with thee? We have not seen her in some days. Thou cannot say she is still busy at the castle. She always made time to visit me."

Crispus drew in a quick breath and looked from one to the other. He opened his mouth to speak, not knowing what to expect. "Your Highness, ladies, your anxieties are understandable, as the situation is grave, but you should not think it a defeat. While loss of life in time of war is unavoidable, I feel ... " He paused to smile. " ... such a great peace. Please, be comforted." He turned to Lady Elizabeth and reached out his hand to her. "Lord Toldar is safe." To Lady Bethalyn, "Lord William, Young Will and Lady Jael – I believe they are all quite safe."

Lady Bethalyn frowned. "How is it that you name them together?"

"Lady Jael rode out to warn of an ambush, but she was ... ah ... " Too late, he noticed Lady Elizabeth's chagrin as she flailed the air with her hands to try to stop him. He took a breath and continued. "All but three of the young men who rode with Young Will perished. The others, upon orders from Young Will himself, returned and as you know, set off the avalanche that closed the pass. While this provided for our safety, it has also rendered Young Will and Lady Jael's return impossible."

Lady Bethalyn sat forward on her chair so suddenly, she startled Lady Blessingstock. "What folly is this? How could she ride out thus? Where were the men? Why did she not send one of them?"

Lady Elizabeth rose and went to her. "Mother, please do not excite yourself so."

Lady Bethalyn glared at her daughter. "You knew of this?" It was more statement than question. Lady Elizabeth knelt beside her mother and spoke softly. "Lady Jael sent a note. I did not want you to worry. I thought she would return quickly and you need never know of it."

"But why would she even consider such a thing? Foolish – foolish girl! We have a house filled with servants, warriors – "

"Your Highness," Crispus said, "if I may, Lady Jael is a bit impulsive, but she is also very wise. We must trust to her reasoning. Whatever purpose drove her forth, I believe 'twas best. Perhaps Young Will needed her. She is quite skilled as a healer."

"It is all too shocking, and as for need, we have need of her here as well."

"Oh my dears," Lady Blessingstock said. "Why dost thou fret and carry on so? It is obviously God's plan that has occurred. Now let us settle ourselves and believe the best. During the magistrate's tirade, I dressed as a servant and worked¯"

Lady Elizabeth quickly interrupted her. "Please, Aunt, not now."

Lady Blessingstock stared back at her for several long moments. She looked from one face to another and then reached over to pat Lady Elizabeth's hand. "Quite right." She turned to Crispus and nodded her head. "Master Crispus, please may we continue? We need God's word to strengthen us, we need prayer and then I will ring for tea, how will that be?"

Crispus began to quote words from memory, finishing what he had begun earlier. He spoke quickly. Lady Elizabeth returned to her seat and folded her hands in her lap. Lady Bethalyn closed her eyes.

"As to the rest, my brethren, be strong in the Lord, and in the power of his might; put on the whole armour of God, for your being able to stand against the wiles of the devil, because we have not the wrestling with blood and flesh, but with the principalities, with the authorities, with the world-rulers of the darkness of this age, with the spiritual things of the evil in the heavenly places; because of this take ye up the whole armour of God, that ye may be able to resist in the day of the evil, and all things having done – to stand."

He ended with a prayer and in the silence that followed, he heard the cooing of the doves nestled in the eaves near the chimney. Outside, where the sun reflected off of the glistening snow, children played, their voices carrying across the great white expanse. Beyond the vale, he knew many lives hung in the balance as the dark clouds of evil threatened, but here, peace reigned. The women of the household of Wrenook breathed deeply its refreshing fragrance and settled in to wait out the storm.

The abductors made camp that night in a well protected cove similar to the one Jael had camped in so long ago. Hidden in the midst of their tethered horses, she waited for just the right moment to approach. One of the men had built a fire beside a quiet stream. He butchered several conies and dropped them into a pot with herbs from his supply. The fragrant smell filled the close canyon.

Jael's eyes moved from the cook and his fire to the surrounding area, silently placing each of the nine men. Last, she checked the dark overhang of rock, just above the horses, where she knew Young Will lay waiting.

She closed her eyes and worshipped God. "In Your hands," she whispered. As she stepped forth, she spoke words in the ancient tongue to reassure the horses and keep them quiet.

The cook stirred the pot of bubbling stew, breathing in its aroma. Afterwards, he crouched near the stream. While his back was turned, Jael drew near and dropped a fistful of powdered endergazen into the bubbling pot. She cast a quick look about her, saw no eyes watching and stirred the stew again before moving away to the place where Adrina sat, still bound hand and foot. A guard stood near her, his back to the wall.

Jael crouched near Adrina and leaned forward until her lips were close to Adrina's ear. "Adrina," she whispered. Adrina's eyes grew large.

Jael kept her eyes on the guard. "Do not be afraid, help is nigh."

Adrina swallowed hard and lowered her eyes.

"If they offer you food, don't eat it – or at the least, eat very little." Then Jael stood and backed slowly away, watching for movement around her. Beneath her foot, a twig snapped. The guard turned, he strained his eyes to see into the darkness. At the fire, an ember glowed and popped loudly, sending sparks into the air. He relaxed and turned away again. Jael stood still as stone until certain of her safety.

The cook scooped up bowls full of stew and handed them out to the men. While the guard walked to the fire to get food for himself and his prisoner, Jael retreated into the shadows and found the trail out of the canyon. As she passed by, one of the horses whinnied and tossed his head. The others stomped and snorted as they sensed her presence. She stepped quickly through their midst so her prints in the snow would be obliterated. A sentry strode forward, his weapon drawn. He raised his nose into the air like an animal sniffing the breeze.

Jael found Young Will at attention, his sword drawn, his eyes on the last sentry. She touched his hand and he turned.

"That's uncanny," he whispered. "I never discerned you at all." They sat down, their eyes on the campsite. He leaned close and whispered, "You were successful?"

"Aye, and I gave a warning to Adrina as well. I do not know what she thought of it." She grinned at Young Will and shrugged. "Voices speaking out of empty space." Jael was almost giddy with the success of her first mission.

"Perhaps it will lend credence to your message," he said with a crooked smile. "How long must we wait?"

"Within the hour they will grow quite weary. I am concerned about this outer sentry, however. I did not notice that he ate."

"There, someone carries a vessel to him. I will watch to see that he empties it. I may have to use this yet." He rose slightly to put away his sword. "Now we must discuss the next stage of our mission."

"I will go straight to Adrina and loose her bonds," Jael said.

Will nodded. "In the meantime, I will release the horses and scatter them."

"You'd better save out one for Adrina, unless you were hoping to carry her on yours." She cast a mischievous glance at him. He narrowed his eyes at her.

"I will keep one of their horses."

They watched in silence for a time before Young Will turned back to her. "You have not told me how you do ... ah ... what you do."

"I cannot really say, other than to tell you how it happens, or perhaps how it began." She held his gaze. "It happens when I meditate."

"That's some powerful meditation then, Lady. While you are transparent, do you walk normally or can you fly?" He waved his hand in front of his face, as if to punctuate his last question.

She chuckled. "I do not fly, Young Will. I must walk as you do." Though she did sometimes move swiftly. No need to tell all.

"So is it like the disappearing trail? Do you think the two things are related?"

She frowned. "It does feel a bit like the disappearing trail and as for being related, that remains a mystery. I have no memory of my father or anyone else in my family relating such an occurrence."

"That does not mean it did not happen."

"Yes, though it seems I would have been told, but my father – as he lay dying – he was barely able to speak. He meant to teach me so much more."

Young Will's eyes searched her face. "That must have been awful for you."

Jael was quiet. She had never spoken of it to anyone, not even William. *Too awful for words.* She watched the camp.

"You have never said, Aunt – what happened to Deborah – your grandmother?"

His words were barely audible. Jael was taken by surprise. She had not thought about Deborah for a long time. "She ... went away."

"She left you – all alone?"

Jael turned to look at him, observed the expression of his face. "She died."

For a long time, they said nothing. He settled back against the cold canyon wall and watched in silence.

Finally she spoke, and it seemed to startle Young Will. "I think it must have been her heart. I thought, at the time perhaps it broke, as they say." His eyes were on her as she continued, "I did all I knew to do. I prayed, I begged God, just as the two of us – Grandmere and I – had done for my father."

She drew a deep breath and released it slowly, watched the vapor leave her lips. It appeared to crystallize in the frigid darkness, lit only by the reflection of moonlight on snow. "She wanted to go, I think. 'I dinna wish to leave ye, lass,' she said to me, 'but I am not so strong as I used to be, and I find I kinna go on.'"

"She wanted me to walk with her, one more time to the thicket. I knew why it was she wanted to go there. Within the thicket, we buried our dead. She said she wished to visit them, but I knew she would stay." Jael turned to look at Young Will and wondered, for a moment, whether he regretted having asked her such a question. When he did not speak, she finished her narrative. "I left her there, as she wished. 'Sing me a song, my love,' she said, and so I did. I went as far as the brook and I sat down there beside the water. I waited and I sang. I sang all of her favorite psalms and songs – everything I could remember. Just as the sun rose, a gentle peace filled my heart and I knew … she was gone."

"Were you not afraid, Aunt?" he whispered. "Being left there, all alone."

She smiled into his eyes. "She was free of pain. To see her own son suffer so. It killed her. She died a thousand deaths that night."

"I am sorry, Aunt, if I have caused you discomfort, I feel I may have overstepped – "

She laid her hand on his arm. "Nay, you did not. I am glad I have spoken of it. I am glad it was you." She smiled into his eyes. "For you will make a fine tale of it. A heroic epic. They will sing of it around the campfires and Deborah will live again. She would be proud nephew, she would be very proud, indeed."

Young Will smiled. "You know me well. I have already been forming the words in my mind as you spoke. I shall try to do her honor."

She looked away again, her eyes drawn to the fireside. "I believe they tire. The time draws nigh. Have you taken a count?"

He stood slowly. "One of them has walked into the darkness."

"I will watch there, if you want to check for the others." While her eyes stayed focused on that dark corner, she continued, "Did you notice if Adrina ate?"

"I could not see; they stood in shadows." As he spoke, one of the men stumbled and nearly fell. Then he sat down and leaned back until he was flat on the ground. "One down," he whispered.

They counted eight who were either already asleep or well on their way. Still the one who had entered the darkness had not returned. Finally, Will moved forward. "I will go check on that one. You make your way to the Princess."

Jael glanced at him and smiled. "She would not like that name."

"All the more reason to use it." He gripped her arm and paused. "Take care, Aunt. I would not want to lose you."

She smiled up at him. "I love you too, Will."

He bowed his head to her and moved away.

She climbed down on the opposite side. Before entering the campsite, she stood quite still and closed her eyes. Once inside her protective cocoon, she lost track of Will, but knew that he would be watching out for her. Swift, but cautious, she made her way around the perimeter of the camp to the place where Adrina sat, wide-eyed.

"I am here," Jael whispered, reaching out for Adrina's hands. She quickly cut through the cords and then moved around to her feet.

Adrina looked about her and whispered, "My lady, how is this possible? How is it that I cannot see you? Are you ... dead?"

Jael could not help the laughter that bubbled up, though she did manage to keep her voice low. "It is a gift, dear one. You must thank the good Lord, for it is His doing entirely. Do not be afraid, soon you will see me and another, who is most concerned for your safety."

A soft intake of breath preceded Adrina's response. "Will has come?"

Jael looked into the girl's eyes. "Aye, he has and is most eager to see you. Now come, we must get away quickly." Already, she could hear a noise among the horses and knew that Will must be there, setting them free. As she turned, it was not Will who stood there, but another of the abductors, his evil eyes bearing down on Adrina. Adrina paled and took a backward step. The man shot forward, almost throwing himself at her, all the while crying out in his guttural tongue. Still unseen, Jael placed herself between Adrina and the man. Her knife sunk into the soft flesh just below his ribcage.

"Run!" she cried.

Adrina ran as fast as she was able, which was not very, since she had been bound for so long. When she stumbled, Will caught her up in his arms. He looked about for Jael.

"Where are you?"

"I am right behind you!"

The fallen sentry did not move, so Jael assumed that his wound, together with the herb, had done its work. She pushed on, trying not to think about what she had done and trying hard to hide the fact that he had caught her with the end of his sword. She kept a constant pressure on her side, not knowing how badly she may be hurt. When they finally made it to the horses, Will lifted her almost effortlessly into the saddle. Adrina sat upon a sleek Arabian that had belonged to one of the abductors. The other horses had scattered. Young Will mounted his horse and led them down a winding trail towards Duflec. They would need to travel most of the night.

Jael placed her hand inside her garments, endeavoring to discern the extent of her injury. It was bleeding a bit more than she liked. She reached into her saddlebag and pulled out a soft bundle. Working with one hand, she managed to open it and sprinkle the dried herbs into her other palm, while doing her best to hold on. She pressed the herbs into the wet cloth of her undershirt and pressed it tightly against the wound. Then she tightened her outer garments and wrapped the rawhide belt around her waist and secured it.

"That will have to do for now," she whispered. Her vision blurred with the acute pain.

Adrina's mind ran along very different avenues. She could not stop thinking about the things that Jael had spoken to her. " … another who is most concerned for your safety." She watched his back as he rode before her, now and again darting a glance over his shoulder. She would not meet his gaze. Ever since that first day in the library, she had thought about him. Each time he came into a room, she would blush.

On the day he and Crispus had confronted her about their suspicions regarding her heritage, she had run from the room, unable to look at either of them. Now she wondered whether they may be right and almost hoped it was true, for she had heard of the strictness of the queen. Lady Bethalyn would never allow her precious grandson to marry a commoner of unknown origins.

Still she resisted the thought. *I will not allow my hopes to soar, only to be dashed in pieces.* She turned to look behind her where Jael rode. The lady's head was bowed. "You must thank the good Lord." Jael's words came back to her. Was that what her ladyship was doing now?

Chapter 23 – Wild River

Jael's head swam as bile rose in her throat. She would not be sick! She twisted the reins around her fingers and drew in a ragged, pain-filled breath. She and Adrina were waiting while Young Will ran ahead to spy out the entrance to the stronghold at Duflec. She squinted into the waning light. The settlement stood in silent splendor, heavy drifts of snow giving the impression of abandonment.

Young Will returned and mounted his horse. As Jael drew up beside him, he said, "They're well protected. Best to ride in as though unaware of their tactics." He urged his horse forward. Jael and Adrina followed.

A light flashed in the distance as a sentry lit a torch. On the opposite side another torch was lit. Within moments the three visitors were surrounded. Young Will dismounted as an elderly man stepped forward and bowed.

"Beg pardon, young sir, but we has to take care these days. Us is all alone here, mostly old men like me," he nodded to a growing throng of onlookers, " … and them womens and childurns."

Young Will dismounted. "Do not apologize, sir. I am well aware that every able-bodied man has gone to fight."

They gripped forearms and the man bowed towards Jael and Adrina. He straightened and cocked his head to look up at Young Will. "Orly Ginterman at your service, sir, we offer ye sustenance and the warmth of our fires, if ye would but come inside. There ye may give us what news ye have of the outside world."

"Pleased to make your acquaintance, Orly Ginterman, I am Will Morgan. We will gladly accept your offer and ask that ye give shelter as well to our mounts."

The elderly man waved his hand and two young boys ran forward to lead the horses away. Young Will helped the ladies to dismount and gathered their gear. Together, they followed the man inside.

Near the entrance, Young Will leaned in close to Jael. "You walk so slowly Aunt," he whispered. "You are too tired, I think. I will ask for a bed, that you may rest."

She shook her head. "Nay, dear nephew, I'll be all right. A bit of nourishment is all I need." *Along with a goodly dose of herbs.*

Jael found a seat in a dark corner and leaned heavily against the wall. Her eyes wanted to close at once, and she had to fight to stay alert. Adrina drew near. "My lady, are you truly all right?"

By now, she could not even nod and her tonque felt swollen. "Tired ... only tired, is all." After Adrina left to help the woman of the house, Jael rummaged through her saddlebags looking for herbs. Her hands shook violently, making the search more difficult. She finally found what she needed and held it in her lap until Adrina returned with a steaming cup of tea. Jael remembered the native tea here. It was strong but quite restorative. When Adrina had gone again, she dropped a few leaves into the hot liquid and stirred it slowly. When she had taken a drink, she sat back and leaned her head against the granite wall of the cavehouse. Though frigid and damp outside, the interior of the cave was cozy and warm. The warmth soon took its toll on Jael.

Young Will smiled to see Jael napping. His eyes found their way to another face, so like hers. It was good to have Adrina near. Though she kept her eyes averted as she draped a pelt over Jael, he thought he detected a slight rosiness in her cheek. She was aware of his attention.

Orly Ginterman approached, holding a stool in each hand. He set them down before the fire and motioned for Will to sit. "So tell me young man," he said, "how goes the battle?"

Will sat down on the rough wooden stool and faced Orly. "I do not know, for I have been in Cragmorton until recently."

Orly creased his wooly brow and rubbed his chin. "Cragmorton? I seen a man not long ago o'Cragmorton, a tall young man by name of Toldar."

Young Will smiled. "He is my uncle."

Orly jumped up and bowed again. "Then ye are of the royal house and here I have ye in me humble old hovel."

Young Will shook his head. "'Tis as good as a castle and even more so, for it is warm and the food smells quite fine. You'll hear no complaint from us, sir."

Orly nodded toward Jael. "Not from that one there, for sure and certain. He's a bit fagged, I think. Shall we get him to a bed?"

Young Will smiled at the reference to his aunt. If not for the man's assumption, he surely would have introduced her as female. "Nay sir, we have not long to rest. We must away ere the dawn." He lowered his voice. "And I must warn you sir, we may be followed. Those who would track us could be quite dangerous."

"Aye well, we have come against worse, I can tell ye that. Ye go by the river then?"

"Aye, sir and were hoping to leave our horses under your protection, though you may want to lose one of them. I'm afraid it was ... ah ... borrowed from those who track us."

Orly leaned forward, his hands upon his knees and laughed out loud. "Borrowed, is it? Well, we shall give it a good home sir, where no one will soon find it. Ye needn't worry over it. We is used to such here."

Adrina tried to be discreet as she ate the food given her. She was so hungry, and it felt so good to eat. When she had finished, she went again to check on Jael and found that she had not eaten her food. Adrina raised the cup and looked at it, noticed the strange leaves floating in the bottom. She frowned. *What herb is this?* A soft step behind her brought her head up. Young Will stood near.

"I'm afraid we must waken her." His voice was low. "Dawn approaches and we must be on our way."

Adrina bit her lower lip, wondering whether to speak her concern, but decided against it. She nodded and turned to Jael.

Jael woke to Adrina's nudge. Her eyelids still heavy from sleep, she peered about to see whether they were alone. "I must have dozed off."

"Yes, my lady, you did and you have not yet eaten." Adrina held a wooden bowl in front of Jael's face. "I think you should at least try to take a bit of this porridge. It is quite palatable."

Jael sat forward and picked up the spoon. "I remember the porridge well. I stayed here some time back you know."

Under Adrina's gaze, Jael took careful, tiny bites of the porridge. Adrina lifted Jael's cup to her nose and sniffed the contents. "Why have ye a need for drumwort, my lady?"

Jael glanced around the dimly lit room before whispering, "Say nothing of this to Young Will. I am all right, just in need of a – "

Adrina tilted her head sideways. "Blood thickener? I know what it is, my lady, and I know its uses." She turned away and asked the woman of the house for water and cloth to use for bandages.

The woman covered her mouth with her hand. "Him is hurt my lady?"

Adrina nodded.

The woman led them to a smaller room behind the fireplace. "Here you will have more privacy." A few minutes later, she returned with a basin of warm water, a cloth for washing and another length of cloth to use as a bandage. Her gaze slid over Jael and her brows knit together in a frown, but she made no comment. She pulled a curtain across the opening and left them alone. Adrina helped Jael to sit down on the bed.

"I do not know how to thank you, Adrina."

Adrina leaned back and looked at her. "You wish to thank me? 'Tis my fault that you are injured."

Jael slowly removed her outer clothing. "No, it is not. It was through no fault of your own. You stood in my stead there. It should have been me."

"Let's not argue particulars. I am as grateful to you as can be for what you have done."

As Jael removed the blood soaked shirt, Adrina drew in a breath. "I hope you do not have internal damage, my lady. If you are bleeding within, you could ..."

Jael paused and their eyes met. "Do not say the word. I will not. I have drunk enough drumwort to stop whatever damage there may have been."

"Aye, if you do not jostle it overmuch. You must be careful."

Adrina cleaned the wound and packed it tightly, wrapped it with the cloth and tied it off. Then she helped Jael back into her clothing. Once she was on her feet, Adrina picked up the pan of soiled water and the rag and led the way out into the other room. Jael gazed about, hoping the men were still out. The woman of the house came immediately and took the pan and the rag. She set them aside and bowed.

"Is there anything else ye need, ladies?"

Adrina and Jael exchanged glances. The woman had sharp eyes. She was not fooled by men's apparel.

"You have been most accommodating," Adrina said. "We are so very grateful for your help."

Jael touched the woman's arm. "God bless you."

The woman bowed again. "It be an honor, Your Majesty."

A chill ran up Jael's spine at the words. The woman knew exactly who she was. "May I know your name?"

The woman smiled behind her hand and lowered her head. "I am Berta of Ginterman."

Jael nodded. "I will not forget your kindness, Berta of Ginterman. May your life be blessed."

As they passed through the doorway, Jael leaned close to Adrina's ear. "Please say nothing of my injury to Will. I do not want him overly concerned."

Adrina gave her a stern glance. "You do not have to worry on that head, unless you grow weaker. Then I will have no choice, my lady."

From Duflec's outer walls, Jael and Adrina followed as Will led the way to the river. "The snow is not so deep here," he said over his shoulder. "It will be easier going. Have you heard anything, Aunt? Are we being pursued?"

Jael was embarrassed to say that she had not thought to try. Will eyed her closely.

As Adrina passed, he said, "I do not like the grayness of her complexion. She is too weary." He stepped forward and offered Jael his arm to lean upon.

She looked up at him. "You know I can hear you?"

He smiled as she accepted his help, then closed her eyes and turned her head about, listening. After several moments of silence, she spoke.

"Footfall upon hard rock, no words pass ... " Her head jerked up to observe the sky. "They are some distance yet. We shall easily escape them upon the water – " Her voice broke as she was taken by a sharp pain. Her eyes glazed over and she nearly fainted. Young Will caught her up in his arms and set her down on a nearby boulder.

"Aunt, what is it?"

Adrina rushed forward and opened her mouth to speak, but Jael caught her eye and shook her head. She swallowed and pushed her hair back. "I am well enough, dear nephew, and will be just fine sitting in a small boat. Is it nearby?"

"Aye, but are you certain? My uncle will never forgive me if I let anything happen to you."

"You needn't worry. I will last." Her eyes held his. "There is nothing that will keep me from his side."

"I believe that at least. Allow me to carry you then." He did not wait for a reply, but lifted and carried her.

The noise of the water soon drowned out all other sound.

"It is too loud," Jael said to Will.

"Aye, it runs high. Our journey will go all the faster can we manage to stay afloat."

"We will manage."

He looked at her and then back at Adrina. "I hope you are a swimmer, my lady."

From her perch in his arms, Jael could see Adrina. She had to run to keep up with Young Will's long strides. Jael wondered about her. She said so little. Did she realize how much her life had changed in so short a spell? In Cragmorton she had been an outcast, now she was royalty.

Young Will set down his burden and climbed among the rocks. Here he found the boat exactly as Orly had said. He turned it over and held it in place until the ladies were aboard. Two much-used oars were attached to the sides. He untied them and laid them on the bottom of the boat. When everything was ready, he pushed the boat into the water and jumped in. He had not a moment to lose as the swiftly moving current caught and carried them out into the center of the river. There he stayed with little trouble until they hit the first of the rapids. Adrina's eyes grew large at the sight. Jael often squeezed hers shut as wave after wave of pain shot through her body.

It was not only pain that she fought, but nausea and an overall feeling of malaise. This worried her, for she feared infection. She steadied herself somewhat and forced her eyes open. The river was rough and cold. They must stay afloat. She had little confidence that she could survive a dunking in her present condition.

Adrina kept a constant vigil, watching over Jael. After the first rapids were behind them, the two sat together in the bottom of the boat. Jael leaned heavily upon her and sang softly in the ancient tongue, to shore up her strength.

Several times, Jael saw Adrina raise her eyes to watch Young Will's struggle against the river. The time would come when those two would admit their feelings for one another. As another sharp pain struck, she sincerely hoped to be around to witness it.

They had been on the river for several hours when they entered calmer waters. Adrina's eyes drank in the unfamiliar scenery. Great old trees spread their gnarled branches over the banks, some still dropping golden leaves upon the water. The sky above those overhanging limbs was white with clouds. Before day's end, snow began to fall again.

As the light faded, Young Will scanned the banks of the river, searching for a good place to make camp. He finally brought the boat ashore upon a sandy beach and only then did he notice Jael. His face went ashen as he drew near. He dropped down upon one knee.

"She has been unconscious for some time now," Adrina said.

His eyes were accusing as he looked at her. "Why did you not tell me?"

Adrina swallowed. "She made me promise not to."

Young Will lifted Jael and carried her the short distance to a suitable campsite. There he laid her gently down and turned back to face Adrina. "You have some knowledge of the healing herbs, I believe?"

"Aye sir, but … her illness stems from an injury. I wanted to tell you, but she would not allow me."

His eyes narrowed, his voice was stern. "What injury?"

Adrina was unruffled, for she had expected a negative reaction. She kept her voice even and low, hoping to calm his frazzled nerves. "At the last, when I was attacked, she stepped between the attacker and myself. She took a blow meant for me." Her eyes filled with tears as she gave the account of the skirmish.

Young Will moved near and reached out his hand, but did not touch her. "Do not trouble yourself, my lady. It was in no way your fault." He turned away and set about making camp. When he brought wood, Adrina made a fire, freeing him to find food.

While he was away, she dressed Jael's wound. It looked clean. She gave a relieved sigh. There did not seem to be any infection, which spoke well of Jael's early attention to it. Adrina found herbs in Jael's saddlebags and a small cast iron dish among Jael's things. She went to fetch water for tea and settled it among the embers to boil.

Adrina was attempting to feed Jael a bit of the tea when Young Will returned. He wrapped several cleaned fish in riverweed, and buried them in the ashes.

"The wound is clean," Adrina said. "There does not seem to be any infection."

Young Will leveled his gaze at her. "You are worried about her."

She nodded. "I am concerned there may internal damage, otherwise she would not be so ill."

He dropped his head in his hands and sighed. "I do not like this. We have yet a long distance to cover. We are far from any friends. Had I known of this, I would have left you both at Duflec, where you would be safe."

Adrina gazed up at him. "I am sorry, sir. It is fully upon me."

He frowned and cast a look at Jael. "Nay, it is that willful lady there." He stood still for a moment as though contemplating their choices. He turned back to Adrina.

A wry smile softened his expression. "She is strong and will no doubt make a full recovery. Were she able, she would order me to deliver her to my uncle."

He gazed into Adrina's eyes until she could hardly breathe. Here was the reason she usually tried to avoid his gaze. She forced herself to turn back to Jael and check her brow for fever.

Chapter 24 – A Gathering of Eagles

King George, along with his advisors and highest ranking officers, descended an ancient stair to the beach below the stronghold of Coldthwaite. William's men were assembled there, awaiting the king's orders. Among them were horsemen, archers and infantry, armed with shields and swords. These were the best of the North, gathered from every region of its vast kingdom.

William dismounted and approached his father. A strong grip of fists and a long, penetrating gaze passed between them. George Horatio could hardly speak for the feelings that pressed in upon him. He held his head high and addressed the assembled men.

"I thank God for you, and that you are ready to defend our great land. Your brave stand will not go unnoticed by our great God. He will defend you as you go forth this day into battle against a dark enemy. For it is against powers and principalities that we battle, and He shall give us strength. Be strong, be of good courage, brethren. This battle shall not fail. We shall not be defeated."

He ended his speech with a strength that he did not feel. He stood back amid their wild huzzahs and scanned the ranks. His chest swelled with pride at the sight of them. Upon the ramparts and porches of the castle, the men of Coldthwaite stood, matching cheers and huzzahs with their own. Flags were lifted up alongside mighty swords. William saluted his father and then mounted his horse. William and Toldar rode with the advance force to lead them into the field of battle.

King George Horatio stood at attention, to honor the men with his presence. After they had all passed, he crossed the pebble strewn beach and climbed the steps carved into the cliff. Several times he had to stop and rest.

Eldred signaled to one of the pages. "Your Majesty, allow me to call for a chair." King George turned to look at him, blinking hard against the throbbing pain in his head. "I will rest a bit and then go on." He leaned against the granite wall. "It is only this headache. It will not leave me."

"I will send for the apothecary at once Your Majesty, by your leave."

King George pushed away from the wall and resumed his upward trek. "You may do that Eldred, with my gratitude. I must be able to stand before the enemy."

$\mathfrak{S}$everal miles away, Din Glun and his army made ready for battle. They assembled weapons of war, great tree trunks gleaned from the nearby forests to use as battering rams. Cauldrons of fat bubbled on great fires. Massive hide-filled balls would be soaked in the oil, set on fire and launched into the air. The men rolled them onto oxcarts for delivery to the front, along with huge caches of weapons.

They blackened their faces and dressed the backs of their heads with wildly painted masks to confuse the enemy. They decorated hard leather shields with the skulls of their foes.

Din Glun rode forward to make certain everything was done according to his orders. This would be the last time he would show himself. Afterward, those who wore his armor would ride in the midst of the men. He would stand upon a high hill and watch the battle.

$\mathfrak{W}$illiam and Toldar rode out to check the progress of the enemy. Throughout the long day, the good men of the North stood their ground, waiting for whatever must come. They kept a vigilant watch over the great horde whose faces were painted black.

Toldar gazed down upon them. "They have painted their faces to match their hearts." "Aye," William answered as he turned his horse around. "At least we will know our enemy. There's no mistaking who is who."

Courin met them as they rode back into the main camp. "Rondar has come," he said.

They dismounted at once and followed Courin to a secluded area set aside for them. Rondar stood as they approached.

"Good sirs," he said, addressing them as ordinary soldiers.

William bowed his head in greeting. "It is good to see you again. I had about given you up."

"I disengaged myself from their ranks some days ago. I knew 'twould not be easy, but I did not wish to wage war against my own."

"I am grateful for that at least," William said.

Toldar smiled ruefully. "One less in their ranks, will you even be missed?"

"At some point, I may've been missed. I fell overboard into Verani Basin. The moon was dark and no cry went up."

"What have you for us, then?" William asked.

"I think by now ye know his habits. However, ye may not know that he has dressed all of his commanders in identical armor to his own. Their horses resemble his also. Even those under his command do not know the difference. In reality, he keeps watch over the whole affair, beginning to end. He is encamped upon Ibor Hill."

William looked at Toldar. "That is good information. You are certain? It is not another ruse?"

"Aye, sir. I have seen the preparations with my own eyes." He stepped nearer and spoke directly to William. "There is more, good sir. He sent two raiding parties into Cragmorton. The first never reported back, so he sent a second. He sent them to bring back your women, sir, alive."

Jael's words from his vision returned to William and he cast a glance at Toldar, who was obviously agitated.

Rondar continued with haste. "No word had come from either party when I left. Benabi went out just ahead of the second raiding party, intent on giving a warning. He did not return."

Toldar was ready to set off at once for the enemy camp to find Din Glun and see whether he kept any ladies captive, but William stopped him with uplifted hand. "Hear what I have to say first, brother. Yesterday morn as I was in prayer, I saw a vision. I believe it was a vision – or perhaps a dream – though I do not think I slept. I saw my lady Jael and she spoke to me. She told me that Din Glun would attempt to convince me he had captured her, but I must not believe it. She assured me that she was safe and I would soon see her."

Toldar scoffed. "A vision, brother? You are strongly persuaded that this is fact?"

"It was quite real and yes, I am strongly persuaded." He turned back to Rondar. "Is there any way to secure proof?"

Rondar looked from one to the other. "I am at your command, good sirs."

William strode forward, deep in thought. "None but the closest advisors would know."

"Or his personal servants," Rondar said. "They would be with him upon the mount."

Toldar frowned. "Would that not be where he kept prisoners?"

Rondar shook his head. "He is devious, sir. He may keep them hidden almost anywhere, even in nearby villages."

William pushed his fingers through his hair and turned to face Rondar. "We cannot spare men to spy them out and I would not risk sending you back into the midst."

Rondar nodded. "I will ride out and see what I may learn. I will keep a distance between myself and any of that army. I do not wish to be found by them."

Toldar gripped the hilt of his sword. "This is surely not all you intend, brother? The very thought – "

William laid his hand on Toldar's shoulder. "You know I would not risk them, brother. I am convinced it is a ruse. He will only toss out that ring if he is desperate to win. It will go best for us if we can have the facts. Proceed, Rondar."

As soon as Rondar left, William strode back to his horse. "We must stay on target, Toldar. We cannot let ourselves be distracted, else he has won. Not one among our dear ladies would wish that." Just as he went to mount his horse, he cast his eyes upward. Overhead, three eagles circled. "Look there, brother. It is a sign, do you doubt it?"

Toldar shook his head. "I cannot. Rarely does one see such a sight. One eagle – two, maybe – but never three together."

Chapter 25 – The Company of Friends

Just before dawn, Jael awoke, sat up too suddenly and immediately wished she had not. Her head swam and she was nauseated. She could not get far, but managed to move a little distance from camp. She had not eaten in two days, so there was little to come up. Pain wracked her body as she heaved. Adrina, awakened by the soft sounds, rushed to her side and pressed a cool, damp cloth to Jael's forehead, then helped her back to the fire. Young Will was just returning from the water and strode quickly to them.

"She is awake," he said.

Jael gazed into his eyes. "I take it I have rested?"

"It was more than rest that took you, lady. I am not pleased with you. You should have told me of your injury."

Jael darted a look at Adrina, who turned away. "I was afraid you would halt our journey. I feel it is most imperative that we continue."

"So you have said, repeatedly, but I will not proceed until I have seen you take food."

"I am a little hungry. Have we anything to eat?"

Adrina smiled and built up the fire. Will brought more fish from the river. "I found these waiting about for us. They were a bit sluggish from the cold."

He cleaned them and hung them over the fire to cook. Adrina brought more water for the herbs. "The wound is clean and appears free of infection," she told Jael. "Do you think it is only that you have gone without food?"

"I am not feverish, but my head aches and I am a bit dizzy. Perhaps it is the lack of nourishment. I think you are right, it is some days since I have taken food."

Will smiled at her as he handed over a chunk of freshly roasted fish.

"I'm sorry I don't have anything else to offer you. Not even a bit of bread. I remember well your fondness for stonebread."

"Ah, with clotted cheese," she said, "but this is quite substantial, thank you." After eating the fish and drinking a little of the herbal mixture, Jael felt better. Except for soreness around the wound, she was somewhat recovered.

The day started with a mixture of sun and snow, which leant a strange beauty to the otherwise barren scene. The trees were devoid of leaves, being of a deciduous variety. Jael was pleased to find nut trees among them and spent a few minutes gathering some. These would provide nourishment along the way. Will seemed happy, almost chipper. Jael watched him with interest. Was it relief over her recovery, or … she turned her eyes to Adrina, who hummed as she worked. Jael smiled.

When it was time to go, Young Will loaded the boat. "Another day upon this river will put us at the basin."

"Within sight of the Haven," Jael said.

He pushed away from the shore. "Aye."

Jael turned to smile at Adrina. "I heard you speak the words of a favorite psalm of mine, 'Though I walk through the valley of the shadow of death' – "

"'I will fear no evil.' I spoke it often during my captivity." Adrina glanced towards the front of the boat. "I have not so many committed to memory as you."

Jael leaned her head back as tiny, wet snowflakes drifted down. "I grew up singing the songs of the ancients."

"Is that how you learned the forbidden tongue?"

Jael shrugged, noticing the slight turn of Young Will's head, as if to hear her answer.

"I have spoken it as long as I can remember."

Again, Will glanced over his shoulder. When he spoke, his voice echoed over the surface of the water. "I knew a man once, who spoke a similar tongue – among many others, I might add – he came from a small isle south of here, in the midst of the Great Sea."

"Of Milos, Young Will? Is this the isle of which you speak?"

He glanced at Jael again. "You know it?"

"Aye. We had a visitor of Milos when I was but a child. He spent many days in the Haven, communing with my father."

Young Will turned back to the front and paddled in silence. Jael had all but forgotten the conversation when he said, "I cannot remember the man's name, but I'll wager he was the same man that visited your esteemed father."

Jael cocked her head. "I do not remember his name either. He had a beard, mostly white. I did like him. My grandmother was quite fond of him as well. I do believe she would have gone with him, had it not been for … me."

Now Will swung completely around to gaze upon her fully. "You do not mean it? It must have been the same man." He chuckled. "It was your grandmother." He twisted back and plied the oars again. "He spoke of a beautiful lady he had met in a remote region. She played most skillfully upon the lyre and sang like a bird. He missed her sorely."

Jael smiled at his description of her grandmother. "I believe it must have been she. You have a very good memory, nephew."

Adrina leaned close to Jael. "So we draw near the place where you were born?"

"The other side of the Verani Basin, near the foot of the great falls is Verani Haven. That is where I was born and spent most of my life."

"You've heard tell of the disappearing trail?" Young Will said to Adrina.

She glanced up at him. "I have heard it spoken of in tales of the Rogan. I did not believe it, however."

"Oh you may believe it, for here sits one who has often walked its length and evidently, carries its powers within."

Adrina looked at Jael. "Is this the secret then? I have had little opportunity to question what happened back there."

Young Will chuckled softly. "Oh you'll get no answers from her."

Jael glared at Young Will's back. To Adrina, she said, "In truth, I do not know how it happens, only that it does. I would prefer that it remain a mystery. Already it seems, too many know too much."

"It is bound to happen, Aunt. Such news travels fast."

Jael changed the subject. "I see an island up ahead. Do you think we could stop there?"

"We have been at this for over half the day, I suppose I could stretch my legs a bit." They soon arrived and Young Will scouted it out before allowing the ladies free reign. "We must not forget there are enemies about."

Jael could not forget. She sat in silence for several moments, listening. "I hear little near at hand, beyond the bubbling of the water." She raised her eyes to Young Will's.

His brow creased. "What is it, Aunt?"

"A distant sound of drums, preparation for battle … " her voice trailed off.

He moved near and laid his hand upon her shoulder. "Do not be troubled, Lady. We must have faith."

She did not know whether it was realization of what lay ahead or the remnants of what lay behind, but she felt weak and vulnerable, even emotional, totally unlike herself. It was unsettling.

Adrina moved near and helped her back to the boat. "You are tired, my lady, you have only just overcome a grave injury."

A few minutes later, they were on their way again. The Ishcairne would soon widen at the point where it emptied into the Verani Basin. Jael tried to concentrate, tried to keep her mind clear of the anxieties that constantly pricked at her. She touched her side and was relieved to find it barely sore. Her ordeal must be emotional in nature. She began to sing in a low tone at first, but then was encouraged to lift her voice a little. She sang the favorite song of her childhood, to greet the Verani as they drew near its familiar shores.

Chapter 26 – Dragons

On the third day after the arrival of the northern armies at Coldthwaite, the sound of a ram's horn echoed upon the ramparts of the great castle. Down on the tidal plain, battle was imminent. As the dark warriors approached, cringee crabs scattered in all directions over the pebbly beach. William ordered Solis and his men to lay in wait, hidden from sight in caves and crevices. Once the enemy had passed, they would begin their onslaught, raining down arrows upon the rear flanks.

The dark warriors assembled themselves in long lines, making a great show of strength. Their officers galloped about on horseback, shouting orders. Dressed like any other cavalier, William and Toldar watched from a safe distance atop a high cliff overlooking the sea.

Toldar leaned forward in his saddle and nodded toward the scene below. "Do you see them?"

"Aye," William said. "I've counted perhaps ten so far. It is as Rondar said."

"What plan have ye then?"

"Rondar has not yet returned, so we cannot know where the enemy hides. We must concentrate our forces on these and trust skill over numbers again."

Toldar raised himself and gazed at William. "It has always been our strength."

"With God's help, it shall once more. Be ye ready, brother?"

"Aye, brother, go with God."

William touched his brow with his fingertips. "And you also." He returned to the castle grounds; Toldar rode to the valley where Courin led the infantry.

Another blast of the ram's horns sent the dark warriors forth, crying with a loud voice, shields high to stave off the many arrows of Toldar's archers. The infantry advanced ahead of the cavalry to clear the way for the battering rams.

Swords and spears flashed in the early morning light. Courin's men fought valiantly. Solis and his men continued to hack away at the rear flanks and succeeded in scattering a good number of weary foot soldiers.

William made a wide circuit to encourage the men and did not hesitate to climb down off his horse and join in whenever necessary. He caught an especially fierce warrior off guard and felled him with one blow. In the lull that followed, Solis approached.

"They seem to have little heart for battle," he said.

William retrieved a young patriot's sword and held it out to him. "Do not be fooled into complacency, Solis. It could be another deception."

Solis wiped sweat from his brow. "They are the trickiest devils I have ever come against."

After many well-matched skirmishes, the black army managed to push forward but a little. Late in the day, they drew back to gather their forces. The northern army was exhausted, but there were dead to bury and wounded to tend.

William strolled among the men, offering comfort where he could. He found a few of the Coldthwaitian women there also, tending the wounded. His thoughts ran to Jael and he did not interfere with them. This is exactly where she would be, if she were at Coldthwaite.

Weary, he climbed the steps to his father's room where King George paced to and fro before the fire, his hands clasped behind his back. He halted when William entered.

"Pastor Emrich has just left me. Many have died this day."

William stood at attention. "Aye – on both sides, Father."

"That is little comfort." The king shook his head and sighed. "It chafes me hard to stand by and do nothing as my countrymen fight."

"It is their duty to fight, as it is mine, Father." William's voice softened as he watched his father's face. "I can only imagine how you feel. It would chafe me as well, but you must remain here. The men look up and see you on the ramparts and it gives them encouragement."

"Much more so did they see me in the fray."

William shook his head. "I cannot agree. We have discussed this before. I would not risk you." He turned and walked to the large oaken table where many parchments lay scattered, leaned on the palms of his hands and dropped his head. "We cannot all be on the field, Father. If no one of us survives, where would the kingdom be?"

"Where will the kingdom be if there is no heir to the throne?" King George dropped his head into his hands. William raised up to look at him.

"I do know your anguish, Father, but how would it aid the kingdom to see you brutalized on the field of battle? You have observed the conflict, do you feel physically able to contend?"

The king pressed his fingertips against his temples and drew in a jagged breath. He dropped his hands and turned his gaze upon his son. "I know the truth of what you are saying, but it does not lessen the burning pain of it. My eyes ache from the watching. How much blood must be spilt?"

William stood and faced him. "This enemy will be defeated Father, and soon, I believe."

The King's brow knit as he contemplated his son's words. "Pastor Emrich said he dreamt of a great lot of sea dragons. They came ashore and trampled the enemy underfoot. What do you think of it?"

"Perhaps Pastor Emrich has eaten some bad beef," William said with a wry smile. In two long strides, he closed the space between them and laid his hand on his father's shoulder. "Father, do not be troubled. We have been in dire circumstances before. God is for us and He will not allow us to be put to shame."

When his father did not respond, William took a good look at him. He seemed to have aged ten years in two summers. His hair was grayer and his eyes were red and puffy, his complexion pale. A lump rose in his throat. "Father, I must spend time in the chapel. I need direction for the morrow."

The king searched his eyes. "Speak to Pastor Emrich then, see what you think of his dream."

William clasped his father's forearm and dipped his head. "I will do that, Father." He picked up a lamp and crossed into the main gallery on the way to the chapel. Here, an unfamiliar sight caught his eye. He lifted his light and examined it. One lamp was not enough, so he lit a candelabrum. It was Master Abraham's tapestry. He touched it with his fingertips. "Fine work," he whispered.

How many days must it have taken to work so fine a picture? He smiled at the likeness of himself and his lady. She wore the dark blue cloak and just the barest of halos was cast about her bright hair. William shook his head. She would not like that. His eyes found at last, the pair of doves resting upon the cornice of the castle, gazing out over the kingdom. It was a small thing, but it pierced his heart. *God speaks sometimes in whispers.*

After dousing the extra candles, he proceeded to the chapel.

Pastor Emrich had written the details of the dream. "It was so real," he said, using his hands in grandiose fashion to emphasize his words. "The dragons had great white ears that fanned out on either side and they swam very fast. Fire came out of their mouths and as they made land, they walked with powerful steps. Their tails lashed about, sweeping over the earth and with their tongues, they licked up the blood of their prey."

William was impressed. "That was some dream, Pastor. What is your impression of its meaning?"

"A great army comes over the sea … " he paused for a moment, " … to wreak havoc, I do not doubt. I only hope it is for us and not against us. Though I cannot think who it would be."

"Dragons. If only Lady Jael were here. No doubt she would know."

Pastor Emrich nodded slowly. "I thought His Highness would know, he is usually so discerning."

William frowned. "He is distracted of late."

"With good reason and his health is not good."

William narrowed his eyes at the pastor. "His health – he said nothing to me."

"Nay, Lord William, you know he is a proud man. He would not say, but he is not himself." He rolled up the scroll containing the dream. "I do not think he sleeps well."

"That explains a lot. He is greatly troubled and wishes to be in the fight."

"I have seen it as well. I had decided it was best to pray and not to advise on such a subject. I have to say, he is a much easier man when your mother is in residence."

William cast a wry smile at the pastor.

Pastor Emrich nodded his head. "I will leave you then, my lord that you may address your Heavenly Father." He bowed, then made eye contact with William. "May you find what it is you seek."

"Thank you Pastor. Go with God." William knelt before the altar and bowed his head.

The night watch called twice before William exited the chapel. On the way, he stopped to comfort the anxious guards. Never in all their days had they seen an enemy so bold as to come near the gates of Coldthwaite. It would set the heart of any man to quaking. As he strode away, he sang.

"Lift up, O gates, your heads,
Be lifted up, O ancient doors,
Doth come the king of glory!
Who is this – `king of glory?'
Jehovah – strong and mighty,
Jehovah, mighty in battle."

Even before dawn's light spread across the sky, Benabi stood outside William's tent. He was dressed in the traditional garb of the Milosian warrior – billowing trousers bound tightly at the waist and ankles and snug leather vest over a black shirt.

William grasped Benabi's forearm. "What news have you?"

Benabi sliced the air with his arm. "Look out and tell me what you see."

Out upon the waters a hundred great ships stood at anchor – all bearing the sign of the dragon. As he beheld the sight, William bowed his head in silent worship. He raised his eyes to connect with Benabi's.

"For just such a miracle I have prayed and only last night, was assured of its coming."

Benabi stood, his feet spread apart and a palm resting on either hip.

"Each of those vessels carries one hundred warriors ready for battle, my lord."

William smiled at the traditional stance of the Milosian warrior. As Benabi's words sank in, he turned to gaze at the ships, mentally calculating the numbers.

Benabi gestured to a servant standing nearby and looked back at William. "Where would you have me send them?"

When William entered his father's chamber, he found Eldred helping him into his armor. William stood to one side to allow Benabi entry. The king's eyes widened. "Benabi – is that you?"

Benabi bowed before the king. "Yes, Your Greatness, it is I. And you ... I hope you are well?"

The king sighed. "As well as may be."

"Father, please allow me to interrupt," William said. "If you will only cast a glance out of your window."

Dawn lent an ethereal glow over billowing fog, but between puffs of vapor, the dragon ships appeared like ghosts dancing on the surface of the water.

"What in the … ?" King George turned his head to gaze first at his son and then at Benabi. "Is this your doing, Benabi?"

Again, Benabi bowed. "The Milosians and their allies are at your service, Your Majesty."

Under cover of thick fog, the Milosians disembarked and marched ashore. Upon the high reaches, Din Glun observed their progress. He knew the sign of the dragon quite well. He would wait just a little while longer, and then he would play his trump card. He did not fear the massive army of the Milosians, any more than he feared these heathen northerners. They meant little to him. He lifted his staff, shook it at the sky and cried out.

"I am the most powerful man upon the earth, I will do battle and I will triumph!"

Toldar stood on an outcropping of rock, straining his eyes against the mist that lay heavy over the blood-strewn battlefield. Until it lifted, the black army would not blow its horns. He could see neither the coast or its shores, but a sound reverberated through the vale as the sentries sent out the report.

"The Dragon Ships of Milos have come," they said.

Close on the heels of this news came a song. Toldar smiled. Most among Din Glun's men would not understand its words.

The same psalm William sang in the halls of Castle Coldthwaite was now being sung by his men. Their voices drifted over the valley and through the mist, to echo on the surrounding hills and water. In the dales, Solis' men took it up. Soon the Milosians heard it, and those who spoke the language joined in the song.

As the mist cleared, Toldar watched and marveled. The sound struck fear in the hearts of the black warriors, but they appeared unable to move. They were hemmed in on all sides. There was no alternative but to fight. The dark army would never surrender. In the frosty air of early morning, the ram's horns blew. Toldar ran down the steep incline, mounted his horse and rode swiftly to the battlefield, ready to join William and the energized men of the North.

Still it was no short work. The black army wielded their great strength, refusing to give up easily. Toldar and William fought side by side. At one point, they stood back to back, against almost overwhelming odds when the enemy made a strong push for the castle walls. As great stones flew over their heads, they fought with renewed vigor.

A few of the stones hit their mark, crashing into the heavy walls of Coldthwaite. Flame-tipped arrows followed. Fires jumped at their landing sites, sending the warriors stationed inside scurrying to extinguish them.

The Milosian army pressed in on all sides and finally cleared a path to the sea. They captured scores of black-painted warriors. They would return them to their homeland to reap the consequences of their sins. By the end of a long and exhausting day, the outcome of the battle was clear.

Benabi stood before King George along with William, Toldar, Solis and Courin. "A message was carried down from Din Glun, Your Majesty." He bowed to the king, then in turn to William and Toldar. "My lords, by your leave, I will translate."

"Please, sir, do so at once," King George said.

Benabi unrolled the parchment. "To the infidel king," he read. "The golden-haired lady sorceress dwells with me now. If the son of the infidel king wishes to reclaim her, he must meet me upon the battlefield."

The men shot worried glances at one another while King George gazed into the fire. Without turning his head to look at him, he asked, "What think ye of this, my son?"

William met Benabi's gaze.

Benabi gave a quick shake of his head. "I advise against it, my lord."

William shrugged his shoulders. "I will not do it, for he does not have my wife."

Solis moved forward. "He does have someone, my lord – we have seen her."

King George spun around to address William. "Do you know of a certainty that he does not have Lady Jael?"

William rubbed the back of his neck. "As certain as I can be." He exhaled and looked from one face to another. Would they believe him?

"From her own lips I have heard it, though I cannot say how."

King George frowned into the fire. One hand rested on the hilt of his sword; with the other, he smoothed his beard. "Then it must be so. For I know, were there a way, she would speak to you. Ha! – sorceress – he calls her a sorceress." He chuckled. After a moment he turned back to his counselors. "Who then does he have? And what harm would come to her – whoever she is – if we do not answer this?"

"None if we do this correctly, Your Majesty," Benabi said. "If I may be so bold as to answer."

King George nodded. "Do your best my friend, and we will listen. What is your plan?"

Chapter 27 – To the Gates of Hell

In full armor, William and Toldar watched Din Glun's forces gather in the valley below them. Lodan snorted and stamped the ground as riders broke away from the main force and approached. One among them wore Din Glun's armor. A lone warrior stayed by the woman to guard her as the leaders faced one another.

Through an interpreter, Din Glun spoke. "You have made a wise decision, thou son of the king."

Lodan pranced again and William tightened his grip on the reins. "What choice had I?"

When he heard the translation, Din Glun turned his head to one side. His black eyes swept across the ranks before him.

"State your terms," William said.

"My terms? Oh you mistake me, esteemed Prince, I only wish to return to you your sorceress wife. I have no further need of her, though I must say, I did enjoy her … entertainments." He threw his head back and laughed. "You have won, you see?" As his words were translated, Din Glun wrapped his fingers around his lance, spat out a stream of black liquid and wiped his lips on the back of his other hand.

William made no response to Din Glun. When Toldar's hand found the hilt of his sword, William held up his hand.

Din Glun made a gurgling sound. "Ah, I see – you do not trust me – how pleasing. I thought you would not." He signaled with his hand and the warrior who waited beside the woman reached forward and pulled the cord that bound the woman's cloak. While everyone watched, the cloak fell away, revealing a garish, painted face upon a straw figure. The flaxen braid was affixed to the head of a dummy.

William jerked his head back to look at Din Glun, who glared at the figure and then turned angry eyes upon the man who had loosed the rope.

Benabi removed his helmet and bowed to Din Glun. Before anyone could react, Din Glun sent his lance deep into William's chest, jerked his horse around and disappeared into the midst of his men.

Benabi ran after Din Glun, sword drawn, but in the din and confusion that followed, Din Glun disappeared into the mist. Toldar joined Benabi, but they were bombarded by look-alikes and lost track of the real Din Glun.

His hands at his side, Benabi stared after the retreating enemy. How could they have lost the man again? Din Glun had seemed exultant, no doubt because he had killed the heir to the throne. Only a few of his warriors survived to ride with him, however.

Toldar and Benabi returned to the vale of Coldthwaite. The valley was littered with bodies and still the Coldthwaitians and Milosians fought side by side. When they returned to Coldthwaite Castle, a guard ushered them into the king's drawing room, where they stood in the presence of King George Horatio. Soon after their arrival, Solis entered, followed closely by William.

William crossed to his father and grasped his forearm. Their eyes locked for a moment. Benabi stepped forward and addressed William.

"It is good to see you, my lord. I hope your young captain survived also?"

William averted his eyes. "Courin has fallen, Benabi."

Benabi shook his head. "I am very sorry to hear it."

"He knew the risk," King George said. "His great courage in taking William's place will be highly honored."

William looked into the flames. "It was a good death, as we are so … fond of saying."

The king sat down in his chair and sighed. "Had Courin not stepped up, it would have been you. I could not have borne it."

William spun to face his father and started to say something, but instead gave a curt nod and strode from the room, with Toldar right behind him.

King George did not call after them. Emotions ran high and he knew his son would soon conquer them. He looked at Benabi. "I am sorry for his abruptness, Benabi."

"You need not apologize, Your Highness. As a leader of men I understand his feelings completely. It is never easy to lose one's right-hand man." He stood solidly before the king, his feet apart, and arms behind his back as was custom in his own country.

King George nodded his understanding. He hated to lose a good man too, and Courin was one of the best. He tugged his mind back to the present and realized Benabi still stood before him. "Forgive me a wandering mind, Benabi. What have you come to say?"

"I have come for two reasons, Your Highness. On behalf of my captains, to say that they will be leaving your harbor at first light, and on my own behalf, to let you know that Din Glun shall not escape. We will follow him until he is found. You need have no worry on that head."

King George sighed and settled into his chair. "I do appreciate your saying it, Benabi. I have thought of little else since I heard of his escape – would that I could run him down myself!"

"I am certain you would like nothing better. God be with you, Your Greatness, I hope to see you again someday." With that, he bowed, then turned and left the room. For a long time after, stillness reigned in King George's study as he sat staring into the flames.

William and Toldar went directly to the stables where grooms readied their horses for a long journey. While Toldar packed his saddlebags, William sat down to clean his weapons. Benabi joined them there after he had taken leave of the king.

"Are you certain it is wise, my brother?" Benabi asked William.

William checked the blade of his long sword and scrubbed at another spot. "I have followed after that man for too long. I know his ways. I do not intend to let him get away."

"I assure you, neither do I," Benabi said. "I know him better than most, having served under his command."

"I am well aware of that, Benabi." William stood and sheathed his sword. "Surely you can see my reasoning? If allowed to get away, you know he will return."

"There is little doubt of that. He will not be humiliated in so public a fashion." Benabi nodded. "Aye, he will do his best to make retribution."

William gazed intently at Benabi. "I will not be satisfied until I see his destruction."

Benabi drew in a deep breath. "I only wanted to be certain you knew the risks. You are, after all, the only son of your father and heir to the throne. I do not doubt that your esteemed father would not approve."

William smiled at Benabi. "Then we are alike, for I do not doubt it either, just as your own esteemed father would not approve."

Benabi bowed his head in acquiescence. "You are right." He turned to address Toldar. "And you mean to accompany him?"

Toldar lifted his head and eyed Benabi. "That had been my intention."

"I do not think it wise," William said while observing his brother-in-law's expression. "He must return to Cragmorton at once."

"Ah, the City in the Clouds," Benabi said. He set one foot on an upended bucket and gazed from one to the other. "Aye, it is a fair prospect, but I heard it was closed to all traffic until spring thaw."

Toldar's jaw muscles bulged as though he bit back a swift retort. He strode to his horse and busied himself with tightening cinches and checking the animal's hooves.

William glanced at Benabi. "You heard correctly. Toldar will accompany us until then."

Toldar cut a loose string hanging from one end of his blanket and turned about as he slid the knife back in its sheath. He continued his forward movement until he stood an arm's length from Benabi.

Benabi grinned and bowed his head. "No doubt there has been some contention between you concerning this." He addressed Toldar, "Perhaps your lady wife could rule in your stead."

There was absolute silence as William and Toldar contemplated that remark. Toldar's eyes swept William's face, and they both erupted into laughter.

"No, my good man," Toldar said with a smile, "I do not think that would be wise. My 'lady wife' is beautiful and of a good nature and I do trust her to raise our children well, but I would never entrust a region to her care."

"She would quickly bankrupt it," William said, "redecorating the castle and outfitting the servants."

A groom brought the horses forward. Toldar made one more adjustment to his saddlebags and mounted.

William faced Benabi. "Will you join us now, or do you sail with your men?"

"My horse awaits me yonder." Benabi signaled his groom. "You do not speak with your father?"

William mounted Lodan and turned him about. His gaze rested on Castle Coldthwaite, where he knew his father watched for their departure. "I have already made him aware of my plans. He does not agree with me. He wishes for me to remain here, but he has given me leave to go."

Benabi nodded his understanding. "I see."

Toldar looked pointedly at Benabi. "I believe it was the part about the gates of Hell that convinced him of your … er … resolve." His eyes flicked to William, the hint of a smile curving his lips.

Benabi arched his brows at William. "My lord?"

"I believe I said, 'I will not stop though I must follow him to the very gates of Hell.'" Lodan, eager to be off, leapt forward. Toldar slapped his horse's flank and followed along behind.

Benabi chuckled as he mounted his horse and set out after his friends. "Then I do most heartily join you in your quest, my friend, though I hope it does not take us quite so far as that."

Chapter 28 – Sanctuary

A familiar sound greeted Jael when she awoke from a nap – the voice of the waters – the great cascade of Verani. She could not see it yet, but she could hear it. She looked up at Young Will's strong back as he paddled across the calm basin. A cold mist hung over the water and here and there, golden leaves still clung to the branches of the trees. Beside her, Adrina stirred and sat up. Young Will turned and looked back at them. "I will make for shore so we can stretch our legs."

From their landing place, Jael could look out over the vast expanse and see the Haven in the distance, shrouded in mist. Young Will clambered about bringing the small boat ashore. A sound caught her attention and she spun about. In a moment, he was beside her.

"What is it?"

She turned her head slowly, watching and listening. "There," she whispered, pointing toward a bend in the river. "A movement – it is the form of a man. I cannot make him out."

Young Will gripped his knife. "Take cover, ladies. I will spy him out."

Jael moved forward. "Why do you not let me?"

The muscles of his jaw tightened and his eyes flashed. "No, Aunt. I cannot risk you."

Adrina gripped Jael's arm. "My lady, you are not well."

Jael opened her mouth to object, but the look in Young Will's eyes stopped her. She stepped aside. "Perhaps you should go. We will remain here."

Young Will frowned at her. "I'll go find out. You two remain here."

As he walked away, Adrina bit her lip in an attempt to stay the smile. Jael chuckled softly. "Do not be afraid to laugh at him, Adrina. In this way, we keep our men humble."

Young Will stole through the trees along the shoreline. The smell of fire drew him to the edge of a small inlet. On a bit of sandy beach, a dark figure crouched before a flame. Young Will took cover behind a large tree trunk. The man stood and turned about, as though alerted to a presence. Young Will held his breath and then relaxed. It was Rondar. He slid his knife back into its sheaf and waited until Rondar turned back to his task before stepping away from the tree and calling out.

"Rondar! Will Morgan wishes to approach your fire."

Rondar jumped up. When he saw Will, he relaxed his stance. "Young Will! Ye fair stopped me heart – draw nigh." The two men gripped forearms and Rondar waved for Young Will to sit. "What brings ye to the wilderness?"

"I was wondering the same of you."

Rondar slid the point of his knife along the belly of a fish. "I seek the whereabouts of the Lady of the Haven."

Young Will folded his arms over his chest. "Then you have found her, for she accompanies me to Coldthwaite."

Rondar's eyes snapped to his. "She is with ye? Her husband seeks her, for the dark enemy claims he has her."

"He very nearly did, or someone like her at least. They are both with me now. I go to my uncle."

Rondar shook his head. "I doubt the wisdom of that just now. Should the enemy get his hands on her – "

"He will not."

Rondar grinned as he threw another stick on the fire. "I don't doubt ye have run up on some of his men."

"Aye, it was necessary to free the lady." He chuckled. "We left them sleeping rather soundly, all but one. He may have been dead."

Rondar eyed him. "Ye are alone excepting the women?"

"Well … yes … Lady Jael is dressed as a man, but it does not really hide – "

Rondar laughed and slapped his knee. "She learnt naught the first time? Where is she now?"

"They wait where we came ashore."

"Ah, ye go by boat? Then ye certainly should not go on, for the danger is very great. The war is on and some of the enemy have already scattered. These waters may be infested with 'em."

"I will speak to my aunt." He stood to his feet and Rondar with him.

"Bring them here. I have these several fish. I meant to smoke the extra, but could easily share them. I don't doubt ye are hungry?"

𝕵𝖆𝖊𝖑 followed Young Will into Rondar's campsite. She had given no thought to her appearance until she saw the look on Rondar's face as his eyes raked over her form. He seemed to find it difficult not to smile.

"If ye really mean to pass yerself off as a man, my lady," he said, "ye'll want to cover yer face and eyes also. Else no one will ever believe ye."

Jael arched her brows at him and feigned anger. "It worked in the past."

Young Will choked back a guffaw. "It only worked the first time because you were so filthy."

Rondar bowed, no doubt to cover his expression. As he rose, his eyes came to rest on Adrina. Young Will introduced them.

"I hope ye will join me at my humble fire," Rondar said. As they sat down, he carefully removed the fish from the coals and served it on dried leaves. Jael ate hungrily. When she had finished, she looked at Rondar.

"Will tells me you were sent by Lord William?"

"Aye, upon receipt of a threat from the dark enemy, saying he had ye. Lord William, he did not believe it, saying he had seen ye or some such." His eyes held hers.

Jael's heartbeat quickened. "He saw me?"

"Aye and knew not how 'twas done, but he insisted he'd seen ye and ye'd told him ye would come to him. So then he sent me for to find ye and know who it was the enemy had."

Jael glanced at Adrina. "They very nearly did have someone."

Rondar gave a curt nod. "Oh, they had someone all right, it was a woman of the plains. I seen her afore I left there. She had flaxen hair somewhat like yours and she was of a height." He glanced then at Lady Adrina. "That seems to be going around."

Young Will finished his repast and threw the leavings into the fire. "How goes the battle?"

"It were a most fierce battle and many lives has been lost. Castle Coldthwaite has suffered a bit of damage, but the fires was small and put out pretty quick, I hear."

At Jael's intake of breath, he shook his head. "Beg pardon, my lady, I ain't used to niceties. I speak plain."

Young Will sat forward. "The castle was damaged? What of my grandfather?"

"Oh he is well, or he was so when I left. Your uncle, he don't let the old man go forth into battle as he wished to do."

"Good!" Jael and Young Will spoke at the same time.

Young Will met Jael's gaze. "Rondar does not think we should continue our journey by water, my lady. He believes the danger is too great."

"But it's the quickest way," she said. "And we do not now have our horses. On foot it would take too long."

Rondar shook his head. "I do not think ye should at all. I think ye should find cover fer yerselves and stay there until it's safe to go. I can carry word back to Lord William."

Jael glanced at Young Will, who sat gazing out over the face of the waters. *If not for the Adrina and myself, he could return with Rondar.*

Her eyes fled to Rondar's face. "You are going on, you say?"

"Aye, my lady – to get word to Lord William." He crouched near the fire and doused it.

Young Will faced Jael. "If only we had our horses, we could take the disappearing trail."

Jael's eyes snapped to his.

"I know it is near here," Rondar said, "but where does it end? Where would ye come out of it, my lady?"

Jael stood and brushed her hands together. "Just below Touri Downs, at river's edge."

Rondar sat back a bit and nodded. "I could get ye them horses, did ye wish to go that way. But go no further than the end." He turned back to Jael. "How long can ye stay within?"

"From one sun to the next is what my father said. I do not know why."

Rondar finished putting out the fire and stood. "It may be that one could not return."

Adrina joined Jael near the water's edge. They crouched to wash their hands of the fish. Behind her, Jael heard Rondar speaking to Young Will.

"There is a ravine near there, ye know it?"

"Aye."

"Wait there. I will come or else send someone. I'll have a better idea of the danger by then. Take care though, as the ravine itself can harbor danger."

Jael shook the excess water from her hands, then smoothed her hair. She waited until Adrina was ready and walked with her back to the campsite.

Young Will was nodding at Rondar. "You said you could get horses?"

Rondar smiled. "Aye, there are many riderless horses about these days. I will deliver them to the Haven. You will have them by break of day." He grasped Young Will by the forearm. "I must away quickly, for there is much to do. I may not see ye again, so I will say good day to ye."

"Wait, Rondar." Jael removed her ring and held it out to him. "Give this to my husband. He will know what it means." Her eyes held his for a brief moment. He bowed and took the ring.

While he packed up his horse, Young Will stepped near to speak with him. After Rondar's departure, they made their way back to the boat.

"What did you say to him?" Jael asked Young Will.

"You do not need to know all things, Aunt."

She opened her mouth to retort, but thought better of it. He grinned as he held out his hand and helped her into the boat. When Adrina was seated beside her, Will pushed out into the water and started across the expanse. The day was far spent and the sun would soon dip below a bank of clouds. There was a promise of snow in the air. Jael gathered the fur cloak closer and leaned forward, suddenly nauseous. Adrina watched her.

"How are you feeling, my lady?"

Jael swallowed. "A little unwell. I do not understand it, one minute I am starving and the next … " Her voice fell away as a thought struck her.

Adrina bent to peer into her face. "My lady?"

Jael looked at her and then at Young Will, who did not seem to be listening, but she knew better than to trust to that. She smiled at Adrina and gave a slight shake of her head. Adrina's face relaxed. Jael turned toward the sunset, and the two sat in silence until they drew near the opposite shore.

Young Will jumped out and pulled the boat ashore. He helped the ladies to alight and secured the oars. "We shouldn't camp in the open," he said. "I believe it will snow tonight."

Jael nodded. "Aye, the scent is upon the air. There is shelter some distance away from the shore."

Young Will drew up to look at her. "I heard that your house had been destroyed."

"Aye, it was and the barn also. The shelter of which I speak is quite peaceful and most certainly still intact." She led them to a bramble thicket and stood just outside its barrier.

Will drew near, frowning at the mass of shrubbery. "Shall I clear a path, my lady?"

She smiled. "You may try if you like, but it would resist your efforts." Without another word, she stepped inside.

"How did you do that? I believe she has tricked us some way."

Jael spoke from the other side of the thicket. "Nay, dear Will, you need only step through, though you must do it rather forcefully. You will find it does not tear at you."

Will tried and found himself face-to-face with Jael. "This is a very strange place." He called to Adrina and she followed him. Jael laughed at her wide-eyed wonder.

Once inside, they stood looking about. The place was green with moss and sloped down to a brook. The other bank was grassy and dotted with trees.

Jael motioned for them to follow her. "It may be a magical place, but it is still open to the weather, so you may follow me." She led them across the brook and beyond the meadow, to a moss-covered ravine where two rocks stood upright. Between them, the ground dropped away. Stone steps led down into darkness.

Jael glanced over her shoulder. "I hope you do not mind the dead, for this is our family sepulcher. It will give us shelter from the weather and whatever enemy may happen along in the deep of night."

"May we have a fire?" Will asked.

"Of course." She looked at Adrina, who had not spoken a word.

Adrina's eyes met hers. "You know I do not mind the dead, my lady. You may remember time was I dwelt among them."

"Aye, she did," Jael said to Young Will. A small entry room held an indentation in the floor. An opening overhead served as a vent. "Here you can start a fire and then we may light the torches which are set about."

"It will at least be quiet," Will said, "unless your relatives are gadabouts."

Jael smiled. "They are not; they are at peace."

After Will got the fire going, he left to bring more wood. Jael lit a torch and used it to light the others. The sepulcher, bathed in the soft glow of fire and torchlight, seemed almost cozy.

Young Will returned with the wood. "We have already eaten, but I may be able to catch a few more fish for the morning, if you ladies will excuse me." He started to leave, but then remembered the thicket and turned back to look at Jael. "How do I get out?"

"The same way you got in." She went to him and took his arm. "Here, I will lead you." At the edge of the grove, she stopped. "See this flat rock? It marks the path. There is another on the outer edge, though sometimes it is covered by weeds. Always make certain no one watches and remember to move forcefully."

He grinned down at her. "I should have little trouble with that, my lady." He stepped forward and disappeared through the briars. Jael called to him. "Do you see the flat rock?"

"Aye, I will remember it, Aunt."

Jael smiled as she strolled back to the cave where she found Adrina walking about, holding a torch.

"I have been visiting your family," she said. "It is something I did when first I came to the catacombs at Cragmorton. I felt much more at ease afterwards."

"I am certain they will not mind. I used to visit them often." She extended her hand. "Here is one who may interest you." Jael led her to another chamber and pointed to the mummified remains on a lower shelf. "Here is Lura Abingdon du Frain, my great-grandmother and your aunt, I suppose."

"Two generations back, that is ... if I am indeed who you say I am."

Jael smiled at Adrina. "Oh, you are. I have no doubt."

Adrina pointed to another. " ... And is this?"

Jael nodded. "Aye, it is – the Rogan, son of Ishiel of Jebuel."

"What a wonderful heritage you have, my lady."

"They are much the same as yours."

"I do not know mine."

"Then you must meet Abraham Worther of Coldthwaite. He is a historian as well as a gifted weaver. He loves to find out family secrets."

"Family secrets sometimes should remain thus."

Jael smiled at her. She was so droll at times. They walked back to the entrance and sat down near the fire. Jael fed the flames another log. She felt Adrina's eyes upon her.

"What were you about to tell me in the boat, my lady – concerning the nature of your illness?"

Jael drew her cloak about her and looked into the flames. "I cannot be certain, but it's possible ... I may be with child."

Adrina's eyes opened wide. "Is this not a wonderful thing, my lady?"

Jael touched her hand to her middle. "If it is true, it is indeed wonderful."

"There is a positive way to know," Adrina said.

Jael smiled. "I do know that, but I ... " at Adrina's puzzled look, she briefly explained.

Adrina tucked her legs beneath her and buried her hands in the folds of her cloak. "I better understand you now, but bloodwort is temporary, surely?"

"In most cases, though prolonged use can be dangerous."

"I did not know it would work thus. I only thought it was used to stop heavy bleeding."

Tired, Jael stared into the flames. "That is its main purpose and it really should only be used for such." At the sound of approaching footsteps, they both rose and went to the door. Young Will held up a string of fish.

"I hope you prepared them already," Jael said.

Young Will smiled and shook his head. "Can you do nothing for yourself?" He hung them from the ceiling until morning, trusting to the cold to keep them fresh. Then he sat down by the fire and held out his hands to the warmth "The snow has started in earnest. Does it snow along the disappearing trail?"

"Most certainly it does, but it will not stay our journey."

"You are determined that it will not, and so it will not."

Jael noticed how Adrina seemed to enjoy the banter that passed so naturally between herself and Young Will. Quite often, Adrina's eyes gravitated towards Young Will's and his toward hers. Jael smiled and leaned back against the wall of the sepulcher.

William heard the shout as he, Toldar and Benabi were making final plans for the day's journey. "Rondar has come!"

A moment later, the tent's door parted and the man entered. He bowed to his superiors.

Benabi rose and crossed to him. "Rondar, my old friend, I had about given you up."

Rondar nodded. "I have been about my master's business." He pulled a small object from his pocket and held it out to William.

William folded the ring into his palm. "You have found her?"

"Aye my lord, and she did ask me to give ye this. She said as ye would know what it meant."

"I do indeed, where is she?"

"At this moment, she is somewhere along the disappearing trail, your highness."

William rose and strode from the tent. On the riverbank, the rushing water soothed his tattered spirit. He knelt on one knee and thanked God for Jael's apparent safety. When he returned to the tent, he found Rondar and Benabi conversing amicably. They grew quiet at his entrance. He sat down and addressed Rondar.

"Where did you find her?"

"I found her with Young Will and a woman by name of Adrina – Lady Adrina, of Cragmorton."

"*Lady* Adrina? But why have they come so far?"

Rondar drank the last of his tea and set the cup down. "'Tis a tale I did not get in full, but I am sure they will tell ye of it."

"No doubt and they go to … ?"

"I told them to wait for me near Touri Downs, in the ravine. I figured 'twas safer there than in the town. I do not like what I seen slinking about the countryside."

"Aye – 'tis true," William said. "When did you promise to meet them?"

"Soon as I was done here, making my report to ye."

William bit back a smile as his gaze slid from Toldar to Benabi.

"Not so far out of your way, my lord," Benabi said.

William used his knife to cut off a chunk of bread. He returned the knife to his belt and dipped the bread in his tea. "I do not think it is. I will turn aside, but you must journey on. I will find you."

"Take Rondar with you," Toldar said. "He is an excellent tracker."

William gazed at Toldar. "And I am not?"

Toldar smiled, but made no attempt to answer. William finished the last of his bread, washed it down with tea and stood. Rondar rose and took his leave from Toldar and Benabi.

Benabi raised his cup to William. "Greet your lady for me, brother. I hope to meet her one day. I've heard so much of her, I feel certain she must be descended of the angels."

William smiled, "You are not far wrong, my friend, and I hope you will meet her someday. I think she would like you."

Toldar followed William and Rondar. "Give her a kiss for me, brother, if you have one to spare."

William chuckled. "I believe I can do that for you, old man."

"Oh," Rondar said to William, "I near forgot – there is one thing more. Young Will made a request of ye."

Along the shore of the Verani, Jael, Young Will and Adrina led their newfound horses. Rondar had been as good as his word. The animals were of a good bloodline, well shaped and in good health. All still carried their former rider's saddle.

At first, Adrina and Will looked often about them, amazed at the appearance of things from inside the disappearing trail. It certainly was a strange phenomenon, beyond their understanding. Granite walls on either side of them rose to the heights and disappeared into the sky.

"Are they only hidden in lowering clouds," Young Will asked, "or do they really disappear at the top? Can one ascend to the top and see out, or could one stand upon the heights and look down at us?"

Jael smiled and shook her head. "Too many questions, dear Will. The disappearing trail requires faith. One takes it for what it is."

"So, you do not know the answers." His teeth flashed as he grinned at her.

She stopped and gazed up into mischievous eyes. "I daresay you would find them out, given the time." She turned and resumed her trek. "These are things I had at times asked my father, but he gave me no better answer than the one I have given you."

When they neared the shallows, they mounted their horses and rode in silence. Jael couldn't stop the memories of a former crossing – for here it was that she said farewell to William for the first time – the first of many times, she thought ruefully.

"How far to the end?" Young Will asked after nearly an hour.

"Half a day's journey perhaps," she said. "I have only followed it out once."

They rode on in silence until they neared the end and Jael stopped her horse. She climbed down and walked slowly forward, holding up her hand to the others. "We must take great care in crossing over." She pointed to a strangely shaped rock. "This is the marker. Wait here and I will see if the way is clear." Jael closed her eyes, took a deep breath and centered her mind. Then she took a step outside the disappearing trail.

She had never stood in this place. Great crags of moss-draped granite hung overhead. Near at hand, water dripped and splashed on rock. A tiny rivulet gurgled at her feet. All seemed quiet in the surrounding wilderness. She was just about to turn and reenter the pass when a new sound entered her mind. Footsteps crunched on gravel. Another and then another, she lost count of how many. She stood still as a statue, let her head fall back and whispered in the ancient tongue.

As she worshipped, the atmosphere changed. It crackled with energy as Jael lifted her arms heavenward. Fully cloaked, she stepped out of the shadows.

A line of foot soldiers made their weary way along the river's edge. Though none spoke, Jael had little doubt who they were. A glimpse of dark skin, rough black hair and beards, foreign apparel; they resembled the men she and Young Will had faced in the Touris.

Restless, Young Will examined the weather-pocked granite of the disappearing trail. Where was Lady Jael? Surely she should have returned by now. He glanced at Adrina, who sat motionless on a rock. Peace. She was like a dove that cooed in the early morning. Made him want to close his eyes and go back to sleep. He returned to his horse and brushed at an imaginary bit of dirt.

"Do you think she's all right?" Adrina asked.

The sound of her voice startled Young Will. He turned to look at her and noticed the whiteness of her knuckles. Apparently, she was not so peaceful. He stepped toward her. "I was just wondering whether I should go and find her, but I would not like to leave you here, alone."

Adrina rose. "I think perhaps you should. Lady Jael is not … well."

Young Will frowned. Could he find his way out? His eyes found Adrina's. For a moment, he lost all sense of time. An odd sound, like a pebble dropping into a pool, penetrated his abstraction. Jael had returned.

𝕵𝖆𝖊𝖑 looked from Will to Adrina, wondering at their expressions. Had she interrupted something? "I saw stragglers from the dark army making their way along the river."

Young Will stepped forward. "The dark army?"

She nodded. "I waited until they had all passed by."

Young Will took her arm and led her forward. "Do you feel it is safe to proceed?"

She glanced at Adrina. "I do, but we must take care."

Young Will brought the horses forward and helped Jael and Adrina to mount. His horse gave him a bit of trouble, but he soon brought it under control. "He's a bit high-strung," he said with a grin. "You lead on, Aunt."

Jael halted at the pass, held up her hand to stop the others and listened. Satisfied, she dropped her hand and clucked to her horse. On the other side, she drew up again and turned about to watch the others. Young Will stopped and stared in amazement at the solid rock wall that materialized once they were clear of the disappearing trail.

They found shelter beneath an overhang, with a view of the main road. Young Will tethered their horses behind a row of fir trees and they all sat down to wait.

"I think we should not light a fire," he said. Jael agreed, so they huddled close together for warmth.

It was fully dark before Jael heard the sound of approaching horses. Heedless of danger, she rushed to meet them. Young Will was fast upon her heels.

She held onto William so tightly he laughed, but made no effort to break free. He gripped Young Will's arm and followed him down the sharp incline to the campsite, Jael at his side.

Rondar built a small fire and made a stew of dried fish and herbs. Young Will and Adrina slept as Rondar kept watch. Jael cared not for sleep. Throughout the long night, she clung to her husband, unwilling to let go.

She buried her face in his chest. "I know it is your mission to pursue Din Glun, but I must admit, I resent it."

William kissed the top of her head and stroked her fine golden hair. "We cannot live freely knowing that he could someday return."

"Aye and it is God's will that you go." She sighed against him. "For what it is worth, I give my blessing and I will pray for your safety at all times."

He looked deeply into her eyes. "Your blessing is worth much and your prayers – I quite depend upon them." He took her hand and slipped his ring back onto her finger. Then he held her palm to his lips and kissed it. "Always know that I love you."

She gazed into his eyes and promised, "I will never doubt it."

He turned away a moment, drew out a bundle and presented it to her, a crooked smile on his lips. "Young Will has requested that I bring this."

Jael held up the dress and cloak and laughed. "He is embarrassed to be seen with me now."

William cocked an eyebrow. "I cannot think why – I quite prefer a woman in trousers – but I believe he thought of your entry into Coldthwaite." He smiled as he bent to kiss her again.

Jael frowned. "I had not thought of that. I will be sure to thank him."

At dawn, they prepared to leave, but they would take separate roads. William had secured safe passage for the women on a ship of the realm.

"It stands at anchor upon the river awaiting your arrival. The journey will be safer and quicker that way," he said.

Young Will advanced. "Once the ladies are safely aboard, would you allow me to join you?" He advanced on his uncle and set his jaw. "You cannot deny me this, Uncle."

William looked long at his nephew. "I would rather say no, but I do have need of you." He glanced at Jael. "I have lost Courin."

Jael's breath caught in her throat. "Oh no – "

Young Will turned away as William wrapped his arms about her. "I am sorry I did not tell you sooner. It is still so fresh an injury to me, I hardly speak of it." He paused and turned his face aside. He drew in a deep breath and exhaled. "He stood in my stead and took a sword thrust meant for me."

No one spoke for a few moments. Jael brushed away tears. Gallant Courin, so good to her when first she came to Corwinder. "He gave his life for you."

She sensed his impatience and stepped back. He was set to pursue the man who had destroyed so many. She would not stand in his way.

William turned his attention back to Young Will. "I would rather not take you away, but I do need a man by me I can trust."

Young Will's brows knit. "What of Toldar?"

"I am sending him to Cragmorton as soon as the pass is clear. Someone must stand as leader there. He will do well and my sister will be glad to have him home. He will see to my mother's safe return to Coldthwaite." He looked at Jael. "So that leaves you and Lady Adrina."

Rondar finished scattering the coals of their fire. "Perhaps it would be best if I lead them to the ship. I will have no trouble finding the trail again."

William nodded. "Is this agreeable with you, Will?"

Young Will gazed at Adrina. "Aye my lord."

Jael squeezed Young Will's arm and whispered, "Say goodbye to her properly, Will."

William glanced at her, his eyebrows raised.

"Trust me in this, dear husband. I know whereof I speak, and I am certain that your nephew will tell you everything, do you but ask."

"You may be sure I shall ask," he said through a smile that made her heart ache. She would dearly miss that smile.

Young Will walked over to the place where Adrina stood, her hands at her side. She raised her eyes to his face. He took her hand in his and brought it to his lips. "I will see you again in Coldthwaite."

She blushed and whispered, "I will await you there."

He dropped her hand, placed his hands at her waist and lifted her into the saddle. With great reluctance he turned away from her. Jael watched him and smiled when she caught his eye. As he passed her she caught hold of his arm.

"By the way, thank you so much for the dress and cloak."

He planted a swift kiss on her cheek and stepped to his horse.

William hoisted Jael into the saddle, then turned to mount Lodan. "You said you left Sandelstar at Duflec?" She nodded. "I will bring him back to you when I come."

"Is that a promise?"

"Aye dear lady, a solemn one." He cast a glance at Rondar. "I give them over into your care, Rondar. Deliver them safely."

"Aye my lord, I pledge my life."

William's eyes were sad as he looked at Jael. "I hope it will not be required."

She wept. In all of her life, she had never wept so hard, nearly doubled over in the saddle, face covered with a corner of her cloak. Her horse followed Adrina's, whose horse followed Rondar's, for Adrina was little better.

A small fishing vessel awaited Jael and Adrina at river's edge. Rondar stayed and watched until the boat was underway, then mounted his horse and rode off.

The day was a brilliant one, the sky a bright wintry blue. The full sun reflected off newly fallen snow. Sunlight sparkled through ice crystals on the grasses. A fresh cool breeze sent them on their way downriver.

Jael had not been aboard long before the sickness returned. She spent most of her time near the railing. Adrina was able to secure some hot water to make an herbal tea for them both. She was none too seaworthy either. The sailors aboard ship seemed to enjoy their discomfort rather more than was necessary.

"They laugh at us," Adrina said.

"Do not let it trouble you. Their lives have been far too serious these past months. If we can provide them with humor, then so be it."

"But your discomfort is not fully due to the boat's – " She covered her mouth with her hand, as if even the thought of the vessel's motion turned her stomach.

"They do not know that. Let us turn our minds to other things and give this good tea some time to do its work."

After a few minutes of silence, Adrina spoke again. "May I ask you something of a personal nature?"

Jael gazed into Adrina's tired eyes. "After all that has passed between us, there is nothing so personal."

"Did you tell His Majesty of your … condition?"

Jael looked out over the shining water. "Nay, he has too many things …

" her voice caught a little at the thought. She had not fully come to terms with Courin's loss. She would not let herself dwell too long on the memory. "I am sorry to be so emotional. I am not, usually."

"I do know that, my lady."

Jael took a deep breath and sipped the tea. After a while she felt able to continue. "My husband must not be burdened with concern for me, and he would be." She looked at Adrina. "His elder sister – Young Will's mother – did not survive childbirth."

Adrina's brow furrowed, but she made no comment. Jael stood slowly and leaned against the rail. She pushed the hood of her cloak back and let the breezes flow over her face. It was invigorating. Adrina soon followed her example.

"I hope ye ladies are feeling somewhat better?" The captain spoke as he approached. Both turned to look at him. Adrina bowed her head slightly.

Jael said, "We are much better, thank you. It is a good day for a sail."

The captain laughed. "Aye it is, and does the weather hold we will be at sea by dawn tomorrow. Three more days of good sailing will bring us within sight of Castle Coldthwaite and the end of a very long journey for ye both, is what I hear tell."

"Aye, Captain," she said. "It was a very long journey."

That night they were given a berth in the Captain's quarters while he made his bed elsewhere. The evening was a calm one, so they both slept well and awoke hungry, but the smell of frying meat soon sent Jael back into the fresh air. Once her stomach had settled, her eyes swept the coast for familiar scenes. By afternoon, wispy white clouds moved in and the air turned much colder. Brisk winds pushed the vessel well on its way and she hoped that by morning, they would see the hills of Corwinder-by-the-Sea.

Adrina was fascinated by her first glimpse of the sea. "It seems to go on forever and its power is magnificent."

Jael smiled at the memories of her first sighting. "I love the sounds of the sea – the crashing of the waves, the call of the seabirds and the barking of the seals."

Adrina's eyes widened. "I have only read about seals."

"Tomorrow you shall see them, for they dwell in large numbers near Coldthwaite."

Adrina pulled her cloak tighter. "Coldthwaite. From the name, one would assume that it is very cold there."

Jael shook her head. "It is of a temperate climate. Aye, surely there are winds from the northern sea that cool it overmuch in winter, but there are also warmer winds from the Great Sea. Though it does snow, it is seldom deep and does not last long."

Adrina frowned. "I shall miss the snow, I think."

"Then you should definitely go to live at Corwinder, for they have ample snows."

"And Corwinder is also by the sea, I hear tell."

"Aye, but only a harbor, a tidal basin. When the tide is out, it is dry sand with pools all about. But when the tide is in, it is completely covered and looks just like the sea."

The ship lurched and Adrina grabbed hold of the railing. "It all sounds so foreign and yet it holds such interest for me. All of these places Will has told me about and now, I will see them with my own eyes. I only wish … " her voice trailed off.

Jael knew how her friend would end that thought, were she able. She placed an arm about Adrina's waist and drew her closer. "We are much the same, you and I."

That night they did not sleep as well, for the sea was rough. Jael was up sick several times. The second day, a chill wind whipped the boat and forced the ladies to stay below. They survived on pelican stew and strong hot tea. Adrina lay abed all day, while Jael paced about the cramped quarters like a caged cat and prayed for calmer seas.

The mists of morning lifted late, so they were unaware that the craggy cliffs of Coldthwaite loomed ahead. When the mists cleared, Jael's eyes filled with tears. She pressed her palms together and tried to suppress her excitement. At that moment, she felt a sudden movement within. She looked at Adrina and smiled.

"I think that I can say with some assurance, I am with child."

Adrina smiled back. "I am glad to hear it, my lady. I had feared for your health."

Jael laid a hand on her abdomen. "Perhaps he knows that he is home."

Chapter 30 – Coldthwaite

Jael's heart beat wildly as the fishing vessel dropped anchor in the cove below the castle. The captain gave orders for a skiff to be launched to deliver the ladies to shore, where the royal guard waited. Jael and Adrina followed the men of the royal guard up the pebbled beach toward a path to the stone steps.

Their captain bowed before Jael. "Come sit by the fire, my lady, and take your rest until a conveyance can be made ready." She met his gaze.

"I would just as soon walk," she said.

The captain's expression was unchanged as he extended his hand toward two leather stools. "His Majesty, the King would not wish for ye to walk, my lady. Ye must wait."

Jael nodded to Adrina and they sat down, warmed their hands over the fire and waited. Jael felt too weary for speech. After what seemed an eternity, a horse-drawn cart was brought round and one of the guards helped the two ladies inside. All along the road, villagers worked to remove debris left over from the battle. As the cart passed by, they stopped and stared.

Jael's eyes filled with tears at the sight of their haggard faces. She glanced at Adrina. "It looks to have been a difficult battle." Many homes had been reduced to rubble.

As they drew near the castle, she noticed breaches in the very wall of the stronghold and remembered the only other time she had made this journey, following her marriage to William. It had been such a happy time, a triumphant entrance. So different from this day.

A brisk, icy wind off the ocean beat against their backs as they stepped down from the cart at the entrance to the castle. Here they were met by Eldred, the king's valet. He bowed and extended his hand. "Lady Jael, I could not believe the report until finally I have set eyes upon ye. I would not even tell His Majesty, the King until 'twas certainty." Eldred ushered them into an interior room where a fire roared in the great fireplace. "He is so sad of late as ye will see, for everyone has gone away."

Jael shook her head to commiserate with the old servant. "I am very sorry to hear of the king's discomfort."

"Oh well, he will be gladdened in heart to see ye." He took her cloak and she introduced him to Adrina. He bowed to Adrina. As he straightened, his eyes lingered on Adrina's face ever so briefly. "How alike she is to ye, Lady Jael, and ye say she is of the northern royals?"

"Aye she is. Now, will you take us straightaway to His Majesty, Eldred?"

Eldred touched his forehead with his fingertips. "Oh no, my lady, I have called for Lady Bethalyn's own staff to come and see to yer comfort."

He meant for them to tidy themselves up a bit before being presented to his master. As he turned away to hand off their cloaks to another, she smiled and leaned in close to whisper to Adrina. "Just let them do whatever they wish. They will wait upon you hand and foot. It was difficult for me at first, but you do get used to it. You are a lady now and they will expect you to behave as one."

"I do not think I will like it," Adrina whispered back as the contingent of maidservants bore down upon them.

"Just remember, they will talk among themselves and their impression of you now will help to form Lady Bethalyn's opinion of you later."

Adrina's eyes widened and a visible change came over her countenance. Jael smiled to see it. Adrina was no fool.

The maids showed Jael and Adrina to separate rooms to coddle and comb them and make them ready.

Jael was glad at the sight of Sharla, who had assisted her before.

Sharla curtseyed. "My lady, it is so good to see ye well and safe."

"And you as well, Sharla. I hope all is well with your family."

"We was threatened, but unhurt. My Dan is gone to Corwinder to give aid there."

Sharla began to comb out Jael's hair. "Who is this Lady Adrina, if I may be so bold to ask? She has a familiar look to her."

"She is a descendant of the Cragmorton royal family."

"But I thought, 'twas said they were no more?"

Jael nodded. "It was said, but it was not the truth. The royal midwife hid Lady Adrina soon after her birth and kept her heritage a secret, even from Adrina herself, till we came to Cragmorton and discovered it."

"Ye must be so glad of heart. 'Twas a blessing to find one of yer own still living."

Jael smiled and closed her eyes as she lowered her aching body into the warm bath water. "Oh, this is wonderful, it has been many weeks since I have had a real bath."

Sharla smiled and began to scrub Jael's back. "His Highness will be so glad to set eyes upon ye. He does pine away for Her Highness. It near breaks our hearts to see it."

Jael opened her eyes. "Does he?"

"Aye, my lady and he wearies himself thinking of his son gone off to the desert and now he has just received word that his grandson has gone along with him. We is that concerned." Another maid entered, carrying more wood, which she added to the fire.

Jael sighed. "I hope he will at least be diverted by our company."

"Oh, he will and when I am finished with ye – but my lady – "

Jael saw that Sharla had noticed the bulge at her middle. Though slight, there was no hiding it. It was not like a normal widening that comes with age, and Jael had never held an extra ounce of fat.

Sharla knelt beside the basin and covered her mouth with her forearm. "Oh my lady, I … I am … glad to see that ye have gained a bit of weight, fer ye were none but a frail thing last I saw."

Jael smiled and touched her lips with her fingertip. "I would prefer that you not noise it abroad, Sharla. It is not common knowledge."

Sharla's eyes were round as saucers. "Then it is – ye are – "

Jael nodded. "Please do keep it to yourself, at least until I have had time to settle in. The king may hear from other than me and that would not be good."

Sharla dried her hands on her apron. "Oh, but he will be so pleased, my lady. As we all will be." She clasped her hands together. "Glory to God."

Jael did not worry about her shape showing through the heavy clothing worn in winter. She could be much farther along and no one would notice. She left word for Adrina to be brought down at once when she was ready and then went alone to see her father-in-law. He was anxiously pacing the main sitting room. At her entrance, he strode quickly across to greet her, nearly suffocating her in his affectionate embrace. This was not the usual decorous greeting but no one seemed to notice. Jael rose on her tiptoes to plant a kiss on his cheek.

"How I have missed you, Father!"

He drew back to look at her. "And I you, daughter, what wonderful news I was greeted with this very morn, that you were within the castle grounds and not only you, but another." He frowned. "Who is this Lady

Adrina?"

"She was born to the Queen at Cragmorton just prior to her death and hidden away by the royal midwife." As they talked, King George and Jael crossed to a spot nearer the fire. She lowered her voice, so as not to be overheard. "She grew up believing she was a bastard child, but in truth she is the true daughter of the last king of Cragmorton. Her given name was recorded in the book of deaths as a stillbirth."

"You are quite certain?"

"Our good friend Crispus found the records, with Young Will's help. Her true name is Lura Corina du Frain, but she prefers to be known as Adrina Grumfeld. When you see her, you will have no doubt of her heritage."

A moment later, the wait ended as Adrina was shown into the room. King George stood speechless for the first few moments. His eyes darted between them. "She could be your close kinswoman so like is she!" He beckoned to Adrina. "Come here, child."

Jael smiled at Adrina. "She is my own kin, since our great-grandmothers were sisters."

King George took Adrina's hand and lifted it to his lips. "I am well pleased to make your acquaintance, Lady, and to be able to welcome you to Castle Coldthwaite, so recently the scene of a deadly fracás." He let go of her hand and glanced at Jael. "I hope you had a safe journey?"

"Aye we did as much as was possible. Once we were freed from our pursuers. Young Will showed himself to be a brave and trustworthy leader."

The king's brow furrowed and he shook his head. "I am sorry he did not wish to return here to me. Would that I had never let him go!"

Jael touched his hand and peered into his troubled eyes. "He so longed to be with his uncle. He thought of little else the entire time."

"I am certain it was so. He is young yet, and ready for excitement. But where they are going … " He lifted his hand to his head and closed his eyes against obvious pain.

Jael caught her breath and stepped nearer. "Father, you are unwell."

He brought his red, watery eyes back to her face.

"I am not unwell, but I do suffer from the headache. I suppose it is the strain of loss." He sat down heavily in a nearby chair. Jael glanced at Adrina and sat down. Adrina followed her example.

King George groaned and stared into the fire. "We have lost a great many, dear Jael. Our fair city is but half of what it was."

Jael leaned forward and touched his arm. "What of Master Abraham, I hope he is well?"

He did not answer for several seconds. "What? Oh, yes, Master Abraham is quite well and joins me oft for supper."

"I am glad to hear it." Observing his distraction, she signaled to Adrina, who rose from her chair and waited near the door. Jael knelt close to the king. "Now if you will excuse us, Father, you need your rest, I think."

He nodded, childlike. "I do, yes." He reached out a hand toward her. "But do not go just yet. I have been thinking, wondering really. What would you advise for relief of the headache? Our physicians are so busy amongst the wounded – "

Jael took his large hands in her small ones. "Of course, Father. I will see to it at once." As she rose to go, she bit her lower lip and frowned. What had happened to him? Was he only troubled, as Sharla had hinted, or was he truly ill?

Chapter 31 – In Times of Peace

It was quiet in the vale of Cragmorton. Almost too quiet for Lady Bethalyn as she roamed about Wrenook for the hundredth time. Outside, upon the snow-covered downs, children's voices echoed. They played in the winter sun anytime it made an appearance. She had to admire their stamina.

She never thought to miss her daughter-in-law. At least the girl had spirit and humor and though she had always looked upon her with a critical eye, Lady Bethalyn had come to admire her.

A bell clanging below drew her attention. She stood upon the landing so she could hear who had come. It was Crispus. She frowned. In the middle of the week? She descended the stairs at once. Crispus' weekly visits helped to keep her sane, but she was curious to know why he came so soon. Had there been news? Was it bad?

Crispus bowed. "Lady Bethalyn, I have come for you. I thought you may like a visit to Cragmorton."

She cringed at the thought of the awful cold. "Why would you think that?"

Crispus touched his fingertips together at his waist. "The boys of Cragmorton will compete upon the Greshne this day. It is most diverting, and Lady Jael always attended. They would be so honored if you would come in her stead."

"Well, since you put it that way, perhaps I could." She turned and hastened to her room, calling for her maids.

Lady Bethalyn felt almost giddy as the horses dragged the sled across the frozen tundra. Fur covered her from head to toe and a woolen scarf hid all but her eyes and a very narrow strip of her cheeks just below them. The sun shone so bright upon the snow that she had to scrunch up her eyes just to see, but it was all such a grand adventure. The sleigh went very fast and the air upon her face felt so refreshing, though the day was frigid.

Crispus smiled at her from his seat, but did not attempt speech over the noise of the journey. It seemed but a short time until the gates of Cragmorton loomed ahead. Around the side of the castle they flew, down to an open area where Lady Bethalyn would be afforded the best possible view of the event. Already a crowd of locals had formed near the place where the boys stood about practicing their strokes.

"What is upon their feet to allow them to move so?" Lady Bethalyn asked Crispus.

He leaned forward. "It is a smooth wooden blade, Your Highness, well honed and polished daily. When they have finished their race, I will have them come and show you."

Lady Bethalyn watched as the boys assembled at one end of the lake, and at the sound of a ram's horn blowing, took off.

Lady Bethalyn held fast to the seat of the sleigh, as if she too were skating. She cast a glance at Crispus. "How do they not fall?"

"Some do, see there?" He pointed as one poor lad fell flat. "They get up again most times. He will try again."

It was over so quickly Lady Bethalyn was disappointed.

"Is that it then?"

"Oh, they will celebrate and then they will show off a bit. They do such wonderful tricks out on the ice. You must stay and see it all."

Crispus leapt down and went to find one of the boys to come and show Lady Bethalyn the special shoes they used to race. He brought back fried pies and hot mulled cider. "These are traditional foods for their festivities, Your Highness."

She sipped the cider and ate a tiny bite of the fried pie. "Quite tasty," she said. At the approach of several of the skaters, she handed the food to a servant.

The young man who had won the race held his shoes up for her examination. She drew her scarf aside. "You are a very talented young man. I think it must take a deal of balance and skill to perform so well."

He blushed and bowed and murmured his thanks, then ran off to rejoin his friends to celebrate his victory.

"What a coup for him on such a day," Crispus said, rubbing his hands together. "The Queen of all the empire has seen him win."

Lady Bethalyn beamed beneath her repositioned scarf. "You make too much of it, Crispus."

Before returning to Wrenook, she accompanied him to the castle and warmed herself by the fire in the small drawing room. "You must be very lonely here these days," she said.

"I do miss Her Ladyship and most especially Young Will, whom I had come to know a good deal. I hope someday to see them again."

She fingered a knot in the fringe of her scarf. "And you are still quite certain that they are ... alive and well?"

Crispus bowed his head. "Oh aye, Your Highness, more so than ever."

She shivered and hugged herself for warmth. "Oh, for the heat of summer, when the snowgate will melt and allow me to escape my bounds."

Crispus' good humor overflowed, and he laughed heartily. "The snowgate! I have never heard it named thus. How apt a term for it and when it has opened, perhaps our friends will return to us and we will hear of the world outside."

He cast another log onto the fire and rose, brushing his hands together. "Now if you are ready, I will deliver you back to Wrenook where they will no doubt be anxious for your return."

Jael stood in front of the new tapestry that hung in the gallery at Coldthwaite, in awe of the finely crafted piece of work. Her eyes misted as she gazed upon the likeness of Lord William, so tall and fine. "Hmm," she said at sight of the halo round the head of her likeness. She arched an eyebrow and whispered, "I cannot like that."

She noticed that Abraham had placed a large body of water in the background, which must be Greshne, but the castle was not Cragmorton. It was fashioned after the stronghold at Coldthwaite, which had a more peculiar shape. Her gaze moved to the eaves of the castle, where sat a pair of turtledoves of purest white. She smiled.

This was undoubtedly Master Abraham's finest work. She must send word to him at once and request a meeting. She stepped to the window and gazed out at the main thoroughfare, crowded with citizens. Just at the top of the hill was the little shop where Abraham crafted his fine tapestries. It was also the place where he stored an impressive collection of historical documents. Jael knew he would consider Adrina a challenge. He would dig out every document that existed regarding the Cragmorton royals and regale any listeners with a long history of their exploits.

Abraham responded to Jael's invitation with an immediate reply that he would be most happy to come. King George was pleased to have him at dinner.

As Jael expected, Abraham was keenly interested in Lady Adrina. After being introduced to her, his gaze shifted from Jael to Adrina and back again. "The likeness between the two of you," he nodded to Jael, "is astonishing!"

Jael took a step forward. "Aye, sir it is, and we would be most interested in discovering more about our connections."

Abraham bowed to them both. "I will take great pleasure in searching out whatever I can find." During the meal, he told them all about the twin kings. "Joseph remained as regent in Coldthwaite, while John traveled to Cragmorton." Master Abraham took a moment to compliment the cook on the wonderful flavor of the braised beef before continuing his narrative.

Jael sipped her tea and turned to Abraham. "Was this the John who was called Twain? William told me of him."

Master Abraham beamed. "Yes! The Cragmortons did call him Twain, because there were so many Johns, you see." He nodded and smiled. "I must dig further and find out more, Lady Adrina. I know there is so much more."

At dinner's conclusion, Jael rose from her chair. "If you would be so kind, Master Abraham, help me to understand the meaning of the tapestry."

His smile, as he rose from his chair, bespoke his pleasure. "Ah yes, the tapestry. How do you like it, my lady?"

She folded her hands beneath her chin. "It is wonderful and I was particularly interested to note that the castle behind the lake was very like Coldthwaite."

He smiled and offered her his arm. "Let us go there and I will explain it more fully." King George ordered the servants to go ahead of them and light the wall sconces and candles, to shed more light on the object of their interest. Master Abraham pointed to the horses grazing in the background. Behind them was something Jael had not noticed, a great waterfall, crowned with a rainbow.

"Verani ... " she whispered.

"Aye, and the rainbow signifies the promises of God. He was surely watching over Lord William on that great day."

"Aye, He was ... but what of the lake and the castle, Master Abraham?"

He smiled and stepped near. "Well, in the beginning it was to be Greshne and Cragmorton." He coughed behind his fist. "Of course, I have never seen either. Therefore, I fashioned the castle after this one, thinking that they may be somewhat alike, being both built by the same family." He crossed his arms over his chest. "Now I'm thinking that it may have been prophetic, for you are here again, you see?"

Jael nodded. "And the doves?"

Abraham tipped his head back to view the doves. "My constant companions of late, they have been nesting in the eaves of my shop." He bowed before her. "I hope they, too, may be seen as prophetic."

"I depend upon it," King George said. "Their very likeness gave me hope in the midst of despair."

Abraham bowed his head toward the king and said, "If I may, Your Highness." At King George's nod, Abraham turned to Jael. "My lady, many years ago, a prophecy came forth that one day a Rogan would sit upon the throne at Coldthwaite."

A tremor ran through Jael. King George drew up beside her and took her hand. "That day is fast approaching, my good friend," he said to Abraham.

Abraham laid his hand on the king's shoulder. "I am humbled to be allowed to witness its beginning."

Jael bit her lip and bowed her head. What would they think when her secret became known? For she had already discerned that the child she carried was male.

Weeks passed, and when Jael could no longer hide her condition, she asked for a private meeting with her father-in-law. She found him in his study, seated in his favorite chair. His feet were propped up and his face was downcast.

As she approached, he asked in a weary voice, "What is it you need of me, Daughter?"

Jael perched on the edge of the chair across from him.

"I have no need that is not already met, Father. I wanted a private audience to give you a bit of good news for once."

His face lit up as his gaze met hers. "You have heard from my son?"

Jael shook her head sadly. "Alas, I have not, though it is the greatest desire of my heart. No, Father. I wanted to tell you that I will soon have to withdraw from you for a time." At his look of alarm, she continued. "I must go into confinement."

For a few moments, he said nothing. The fire crackled and off in the distance someone pounded with a hammer. Jael watched as the king's expression transformed from downcast to radiant. He laid his hands gently upon her shoulders, leaned forward and kissed her cheek. As if that were not enough, he caressed her face in the palms of his hands. Suddenly, he rose and crossed to the fire. She knew he was dealing with strong emotions, so she did not interrupt. She was well acquainted with emotion of late.

He turned about. "I am nearly overcome, as you can see. I am so pleased with the news you bring. When are we to expect this glad occasion?"

She folded her hands in her lap. "I am not fully certain. It has all come about much more quickly than expected. Lady Adrina has her suspicions and of late – " she hesitated. Should she tell him of their suspicions? She glanced up at him. "Well, I am almost ready to agree. We suspect … that I … may be carrying twins."

His jaw went slack. He sat down in the nearest chair, then jumped up again and threw his hands into the air. "Twins in the royal house again – how praiseworthy that would be!"

Jael drew in a quick breath at his exuberance. "We must not be too anxious for it, in case it is not so." She laid a hand upon her abdomen and gave him a mock frown. "But I think it must be, for there are times when I feel as though a battle ensues within."

The king sat back and gave a hearty laugh. He shook his head in disbelief. "This very morn I was so heavy hearted, and now it is all lifted. You have made it so, dear lady." After a moment, he sat forward and gazed into her eyes. He frowned, drawing his brows together. "I think you are right. We will keep it to ourselves – the part about the twins – but it will be glad news in the kingdom." He sat back and shook his head slowly. "They could use a bit of gladness at present."

Jael rose to go. "Will you excuse me, Father? I feel I must return to my room." She bent to kiss his cheek. When she straightened, she gave him a warm smile. "Though I keep to my quarters, you will always be welcome there. Please do not spend too much time alone. Let us be company to you until Lady Bethalyn returns. I know how you long for her."

His eyes widened and he returned her smile as though he were struck by a happy thought. "I will go at once to write a letter by my own hand. The first missive she should receive will give her news of the impending birth of a new grandchild. How happy she will be. When does the thaw come to Cragmorton?"

"The pass will not clear until the last weeks of May, I'm afraid, though sooner if the weather is more warm than usual."

He rose and offered her his arm to escort her from the room. "I will pray for fair weather then, and that will bring my lady to me sooner. How I regret having sent her there."

Jael had heard this sentiment many times over since her arrival and had to agree. Though there had been grave danger, the king would surely have fared better had his lady been beside him.

Toldar spent three long days sheltered in a cave high in the Touris as the spring rains brought a halt to his homeward journey. He was quite alone and did not relish it, since it allowed him too much time to regret parting from his lifelong friend. He was finally able to quiet his troubled heart and turn his mind to what lay ahead. A lovely wife, a son who must be quite of a size by this time and a daughter whom he had never seen, all waited for him at Wrenook. If ever the rains did stop, he would go there. Of course, he would never tell Elizabeth that he had not wished to come home even now, but had preferred to accompany the men in their quest for Din Glun.

On the fourth day, a rock dweller sang its morning song as he awoke, and he knew the sky would clear. He scattered the coals of his fire, packed up his horse and began the difficult climb to the pass.

At Wrenook the leaf buds on the roses had barely begun to open. Its white walls stood out starkly against the dark patches of mud where the snow had newly melted. The shrill voices of children playing on the great porch echoed over the nearby fields which were already showing a verdant green, dotted with woolly sheep.

Elizabeth sat at her sewing and watched her children play at her feet. Nathaniel rolled a ball for his little sister to catch and each time it came towards her, she threw her hands in the air and screamed in delighted laughter.

"What joy is this?" Toldar said, as he approached.

Elizabeth dropped her sewing and jumped to her feet. "I know that voice!" She ran to Toldar and threw herself into his waiting arms.

Nathaniel stood wide-eyed at the man he barely remembered. When recognition lit his eyes, he cried out. "Papa?"

Toldar caught the boy up in his arms and swung him about. Baby Rose gazed up at the tall stranger before her. Her lower lip trembled as she reached for her mother.

"She is beautiful," Toldar said as he took her in his arms. Rose drew back to gaze at him. "Just like her mother." He bent to kiss Elizabeth.

"How I have longed for this day."

Elizabeth caressed his cheek. "As have we all, but we had nearly given up hope. I thought never to see you again."

His eyes held hers. "I wondered that as well, several times." He glanced over her shoulder. "Where is Lady Bethalyn?"

Elizabeth motioned to the children's nurse to watch over them. She held out her hand to her husband. "She is inside. She sits with Aunt Blessingstock who can no longer leave her bed."

Toldar drew in a breath and set his jaw. "Then I have come at a good time, I suppose." He folded her hand into his and drew it into the crook of his arm. "Solis is with me. He will oversee the queen's return journey after he has been assured that all is well here."

They strolled toward the house. Elizabeth stopped suddenly. "Then my brother has not come?"

He shook his head. "Nay, my love, he pursues the enemy." He told her a little of what had passed, and promised to tell her more when her mother was within hearing.

As they continued into the house, she asked, "And what of Lady Jael and Young Will? Have you seen them?"

"Your brother saw Lady Jael but briefly. He sent the ladies on to Coldthwaite and Young Will rides with him."

"Two ladies?" She smiled her relief. "So they were able to rescue Adrina?"

"I believe that was the lady's name." He smiled into her eyes. "Apparently, Young Will is quite fond of her."

Elizabeth drew in a quick breath. "Is he?"

He grinned. "You are surprised?"

"I thought it was Crispus – " She glanced up. "Oh well, who can know such things?" She leaned into his arms and offered her lips to his. "I care not, for my beloved has returned to me."

Chapter 32 – Uncharted Waters

Jael's confinement stretched longer and longer, and as her time drew near, she seemed to increase in size on a daily basis. She got very little rest for the struggle within her womb. She frowned and sighed and thrashed about. Despite her best efforts, she tended to complain too much. Adrina, who was sitting nearby, jumped up and ran to her side.

"What is it, my lady?"

"I am so uncomfortable, I feel as though I cannot breathe." She closed her eyes a moment. When she opened them again, Adrina still stood over her, watching. Jael gave her a wan smile. "I am sorry to complain so much, dear friend." She pressed her hands against her abdomen and frowned. "I do believe they have run out of room, for they have grown quiet."

Adrina gave a short laugh. "Your humor is intact, at least." She ordered that the shutters be thrown open. "The day is bright and glorious, you should enjoy it."

Jael turned her eyes to the window. The bed curtains stirred gently in the salty breezes. "There is air stirring, but I cannot feel it. I am so hot!"

"I could send for a servant to come and turn the fan," Adrina said.

"Oh, it is not that – " She pointed to her swollen abdomen. "There simply is no more room in here." She gave Adrina a wry smile. "How fare my feet? I have not seen them in some weeks."

Adrina laughed as she threw aside the covers. "They are well and send their greetings, my lady."

Jael laughed with her. "You'd best read to me, friend. My mind is going. I am bored to distraction." Jael took up her embroidery again. "I have made so many lovely scarves and pillows. Everyone may benefit from my bounty."

Adrina opened a scroll and began to read a letter sent by Patrick some years prior. Jael found them interesting, especially the references to her husband. "What do you think he meant by calling my husband Absalom?"

Adrina's brows knit in a pretty frown. "Absalom was a prideful young man – over fond of his own looks – a son of David, I believe."

Jael stared back at her for a moment, and then erupted into giggles, covering her mouth with her hand. "Small wonder that William refuses to speak of it."

Suddenly a cry was heard from belowstairs. The door flew open and Eldred stood upon the threshold, his face very red, his breath labored. "My lady – pardon my intrusion, but the king!"

Jael pushed herself up in bed. "What of the king, Eldred?"

Eldred was bent nearly double, desperately trying to catch his breath. "He has fallen, my lady."

"Fallen – what do you mean? Literally?" Since fallen was a term among warriors for death, Jael wanted clarity.

Eldred gulped air. "It was his head again – it pained him so. Then he fell. We cannot wake him!"

Jael fought against the covers to rise and Eldred immediately turned his back. Adrina threw up her hands to stop her. "Nay, my lady, you must not."

Still facing outward, Eldred spoke. "The royal physician has been called, my lady. I will return to His Majesty now and send yer maid to ye at once."

Adrina tried to block Jael from rising. "Jael, you can't be up."

Jael glared at her. "I cannot lie here, while he may be dying."

"He would not want you to endanger your children."

Jael sat on the edge of the bed and gazed into Adrina's eyes. "I must go to him, Adrina. I must do what I can to help him."

Adrina gave up trying to dissuade her and helped her instead. When Sharla arrived, she found a robe to cover Jael and the two women helped her walk out into the corridor. Here they were met by a rather large warrior.

He bowed. "My lady, I been sent by Eldred saying I should come and carry ye to the king's quarters. So with yer permission, my lady?"

The women stepped back out of his way and he gathered Jael up like an oversized baby. He carried her easily down the long corridor to King George's personal quarters. A servant opened the door as they drew near, and the warrior set her down gently upon a chair at King George's bedside.

Jael drew in a quick breath at his complexion – ruddy, yet pale at the same time. One arm hung down, lifeless. She lifted his right arm and pushed it back on the bed, tucked the bedclothes beneath to hold it in place. She stood and laid her hand upon his brow. As Adrina entered, she turned and beckoned to her. "I cannot lean over him. Come Adrina, listen for heart-sounds."

Adrina did as she was asked. She straightened and looked at Jael. "They are weak, and his breath is shallow. From the look of his face, his right side is paralyzed. I have seen it before."

"So also have I." Jael sat down on the chair and folded her hands in her lap to calm herself. She closed her eyes and breathed deeply. She spoke in the ancient tongue while slowly rocking forward and back.

"My lady, are you all right?" Adrina whispered.

Jael blew out a breath, but did not open her eyes. "I am fine. I am trying to calm down and at the same time, think what must be done."

Another commotion signaled the arrival of the royal physician, a proud-looking individual who ordered the room to be emptied at once. Jael did not like this, but she did not want to complicate matters. She and Adrina withdrew to the sitting room and waited. After nearly an hour had passed, the door opened and Eldred came out, his face ashen.

"I do not like it, my lady."

Jael grabbed Adrina's hand and squeezed it. "What is it, Eldred?"

"He will bleed the king, but holds little hope for his recovery."

Jael let go of Adrina's hand. "This must not be allowed to happen." She tried to get up, could not, and shook her hands in frustration. "Help me to rise!"

Eldred gazed from Jael to Adrina. "My lady?"

Jael's voice was reduced to a squeak. "Adrina, will you help me?"

Eldred stepped forward and offered his assistance. "What can you do, my lady? The royal physician, he says 'tis hopeless."

Great sobs shook Jael. "It is not hopeless!"

Eldred kicked open the door and led Jael into the interior room. Lord Ronald Whitestone, the royal physician, stood near King George, about to incise for the bloodletting. Though he had served the royal house for many years, Jael did not fear him. She waddled forward with the help of Eldred and Adrina.

Lord Whitestone paused and looked up. Anger flashed from his eyes. "I thought I told you to clear this room, Eldred. I am preparing to bleed His Majesty, the king, and I do not like an audience."

Jael answered him with far more authority than she felt. "You will not have one sir, because you will no longer serve the king."

His eyes raked over her. He sniffed. "My lady, you are hardly in any condition to make such demands. I do know what I am about. I have served the royal house for forty years – "

Jael took a deep breath to steady her nerves. "And you have no doubt done very well, sir, but now it is imperative that we keep the king's welfare uppermost. He will live and not die."

Lord Whitestone shook his head and closed his eyes. "I fear, my lady, that you are suffering from the emotional trauma of so great a tragedy …"

"Oh do not patronize me, Lord Whitestone, I am not a simpering fool." She would not by any means defend herself and her own medical gifts and abilities to such a man. He was well aware of her reputation and it was public knowledge that he distrusted her and looked down upon her as a "mere" woman.

He turned in stately manner to Eldred and held out his hand. "Dear Eldred, please show Lady Jael from the room, she is growing overwrought and is incapable of making reasonable decisions."

Eldred made no move, but waited for Jael's answer, which came in a steady voice. "Nevertheless, I am making them. The king is indisposed, his wife is from home, as is my husband. That makes me next of kin and at the moment all you have of royalty here. I am not demanding, sir, I am *commanding*. You will leave at once or I will call upon the royal guard."

Out of the corner of her eye, Jael could see that the royal guard had heard and was already at the door. Ronald Whitestone's eyes darted to them as well. His face grew red as he began to pack up his things.

"This is an outrage. She means to cause the death of the king. Do you not see that?"

Jael lifted her chin. "You, sir – with your words – will cause the death of the king." Without removing her eyes from his face, she gave a command. "Guards, please show this man out at once!"

He did not wait to be shown. He stormed from the room. They could hear him complaining all the way out.

At once, Jael began calling out orders to Adrina and Eldred. Within minutes, a tisane was steeping and King George had been stripped to the waist. Jael supervised as the others made a plaster for his chest and arm. They spoon-fed an herbal tea, covered him and kept careful watch over him.

The large servant, whose name was Theo, bore Jael back to her bed, but Adrina and Eldred stayed by the King's side throughout the night. Jael insisted that she be carried to the King's room on a daily basis. It was not easy for her, but she could not stay away. She held onto his good hand, sang psalms and prayed while Adrina and Eldred did her bidding.

On the fifth day, she called Eldred to her room. "Eldred, my time draws nigh. Adrina will take over for me, but you must help her."

Eldred bowed. "I am yours to command, my lady."

"What word has gone out of His Majesty's condition?"

"That he is ill only, my lady, but I cannot say as what that physician has said."

Jael took a moment to think. "Find out for me. I think we must make a formal announcement." She peered up at him. "Who does that?"

"That would be Lawrence, my lady. He will read whatever proclamation you wish to make."

"All right. Find out what you can and then we will make some kind of … proclamation. I do not want the people to panic." She reached out her hand to him. "They must know that their king is still very much alive." For a moment, she thought she detected the shadow of a smile on Eldred's face.

"Aye my lady – and there is one more thing. Master Abraham has come 'most every day."

"Oh," she bit her lip. "I did not know. Please, allow him to visit the king. He may sit with him and entertain him with stories."

Eldred frowned. "My lady?"

"Who knows what the king may hear?" She smiled and shook her head. "You know how he loves those stories."

His brows arched, but he nodded. "I see, my lady, I shall send word to Master Abraham at once."

"Thank you, Eldred."

That afternoon through her open window, Jael heard Lawrence read the proclamation in the public square. She closed her eyes and tilted her head to the side to discern his every word. "His Royal Highness, King George Horatio, suffers from a spell of the heart from which he will recover in due time. Though he is under orders to remain abed until he gains his strength, all decisions are referred to him and he remains in supreme control. The royal house desires your prayers and support during His Royal Majesty's convalescence."

Lawrence was dispatched to ride throughout the region proclaiming the news.

As the bell tolled midnight, Jael's labor began.

Throughout the night, Adrina worked to keep her as comfortable as possible. A midwife attended Jael, along with Sharla and two other maids. As dawn approached, Jael ordered the shutters to be thrown open. "I must have air."

By mid morning, she neared despair. She took a deep breath and blew it out. *I am doing exactly what I warned Elizabeth against, fighting my body.* Weariness and pain had sapped her strength. She turned onto her side, closed her eyes, and breathed deeply. When she began to sing, everyone in the room stood completely still. Sharla began to weep quietly and Florence, the midwife, turned away to the window.

Jael's voice broke as a deep and agonizing pain tore through her. "Help me up!"

Adrina and Sharla assisted her, but before she could get to the birthing stool, the first baby's head broke through.

Florence rushed to help. "Do not move her just yet." After a moment, she lifted a smile to Jael. "'Tis a boy, my lady."

Jael knew it wasn't over. She leaned back upon the pillows to breathe. In another moment the pains began again.

Florence prattled on. "If they are alike, there will only be one birthsack."

Jael leaned forward. "The other one comes."

"Another boy," Florence said, "and they are both connected to the same birthsack." She gave Jael a toothless grin. "They will be alike."

Adrina held one and Sharla held the other. Adrina's face shone. "They are a good size, my lady."

"Yes, they are goodly boys," Florence said. "'Tis a miracle, my lady."

Jael lay back, exhausted. Adrina gave one baby to her and leaned close to wipe her tears away with a soft cloth. "You have done very well, my lady."

Jael could not stop weeping, for she could see such a likeness in their tiny faces. They both resembled their father.

When she had gained control, she looked at Adrina.

"Adrina, go to the king at once and tell him what has passed this night. Tell him that there are twin sons in the royal house again." She blew her nose. "I know he will hear you."

Within minutes, she heard bells tolling all over the kingdom and knew that word had gone out. She closed her eyes and slept.

The next few days passed quickly. King George's condition remained stable, though he did not really improve. He slept soundly and took only a little nourishment. Jael sent orders that a hearty meal should be taken to the room three times a day.

"Eldred may eat it," she said to Adrina, "but always return an empty plate. That way, everyone will be encouraged to think that he is improving, and they will not lose hope." She knew Eldred would be quite happy to assist.

Eldred sent a message by Adrina. "I'm taking my cue from the Lady Jael. All the while I am eating, I talk to His Majesty, and I tell him of all that is happening in his kingdom this day."

When a fortnight had passed, Jael was able to sit upon the great porch overlooking the sea. When she gave orders for the nurses to bring her infants for their feeding, they eyed one another and whispered. "The babes will sicken in the dampness."

Jael smiled. They were unaware of her acute hearing. She interrupted their murmuring, and further alarmed them. "Nay, they will grow up strong in the sea air."

She was on the great porch, taking the air when the royal advisors arrived. She sent the children away with their nurses. The men bowed to her and at her invitation, sat down. Her gaze passed from one to the other. "What may I do for you, gentlemen?"

The nearest one, a ruddy man of middling height, spoke first. "I am Dulac, my lady." He gestured to the men next to him, "This is Vincent, Connor and Renwald. As you know, we advise His Majesty the King and see that royal orders are carried out."

She nodded. "I do know and I thank you for your patience throughout this ordeal." She saw the looks that passed between them. What were they thinking?

"We have come out of concern for the kingdom, my lady," Vincent said. "In the absence of Prince William and Her Majesty the Queen, as well as Young Will, it falls upon you to make whatever decisions must be made. We have several matters which do at this time require your attention."

Dulac sat forward. "I am sorry for the inconvenient timing, my lady …"

Jael waved away his apology. "There is no need to apologize, gentlemen, no one could have foreseen such an event. But you must allow me time to think upon what you have said."

The men looked at one another and bowed their heads. Behind his fist, Vincent cleared his throat and began again. "You are taken aback by the fact that you are in control of the kingdom? Are you not the very lady who sent Lord Ronald Whitestone scurrying away from the castle?" She heard a low, rumbling noise and realized the other men were chuckling. Evidently, the royal physician had few friends.

Jael observed their faces. "That was a different situation. I was concerned for the king's welfare."

"As well as that of his constituents," Renwald said. "You also took vital steps to assure the welfare of the kingdom. You have already shown great leadership abilities, my lady."

"Not to mention your kind attention to the wounded and dying among the warriors, though you were … ah … indisposed," Vincent said.

"Then allow me this," she said. "Give me a few hours only. Come to me again on the morrow. I will meet you in the king's chamber. As for those pressing matters, have you written them down?"

"Aye my lady." Dulac held out a rolled parchment.

She took it from him. "I will look at this and speak with you on the morrow. Go with God."

"And you also, my lady," he said, and the others echoed his words.

Long after they had gone, Jael sat in silence. Many jumbled thoughts troubled her mind. She did not in any way feel confident to step into such an important role, and yet it had fallen upon her shoulders. How had it come to this?

The events of the past few years came to mind, each one leading her solidly forward. It was as if she had been led by a stronger force, an unseen hand. She would have to seek His face and know His will, more so now than ever before. When Adrina joined her later, she found her frowning over the contents of the scroll.

Adrina sat across from her. "You are troubled, my lady."

Jael met her gaze. "I have just been made acquainted with the fact that I am responsible for the kingdom."

Adrina sat back and blinked.

Jael nodded. "It should not come as a surprise, but it does."

"What will you do?"

"I will spend some time in prayer and meditation, I think." At the entrance of Bella with one her sons, she smiled. "Between feedings, of course."

Jael sat at the bedside of the king. She held his hand and prayed. When she looked up at him, his eyes were open, as though he watched her. She touched his cheek and smiled as she spoke to him.

"Father ... I have not seen you since the birth of my sons. I know you have heard the joyous news and in your heart, you rejoice with me for their health. I hope you do not mind, but I have given them names that I felt were suitable. There is no one to advise me in this, but I know if it does not suit, we can make necessary changes later.

"The eldest, I have named William Ferdinand Horatio du Frain. I will call him Freddie. You remember Ferdinand, the young man who saved my life?" She leaned forward and smiled. "It seemed appropriate to honor his memory by naming my first son for him. The younger I have called Jonathan Justus Rogan du Frain, for my father, grandfather and great grandfather. I hope you do not disapprove."

She took a deep breath. What she had to say next was far more serious. "Now I have a few things to discuss with you, and I will begin by saying that I have approached this with much prayer and deliberation." She briefly explained the situation as the advisors had brought it to her. Then she sat down in a nearby chair, and still holding his hand, informed him of her decision. When a knock came upon the chamber door a little later, she was ready for her visitors.

Chapter 33 – United Front

"**Gentlemen,** I have called you to this room in the presence of the king for good reason. After much prayer and meditation, I have a clear vision of what I must do. I stand in my father's place, but he is still the king." She glanced over her shoulder at King George. "He is in complete authority. Know that any decision I make has first been discussed with him." She noticed the looks that passed between the men. She bowed her head for a moment and took a deep breath. When she raised her eyes, she had their full attention.

"I see what you are thinking and I do not blame you for thinking it, but be assured, gentlemen, King George is very much alive, though he cannot respond. He sleeps most of the time, but oft of late, he lies awake and cannot speak. I believe he hears and understands. Therefore, I will tell him what things you bring before me and I will inform him of the answers I receive of the Lord." She willed herself to relax, intertwined her fingers and offered a small smile.

"Lady Adrina, daughter of the late King William Rendwick du Frain, studies the royal records and helps me to find precedents on which to base my decisions. In this, I will also depend upon you, who have more direct knowledge. I realize that precedents will not always be readily available, but I will do my best. Do you have a problem with any of this?"

Vincent stood and bowed. "Nay, my lady, it all seems quite clear."

Dulac nodded his agreement. "Once again, you have shown yourself wise, my lady, and behaved in a way that I believe will maintain stability in the kingdom."

Jael bowed her head out of respect for the older man. "I hope your confidence will always be warranted."

Following her introductory speech, she discussed solutions regarding each point of need, stopping to listen as the men made suggestions and comments. When they rose to go, Jael noticed King George's eyes upon her. She moved to his side, took his hand and bowed to the advisors.

"Please gentlemen, do not forget to pay your respects to His Majesty." Each one drew near in turn and spoke to King George, pledging their prayers and continued servitude. After the men left, Jael bent forward to kiss her father-in-law on the cheek.

"It has been an eventful day, Father, and you must be quite weary. Rest now, and be at peace. I will return to you later." She watched as he closed his eyes. When she knew he slept, she took her leave.

Life settled into a routine after the first few days. Jael endeavored to keep business to a minimum, meeting not more than once a week in the king's quarters. Her inclusion of him in the governmental process seemed to renew his interest in life. He took more food and color returned to his cheeks.

Master Abraham was impressed enough to ask, "Have you introduced him to his grandsons yet?"

Jael tilted her head. "I have not."

"The thought occurred to me as I lay down to sleep last night," he said. "Perhaps if you brought them to him and even allowed them to lie beside him in the bed, as if he were holding them?"

Jael touched her lips with her fingertips. "Who knows but what it may encourage him and give him the strength to make a full recovery." She turned a bright smile on Master Abraham. "Thank you, I shall begin this very day."

King George was awake when Jael brought her sons for a visit. His eyes watched her progress as she entered with Freddie in her arms. "Father, I have brought you a visitor." She presented the baby to him, holding him up in front of King George's face for a moment. With her free hand, she arranged the bedclothes to make room for the baby to lie in the crook of the king's good arm.

To Jael's surprise and delight, a tear rolled down King George's cheek. She dried his face with her handkerchief and smiled into his eyes. "I reacted in similar fashion when first I beheld him. Is he not beautiful?"

The door opened and Adrina entered, holding Jonathan. Jael beckoned to her, took the child and held him up before his grandfather. Jonathan was not so complacent as his brother. He whimpered a bit and threatened to cry.

Jael cuddled him in her arms and comforted him. King George appeared happy, though it was difficult to be certain, because his eyes were filled with tears.

"He is either very happy or very upset with me," she whispered to Adrina.

"I think he is overwhelmed with joy my lady," Adrina said.

In the days and weeks that followed, the king grew stronger in mind and body. Still he did not speak, but gradually, he would lift his left hand in greeting when anyone entered the room. Jael gave instructions to Eldred, and they soon had him up and moving about. He leaned heavily upon his servants, since his right side did not function well and often spent his afternoons sitting up in a chair either by the fire, or when weather permitted, upon the great porch overlooking the sea.

Lady Bethalyn had a very fast trip down the great Verani River in a Dragon Ship owned by the Prince of Milos. She did not really remember who that was, but the honor and distinction was immensely satisfying. She glanced across the deck at Crispus, whose presence was a great comfort. He spoke with Solis and his men as they prepared to disembark near Verani Inlet. The warriors would continue on to Corwinder overland.

At her first sighting of the sea, Lady Bethalyn felt that she was home. Two days later, the Dragon Ship drew into port below Coldthwaite. Lady Bethalyn detected Abraham Worther amongst those standing by as the Milosian general escorted her across the gangplank. The royal guard ordered a palanquin and Abraham walked beside it to the castle. "I was concerned," he said, "lest you have word of His Majesty's welfare from someone who has too little knowledge of the facts, Your Highness."

Lady Bethalyn squeezed her eyes tight and pressed her lips together. *I will not cry. I will not blubber like a weakling and make a spectacle of myself.* She took a deep, cleansing breath and opened her eyes, concentrating on the intricate designs cut into the frame of the palanquin.

"Master Abraham, if you please, do go on. Tell me of my husband's ordeal."

"His ordeal has been great, but by God's grace, he recovers. You will no doubt find him greatly changed, but we endeavor to treat him as we always have." He frowned into the bright afternoon light. "I think if you will take a similar path, you will soon see what I mean."

She nodded her head slowly and wondered why George had been left alone. Where was her son? Why did he not return? Was it possible William did not know? She turned her gaze on Abraham. "Did my son know of this, ere he left for parts unknown?"

Abraham shook his head. "No, Your Highness, he did not. When Prince William left to pursue the enemy, his father appeared to be in health, though troubled, of course – in the aftermath of the battle."

Lady Bethalyn gave a relieved sigh, then frowned as a new thought entered her mind. "Pray, Master Abraham, who rules the kingdom?"

Abraham leaned close. "Your husband still rules … " He nodded his head and smiled. "As you will see."

She was puzzled by a spark of mischief in those gray eyes of his. "What are you hiding, Master Abraham?"

"There are things better left unsaid at present."

Lady Bethalyn certainly understood that. She had been in government all of her life and knew the folly of noising too much about. She nodded as Crispus caught up with the party.

"Come, Crispus, meet Master Abraham Worther of Coldthwaite."

Crispus dipped his head to Master Abraham. "From your name, sir, I assume you are a weaver?"

Master Abraham nodded and the two entered into an animated conversation, while Lady Bethalyn made free to spend the few minutes left of her journey musing over what she had been told. She must prepare her heart and her mind for what lay ahead.

Through the closed door of her husband's chamber, Lady Bethalyn heard Eldred's voice.

"The sea is rough and gray today," he said. "I think we may be in for some rain." As the door opened, he turned and though clearly surprised, quickly recovered and bowed before the queen.

"Her Royal Highness!" Throughout the royal chamber, the servants came to immediate attention, while Eldred moved to his master's side. He bowed his head and waited for her command.

Lady Bethalyn could not take her eyes from her husband's face. She swallowed the great lump in her throat. "Thank you, Eldred. Would you … be so kind as to give me some time alone with my husband?"

He dipped his head and gestured to the others. At once, the room emptied. Lady Bethalyn knelt beside her husband, her face a mask. She would not allow him to see how deeply his condition affected her. She would show him the bravery befitting a woman of her standing. After all, had she not seen him injured in battle too many times to count?

Tears rolled down his cheeks as he lifted his left hand and touched her face with his fingertips. His lips moved slightly and she heard only the smallest sound. All her resolve melted. She caressed his face between her hands and kissed him. Their tears mingled as she laid her cheek upon his.

It seemed as if only a few moments had passed. She heard a soft knock upon the door, made quick repairs to her face and that of her husband before standing.

"What is it, Eldred?"

"Lady Jael has come, Your Highness."

Lady Bethalyn took a deep breath and slowly exhaled. "Allow her to enter."

Jael bowed. As she straightened, she searched her ladyship's face. As usual, Lady Bethalyn seemed cool and calm. "Welcome home, Mother. I hope your journey was not too difficult?"

Lady Bethalyn ignored her question. "Come in, Lady Jael, you do not have to carry on with the niceties. Tell me all there is to know about … " her voice failed and she turned quickly away, returning to her husband's side.

Or perhaps not so calm. Jael brought the queen a chair and then one for herself as well. "I hope you do not mind, I have ordered tea to be brought within the hour."

Lady Bethalyn made no reply, but continued to dab at her eyes and nose. Jael smiled at the king. "How happy he is to have his lady by his side again." She raised her eyes to Lady Bethalyn. "Until his illness, he spoke of little else."

Lady Bethalyn turned red-rimmed eyes upon him, but still said nothing, so Jael continued. "I do not know what you have been told, Lady Bethalyn, but he has had what some would call an apoplexy. When I arrived here, he was suffering terrible headaches and they seemed to grow worse. The day came when he collapsed and was no longer able to speak or to move."

Until the time tea arrived, she described each stage of King George's illness and recovery. She poured the tea and handed a cup to Lady Bethalyn, who asked, "Is he able to … eat … and drink?"

Jael gazed into King George's eyes. "Aye, very well, he has even begun to feed himself a little." He lifted his hand from its resting place on his knee, to illustrate his prowess. Jael glanced at Lady Bethalyn. "He is learning to use his left hand."

Lady Bethalyn giggled at the sight, though tears still stood in her eyes. "Would you like some tea, dear?" she asked her husband.

His lips moved. "Aye," he whispered, after some difficulty. Jael could hardly contain her joy. She covered her mouth with her hands, then glanced over them to the queen. "'Tis the first word he has spoken. He wishes to impress you, I think."

Lady Bethalyn set down her cup with a trembling hand. After a slight hesitation, she took it up again and helped him drink from it. All the while, the king's eyes did not leave her face.

Jael pushed away from her chair. "Please excuse me, but I must return to my sons."

Lady Bethalyn paused, her cup suspended in midair. "Sons?" Her voice hit a sudden soprano note. She glanced over her shoulder at Jael. "I received a missive regarding your impending confinement – " She set down the cup and turned to face Jael. "Sons?"

Jael nodded slowly. "Would you like to see your grandsons, Lady Bethalyn?" King George laid his hand upon Lady Bethalyn's. She turned to look at him and gave an affirmative answer to Jael.

A short while later, Lady Bethalyn's shocked gaze drifted from one to the other of the babies. "I cannot believe it. Dear me, they are so alike. How do you know … which … is which?"

Jael showed her the blue ribbon tied to Freddie's ankle. "We will have to do something different as they grow, I suppose."

Lady Bethalyn bent over them. "They are so like their father." She glanced over her shoulder at Jael. "He has not seen them?" She turned back and fingered Freddie's soft curls. "No, he would not have." She straightened, crossed to her chair and sank into it. "Well, you are full of surprises this day."

Jael bowed her head. "You must be so tired, Mother. May I send your maid to you?"

"If you will be so kind, I am quite weary."

When Lady Bethalyn made her appearance the next morning, she was not so composed. She crossed the floor to the place where Jael had been enjoying a moment of peace as she perused an official document.

"What has happened to my husband's physician?"

Jael blinked at Lady Bethalyn and answered in a calm voice. "I dismissed him."

Lady Bethalyn paced up and down. "Lord Whitestone has been with us a great many years."

"I am aware of that, my lady. It was necessary, I assure you."

"Why? He did not agree with your ideas? He did not like your herbals?"

Jael suspected that the man had corresponded with Lady Bethalyn or in some way otherwise communicated, but she did not say so. Instead, she looked at her mother-in-law and said, "If you doubt anything that I have done in your absence, you may speak to the advisors, for I know you trust them."

Lady Bethalyn halted midstride, seemingly lost in thought. After a moment, she found a chair and sat, clearly troubled. Finally, she spoke. "You misunderstand me, Jael. I know how it sounded, but I do not distrust your word. I only want to understand your reasoning in this matter."

Jael drew back. Her mother-in-law expressing humility? She frowned at the parchment laid out before her and took a moment to consider her answer. She faced Lady Bethalyn. "He came in here with the attitude that the king could not survive." She gave her head a shake. "I was greatly offended. He wanted to bleed the king and though that may have worked for some, I did not feel that it would be right for him. Granted, it was an extremely emotional time …"

"You were *offended*?"

Jael drew up her chin. "By his attitude, yes, I was."

Lady Bethalyn sat in silence for so long, Jael grew uncomfortable. When finally she spoke, it was as if she spoke to herself. "My husband was unable to fend for himself and now he cannot speak. He cannot give his side of the story. Eldred barely speaks to me, he fears me so." She raised her eyes to Jael. "Lord Whitestone sent me a searing letter, filled with oaths regarding how you had 'behaved in so undignified a manner – '" Lady Bethalyn paused, a smile lurking behind her eyes. "Which is something I could readily believe."

Jael quirked an eyebrow.

Lady Bethalyn rose suddenly, and paced the room. "Only you can I trust to tell me the truth." She rearranged several items on Jael's table and stood back to study the effect. "I will send word to Lord Whitestone." She glanced at Jael. "I will inform him that I stand by your decision."

Jael blinked.

"I can see that you have acted in my husband's best interest." She fingered the fringe of her shawl. "We, as the ladies of the Royal House, must present a united front. Otherwise, they will all think they can push us about." She dropped the fringe and pressed her hands together at her waist. "Now – if you don't mind – the king wishes to see his grandsons."

With that, she left the room in great haste, leaving Jael to sort out what had just occurred.

Chapter 34 – Journey Into Day

William sat among a group of weary riders on the crest of a huge wave of sand, one more amidst a growing tide. Lodan knickered and tossed his head as William dismounted. He removed a skin of water and poured a few drops into his mouth, then cupped his hand for Lodan to lick up a few drops more. That would have to do for now. He wiped his hand on his breeches and hooked the water skin around his saddle's pommel.

Lodan's shadow afforded a bit of shade, so he sheltered in it for a moment, leaning heavily against the horse's side. In the far north, the snows of winter would have begun again. Ice would be thickening over the Greshne and the sun would seem far away. He pushed away from Lodan's side and squinted into the heatwaves. Here he stood in a place baked by the sun. Instead of covering themselves for warmth, they covered themselves to shield the heat.

Below them, the pale green water of an inland sea lapped at the edges of the vast desert. Palm trees waved languidly in the midmorning breeze and the strange sounds of the desert greeted their ears. The growling moan of a camel, the tinkle of bells, the sound of the omnipresent wind. Benabi crouched low upon the sand, watching the edges of the settlement for any sign of the men they sought. After a few moments, he stood and waved the others on.

"Upon the edge of the settlement, we will set up camp," he told William. "This is a crossroads. Here we may be able to find information that will lead us to our destination."

William, with Young Will, Benabi, Rondar, and a small band of warriors, had been at this for months now, traveling much farther than anyone had planned. William let his head fall back to ease the weariness in his neck. He glanced about him at men as travel-sore as himself. These few had remained true with a single-minded purpose, to seek out and destroy the enemy known to them as Din Glun. That purpose had sent them across high mountains, over the Great Sea and through rock strewn byways. They'd fought off bandits and hid themselves in caves to avoid encounters with local armies. As they rode into the village, William drew up beside Benabi.

"We can rest here a while," Benabi said. "Our animals need to recover. They are not used to such difficulties as they have recently experienced." He eyed William. "We must recover and refocus as well."

William nodded. "Are you certain we shall be safe here?"

Benabi leaned close. "It will be better if you do not speak your language where it can be heard, but other than that, you will be safe."

The night spread its dark cloak quickly and the temperature plunged. The men encamped round a roaring flame.

"The sky is so different here," Young Will said as he reclined near the fire. "How many miles have we come?" He directed his question to no one in particular.

"I lost track some weeks back," William said. He lay beside his nephew, half asleep.

"We have crossed nearly three thousand miles of the lower continent," Benabi said.

Young Will shook his head. "I wish I had not asked. 'Tis most annoying – riding on and on with no end in sight."

"Aye it is annoying," Benabi said, "but the end is always within sight, my friend, always much closer than you think. We must be ever at the ready to face it. Do not allow your thoughts to waver."

"Your words seem almost prophetic." William's voice was muffled beneath a woolen mantle. He drifted off to sleep.

A few days passed as the men and their animals rested and recovered their health. Then word came that a dark warrior had attacked a settlement just the other side of the inland sea.

William rubbed the back of his neck. "By now he will be gone."

Benabi agreed. "Aye, but we can be fast on his trail, for I have secured a vessel that will take us swiftly over the water."

The small sailing vessel held barely enough room for the band of warriors and their mounts. Benabi, Young Will and William stood in the bow, to take full advantage of the breezes.

"This is a dangerous land and home to many who would not wish to be found," Benabi said with a nod to the horizon. "The mountains are treacherous and full of caves. We must take great care."

William removed his turban to let his hair blow in the wind. "We cannot lose their trail again, we have come too far."

Benabi took a sip of water. "Would that we were as gifted as your lady."

Young Will chuckled. "She would infiltrate their camp and put them all into a deep and relaxing sleep. They would never know what hit them."

William scowled at his nephew. "I still do not like to think of it." Young Will's heroic tales of Adrina's rescue had given him little comfort. He could not think of Jael without concern, knowing she would risk her life so. She was a Rogan, after all and could no more suppress that part of herself than he could restrain his own natural warrior instincts. In one moment, he swelled with pride at her accomplishments, and in another, he cowered in fear for her life. Had she not already suffered? Young Will told him of her sword wound as if it were a thing to be respected.

"She conducted herself as any warrior would," he'd said. "She did not even let on that she was injured until it became obvious to all."

William felt something near panic at the thought of her lying unconscious for hours as a result of that wound. And where was he when she had need of him? He frowned at the sunburned land where he sojourned now, ran his fingers through his hair and rewrapped the mandatory turban.

When the boat made shore on the far side, the men disembarked and set off for the village. They found it much as they had so many other villages and settlements along the way – pillaged and burnt and burying its dead.

"It was the black warrior," one survivor told Benabi. William and Young Will watched as he spoke the unfamiliar tongue, punctuating every phrase with elaborate hand gestures, as did many people in these parts. Benabi translated. "No warning, just a quick swooping down like a fire dragon."

They soon picked up the trail and found two more dead along the way. "I cannot understand this bloodthirst," Young Will said.

William shook his head sadly. "It is beyond understanding."

Benabi crouched beside a set of footprints. "He is cursed, so measures his curse upon all." He lifted his head to gaze into the distance. "They are headed due north."

When darkness approached, the men made the decision to journey on. There was a three-quarter-moon that shed a good amount of light.

It was well past midnight when they found Din Glun's camp in a deep ravine with high rock walls. Sentries stood near the entrance of a cave high up on one side.

Benabi groaned. "I know this place." William stepped into place beside him.

"Those are no good memories, by the sound of it."

"You reckon rightly sir." After a few quiet moments, Benabi continued, "I think our best move will be to trap them, and I have just the thing."

William glanced at Benabi, whose face was illumined by the moon. "Is there no other way out? Surely they would not be so foolish?"

Benabi nodded slowly. "Aye, there is a way out. I know it well. However, we will make good preparations." He beckoned to the men. "Come."

Young Will moaned. "Not another cave. Why must they always hide out in caves?"

William eyed his nephew.

Benabi smiled and said, "Here in the desert, my young friend, caves provide our only cover, and these foothills are full of them." He waved his hand toward the nearest canyon wall. "They serve a dual purpose, as you will see."

William stood looking up at the steep walls cloaked in darkness. The air was filled with the familiar smell of the weed smoked by these foreigners. He did not like it. He frowned and moved ahead, following Benabi's lead.

They left a lookout near the entrance to keep an eye on the sentries and another at the head of the trail. From there they entered into a deep crevasse which issued a cool breeze into the dead of night.

Benabi gave instructions before entering. "We must lead our horses on foot. Just on the other side, we will leave them." None of the horses liked the dark narrow trail, but it took an extra bit of coaxing for Young Will's mount. Finally, he covered the animal's eyes with a cloth and caught up to the others. The place where they tethered the horses was almost completely enclosed by low resinous bushes. Here, Benabi knelt and assembled the things he would use.

William stood over him and watched his progress. As Benabi unwrapped a leather bundle, William frowned. "What is that? It smells quite foul."

Benabi cast a glance over his shoulder. "It is a sulfurous compound which will cause their eyes to water." His teeth shone white in the semidarkness. "They will seek the nearest exit."

William crouched beside him. "But if they run, how will this help us?"

Benabi paused a moment in his work to aim a toothy grin at William. "I have a plan, my friend." He quickly finished assembling the ingredients, bundled them in a robe and tied it. Then he took out a long knife and began cutting branches from the resinous bushes. The scent of pine filled the air. "Imitate me," he called out in a low voice to William and Young Will. "We need a goodly bundle of these."

As dawn approached, William and Benabi found the cave entrance and located the solitary sentry, who was dozing and did not rouse at their approach. Benabi made a swift end to his life. They signaled the others and waited for them to arrive with the branches. Just inside the narrow entrance, Benabi piled the resinous limbs and topped them with what wood he could find lying about. Into the center of this, he deposited the bundled robe. They rolled several large stones near to block the entrance, effectively sealing it.

Their preparations complete, all save William and Benabi returned to the front entrance. At William's signal, Benabi lit a torch and pushed it through an opening in the stones. The brush caught quickly and they dashed away.

The sentries near the front entrance were easily taken, before the smoke and fumes drove the others out. Benabi covered his face and dashed into the midst, crying out and slashing furiously with his sword.

Young Will gaped at his uncle. "The man is crazy!"

"Aye but thorough," William said with a sideways grin. "Try not to kill him."

As Din Glun's minions stumbled out of the cave, they were quickly dispatched by William's men. The main objective was to locate Din Glun, and William and his men were determined not to leave this place without him. As they progressed, a second cave branched off from the first. William and Benabi searched one, while Young Will and Rondar headed down another.

William frowned into the heavy darkness, raised his torch and searched for signs of the enemy.

"It did not take you long to clear the entrance," Benabi whispered.

"He has not so many men these days," William said.

Down a narrow corridor, they made their way slowly, William leading with uplifted torch and Benabi close upon his heels. Suddenly Benabi stopped and grabbed William's arm. He waved his hand before his face and the two men listened. Apart from the more distant sounds of conflict, there was the dripping of water and the unmistakable sound of movement ahead.

Benabi signaled and William pushed forward, more slowly. The sand and gravel beneath their feet did not lend itself well to silent trekking. A groan sounded close at hand and William lowered his torch. A body lay just beneath their feet. If not for the groan, they'd have stumbled over it. Benabi turned the warrior and William brought the light overhead. It was not Din Glun, so they left him lying in the darkness.

From there, they entered a room where the ceiling was higher. The torchlight danced upon the rock walls, giving it an eerie appearance. Stalactites dripped water into small pools in the floor. When William's foot slid on the slimy surface, Benabi's hand caught hold of his arm.

Benabi spoke, his lips near William's ear. "Take care – there is a pit here somewhere. No one has ever found the bottom of it. It is called Bab a hinnom. We have found Hell's gate, my friend."

William swallowed. Great. A cold finger of air lifted the hairs on his forearms. A scraping sound, metal on stone, echoed in the darkness. They were not alone.

Benabi shifted to William's other side and gestured towards the ceiling. William raised the torch, but the ledge was too high and he could see nothing. Then the air was filled with noise – a loud whooshing sound. Benabi threw his arms over his head. "Bats!"

William rushed forward, his torch aloft. Now he knew where to look. He climbed on an outcropping of rock and looked down into utter darkness. He gritted his teeth and pressed forward. Inch by inch, he pushed nearer the ledge. Finally, he was within sight of it.

A familiar smell assaulted his senses before he could make out the form of the man lying there. He scanned the area for pitfalls and glanced at Benabi. "If only we possessed Jael's gift now."

Benabi thumbed his chin. "Ah, but we do, my friend. Cover your eyes." He slid past William, his torch held out ahead of him. A sudden bright flash filled the room with light.

Chapter 35 – The Mighty Prince of Milos

𝔜𝔬𝔲𝔫𝔤 Will had discovered the meaning of Benabi's cryptic remark about the dual purpose of the caves. They were filled with ancient skeletons. "Huh! And some not so ancient," he said, to no one in particular, as he passed a few fresh corpses. By these he ascertained that his uncle had passed this way.

"Beg pardon, sir?" Rondar asked. "I did not hear the last of that."

Young Will gave a soft chuckle. "I refer to the fresh trail left behind by my uncle. We need not worry over burying the dead … apparently."

Rondar jostled his sword from one weary hand to the other. "No – 'deed not, sir – they're among friends, most like."

A few furlongs away they stood, ears cocked, listening for sounds that may lead them to the rest of their party. Rondar moved close to Young Will and whispered, "They'll be quiet till they come across his vileness, keeper of the dead."

Young Will smiled into the darkness at Rondar's remark, but there was no time to reply, for down the way, a bright light flashed. The men moved as swiftly as they dared in the dimly lit cave toward the sounds that came after the flash. Cautiously, Young Will peered around the edge of an outcropping of rock, then inched forward.

𝔚𝔦𝔩𝔩𝔦𝔞𝔪 averted his eyes just in time to avoid being blinded by the flash. He had not a moment to lose. Like a serpent flushed from its pit, Din Glun tried to escape. But the bright light had temporarily blinded him. He hesitated and in that instant, William crept behind him. Benabi twirled a sword to keep Din Glun's attention to the front. A deft swordsman, Din Glun darted between the two men, a lance in one hand and a double-edged sword in the other.

Benabi was every bit his equal and able to anticipate Din Glun's catlike moves. One miss – one wrong move – Din Glun's sword pierced William's side. Burning, searing pain shot through him, but he quickly recovered and jumped back into the fray. Instead of weakening him, the injury seemed to energize William. Power coursed through his veins. Sheer, brute strength allowed him to persevere.

Din Glun soon grew weary of the battle against two strong opponents and made a surprising forward jump, straight at Benabi. He brought his lance about with great force and struck Benabi down. His sword sliced the air with such swiftness, William did not see it in the semidarkness, but he certainly heard it, and threw his body against Din Glun, knocking the breath from him.

William reached Benabi where he had fallen, bloodied from a head wound. Din Glun jumped over his inert body and made for the opening. Just as he drew near to it, Young Will jumped out with Rondar and seven other men.

Din Glun pulled up short, threw his arms into the air and brought them down again, spinning like a dervish. It was as though he wished to do as much damage as possible – as if he knew it was over. So much happened so quickly, William could not follow it. He knew he had one chance and one chance only. He set his jaw. *Holy Father, give me strength!*

With one swift cut, William severed Din Glun's head. His body hit the ground with a loud thump. On the other end of the sword and still shaking from the impact of it, William sucked in air, his eyes scanning the darkness for signs of Young Will. His heart beat so fast in his chest he could barely breathe. As his strength faded, he fell face forward over the top of Din Glun's foul-smelling body.

"**Uncle!**" Young Will screamed as he jumped forward. Rondar and the men joined him. Young Will and Rondar lifted William and carried him from the interior.

"Bring Benabi," Young Will said to the men. With great difficulty, they climbed through the maze out into the bright daylight where sentries had been posted. The warriors who were able assisted those who were not. Rondar and Young Will laid William beside his horse.

Young Will collapsed on the ground beside him and laid his ear on his uncle's chest. "He's alive." Relief left him weak and shaky. He glanced up at Rondar. "What of Benabi?"

"He too is alive sir," Rondar said, "and what of ye?"

Young Will swiped at his forehead with the back of his arm. "I'm all right. 'Tis a flesh wound only. Have we accounted for everyone?"

"Aye sir, we've not lost but a few." Young Will faced the young Cragmorton who had been so faithful.

"You've done well, Andor."

Andor gave a slight bow. "Thank ye, sir."

Young Will stood uneasily. "I do not like it here. Rondar, get the men together. We must remove to a safer place."

"Aye sir." Rondar gathered the men. The bodies of the dead were made fast upon their horses. Benabi and William were set upon theirs. Young Will rode behind his uncle to hold him up, leading his own horse behind him. Rondar did the same for Benabi. There was no time to see to their wounds, and they would not toss them unceremoniously over their saddles.

Young Will instructed the men. "We must find safety and then we can dress our wounded and attend to our dead."

"We are not all here, sir," Rondar said as he turned his horse. "Two are unaccounted for." Interrupted by a sound behind them, Young Will turned his horse. The last two men exited the cave, carrying a large bundle fastened with rope. Young Will gave them a crooked smile and tossed his head. "Give them a hand, Andor." Two other men ran to assist them. They slung Din Glun's body over a horse and fastened down. Young Will breathed a prayer for their continued safety and urged Lodan forward.

They returned to the settlement at the water's edge, where they were given shelter and food. The natives danced around their fire throughout the night celebrating the death of the black warrior.

𝖂𝖎𝖑𝖑𝖎𝖆𝖒 woke to throbbing pain and blinked his eyes. He heard a loud moan and suddenly realized it was his own. Young Will came quickly to his side.

"Do not try to get up Uncle, lest the bleeding begin again."

William groaned. "You are not nearly so fair as my last nurse."

"It is good to see you have a bit of humor left."

William frowned and swallowed hard against the pain. "What of Benabi?" He did not like the look in Young Will's eyes, but the news was not so bad as he feared.

Young Will gestured to the far side of the fire, out of William's line of sight. "He will recover, though he will have an ugly wound scar."

"He will wear it proudly." William tried to roll over onto his side, but pain shot through him and Young Will pressed his hand against his arm to stay him.

"Give it time, Uncle."

William grimaced. "What did you do with Din Glun?"

"The men would bring his body back. There was something said about Benabi needing proof." He spooned some tea into William's mouth.

William pushed a strand of hair from his eyes. "Aye, with so many look-a-likes about, we must be certain that it really was he."

Young Will's face paled in the firelight. "Have you any doubt?"

"No. I judge by the way the man fought." He rubbed his forehead. "It was he."

A sound nearby alerted them that Benabi had awakened and was mumbling something. " … to the gates of Hell!"

William smiled into Young Will's eyes. "He cannot forget that."

Benabi groaned. "Your words, my friend – they come to pass."

"We're on the uphill journey now," William said. "You are still alive, though you've lost a bit of your beauty."

"Ah, do not tell me that." Benabi forced his way up onto his elbow and grinned across the fire at William. "You have your life's love, but I have yet to find mine. If I have lost my looks, what have I to offer?"

"Oh, I think you have yet a little to offer, old friend." At the approach of Rondar, William turned his head and offered his hand. "Rondar, I offer you my thanks, you have done well."

Rondar gripped his forearm. "It is not I who has done so well, my lord. Young nephew here took command in yer absence. He it is who done well."

William laid his hand upon Young Will's arm. "I knew I could depend upon him. He has no doubt saved lives this day."

"I had no choice, Uncle. How could I return, else? My aunt is a more fearful foe than ten Din Gluns."

William laughed, but winced at the pain it caused. "You are right, she is indeed, but I long for her skills as nurse. She would not let me lie in pain."

"I am sorry for that at least. I do not have her knowledge of the plants."

"I will soon take care of it," Benabi said. He sat up slowly and tugged at his saddlebags.

Young Will grinned. "He has a bit of everything tucked away in there."

"Aye he does," Rondar said. "But ye'd best beware of wineskins, which is no doubt what he's after now." He slapped his knee and cackled.

Benabi cast a glance in his direction. "For that my friend, I will save your part for myself."

Rondar chuckled again and shook his head. "There is one thing I need to know afore ye get too well on."

"And what would that be, my good man?"

"Yer real name, what is it?"

Benabi grinned. "Aye, I did promise you that. When 'twas safe, I believe I said." He looked about him. "I suppose 'tis safe now, what think you, Lord William?"

"Safe as can be, I'd say."

Young Will eyed William. "What secret is this?"

Benabi rose, none too steadily and touched his bandaged head with his fingertips. He bowed, waved his other hand out before him and drew in a quick breath at the pain such a move caused.

"I present myself to you, Amonadabib Josan Arronnapolis."

Rondar guffawed. "Now that there's a name."

Young Will's mouth hung open. "The Amonadabib? So you are also a prince?"

Benabi bowed again, laid a hand flat on his chest and said, "Aye, but you – my friends – may call me Benabi. I like it better and it's easier to say."

William chuckled softly. "The Mighty Prince of Milos."

𝔄 very tired, ragtag team of warriors left the settlement a fortnight later. They returned across the water to the city on the other side where the newly mummified remains of Din Glun were put on display. There was no doubt now that it was indeed the very man.

After a day's rest, the travelers set out across the vast desert to the Great Sea, where they could fully recuperate in more opulent surroundings, entertained by the royal family at Milos. William's heart longed for home and the sight of his beloved, a distant star on the horizon with so much sand in between.

Young Will's thoughts were much like his uncle's. "I hope Adrina has waited for me." He swatted a fly and turned to gaze at William. "She is so very beautiful. I fear, lest another catches her eye in my absence. Perhaps she will have given up waiting for me to return." He dropped his head forward.

William gazed at Young Will, whose dark bearded face had aged under the hot sun of the southern regions. He reckoned his own looked much like it. "If she allows her head to be turned by another, she is not worthy of you."

Young Will raised imploring eyes to William's face. "I know you are right, but it has been so long, Uncle. We've had no way to get word to them of our whereabouts. For all they know – " His voice broke.

William stepped near and sat cross-legged beside his nephew. "We must have faith, Will. Without it, we are nothing." He gazed into a sky ablaze with color. "We must believe that our loved ones will know we are still alive." He gripped Young Will's shoulder. "She will wait. If she truly loves you."

On one side of the sky, the sun was setting. On the other, the moon was rising. William felt as if he was in the middle of the two and being torn asunder. Here he was, counseling Young Will, when his own faith had faltered more than once. The prolonged battle had tried his soul and left bitterness in its wake. Now he wished for time alone to give himself over to prayer. He could not return to Jael in such a state.

Behind them, Andor began to sing and soon they all joined in. "I will lift up mine eyes to the hills, from whence doth my help come …"

As water lapped gently against the hull of the Dragon Ship, William slumbered. No matter how hard he tried, he could not hold his weary eyes open. He awaited the dawn, when he fully expected to see a more familiar landscape, complete with trees and mellow grasses. The call of the loon echoed in his dreams.

Chapter 36 – Dawn of the Daystar

Jael stood alone on the great porch at Coldthwaite. She watched as a sea eagle soared above the surface of the water. A difficult week had left her mentally drained. After a deep breath of fresh sea air, she planted her hands palm down on the cold stone balustrade and prayed.

"Holy Father, I am greatly troubled in my spirit and near to despair. It is all I can do to stand here and call out to you." A single tear coursed down her cheek and dropped on the exposed skin of her arm. She rubbed it away and raised her face to heaven. "I feel as though I cannot go on. My heart breaks and my hope … is exhausted." Her gaze travelled out across the ever rolling waves of the sea, always so mesmerizing.

A bell tolled out there somewhere, and she was reminded of Verani Basin, when the fishers came in. It seemed long since she had seen it. A second winter had passed since William set out in pursuit of Din Glun. She'd had no word from him and fought a constant battle against the fear that she would never see him again.

The sound of a soft footfall spun her around to observe Lady Bethalyn's approach. Their eyes met. Lady Bethalyn dismissed her lady-in-waiting with a wave.

"I hope I do not disturb you?"

Jael bowed her head. "Of course not, my lady." She tried very hard to make it seem true.

Lady Bethalyn halted in front of Jael. For a moment, she said nothing and Jael was puzzled by the look in her eyes. Sympathy?

Finally Lady Bethalyn spoke. "I know that we have not always seen eye-to-eye. And I know … that … it has been mostly my fault." She closed her eyes briefly. "Entirely my fault in truth. I was a bit jealous of you."

Jael frowned. "Oh no, my lady …"

Lady Bethalyn threw up her hand. "Nay, do not speak, please allow me to finish." She took a deep breath and after a few moments, continued. "I now know … my son chose … very wisely. You were … after all … the best one for him." Her long fingers fiddled with the ribbons on her cloak while her eyes swept the horizon. Jael grew quite distracted watching those fingers, for it was several minutes before Lady Bethalyn continued her speech.

" … After the devastation of our homeland," she drew her eyes back to Jael's face, " … no one else … could have stepped in and taken over as you did – not even me. No one else could have brought my husband back from the brink of death. He has astonished everyone with his recovery, and I know we owe that to your assistance as well."

Jael could tell this was a very difficult speech for the Queen, so she held her silence and averted her eyes. But Lady Bethalyn would not allow it. She reached out and turned Jael's face with her fingertips, forcing Jael to meet her gaze.

"Now you are torn and thinking you have lost the part of yourself that belongs only to my son. I must say my faith has wavered at times as well. But not now⊥ for I know as surely as we stand here together, my son lives still. I think if you will set aside your grief, you too will see it." She dropped her hand, but did not otherwise move.

Tears stung Jael's eyes as she fought to maintain her composure. She did see it, had known it all along. She took a deep breath and attempted a smile.

Lady Bethalyn raised her strong chin in the air and said, "Look out upon the high reaches, dear Jael, Princess of the Realm." She took Jael's hands in her own and smiled. "Watch the hills, for he will return and I believe right quickly."

Jael felt as though the heavens had opened and shone pure light down on her. She blinked her eyes to clear her vision. Lady Bethalyn tucked Jael's hand into the crook of her arm. Together they strolled to the balustrade as Jael sang a song learned from Crispus on her journey into Cragmorton.

"I will lift up mine eyes to the hills, from whence doth my help come? My help is from Jehovah, maker of heaven and earth."

As the sun dipped below the dark blue line of the sea, they waited.

Jael gave herself completely to her meditation. How long had it been since she'd had freedom to do so? The children and the cares of the kingdom took all of her attention. When Lady Bethalyn offered to oversee the children's care for a few hours, Jael found herself quite alone.

She stood in the shadows of the great cliff beneath the castle and allowed the sea breezes to cool her face. Her hair hung loose about her shoulders, except for a single braid crowning her head. She closed her eyes and drifted away.

She had tried many times over the last year to find William. She sought him in the night, but he was lost to her. Too far away – too indistinct – she did not know where to go. Then Crispus admonished her and she knew what he said was true. She sought the wrong one. If she turned her heart back to God and sought His face, her spirit would be renewed and in the renewal of her spirit she would find what she sought. Crispus had admonished her, " ... *seek ye first the reign of God and His righteousness, and all these shall be added to you.*"

It may not be what she expected, but in the process, her soul would be strengthened. She could go on with or without William. That last thought nearly broke her heart in two, but it was necessary. Somewhere upon this earth, he still rode, of this she was certain, but she would not waste away in waiting for him. Too many depended upon her now.

As all of her thoughts and cares drifted away, so did the sounds around her. The grayness of the day no longer shadowed her vision. A brilliant light surrounded her, engulfed her and uplifted her. To the world, she had receded into the background. In this state of rapture, she sang in the ancient tongue and her voice carried out upon the wind. She could not say how long she stood there, completely caught up in the spirit, but at some point, she found herself walking farther down the beach than she had ever gone.

Her heart was light, her feet unfettered by the rocks and sand. She moved as lightly as a swan floating on water, soundlessly as a feather on the wind. She lifted her arms and worshipped God with all her heart. She had never felt so free. A newness of life stirred within her soul, and she sang out the words that came to mind. She sang praises to God and danced with abandon upon the craggy beach.

The sun was on its downward trek and the seabirds dipped low on the dark waters. Jael wandered among the mossy rocks of the nearby downs where early spring flowers danced upon the wind. She sat down on a large boulder, snuggled in her cloak and looked out to sea where fishing vessels plied among the waves, their white sails billowing.

Her ears, tuned to distant sounds, picked up something new. She raised her eyes to the place where an unfettered horse ran along the shoreline. Water splashed as the waves rolled in around its legs. Jael smiled to see it cavorting. As it drew nearer, her heart skipped. She sprung from the rock and dashed forward. "Sandelstar!" Her heart rose into her throat and she came to a sudden halt.

If this was indeed Sandelstar, then … could William be far behind? Had he not promised to bring Sandelstar back to her on his return journey? Tears started in her eyes as she cast about, searching for him. Sandelstar ran to her, stopped just short and stretched his nose toward her. He sniffed her hands and hair and tossed his head. She petted him and scratched behind his ear. And then her eyes found the object of her search.

He stood above them on a low overlook, watching her. She felt as though she could not breathe. She forced her legs to move, her feet to step, followed closely by Sandelstar. William was not so patient. He rode Lodan and made short work of the distance. He jumped down before Lodan could come to a full stop.

"Do you often walk alone, my lady?"

Was he real or only imagined? He was so changed. She reached out and touched his rough beard. He smiled. Her mouth moved, but no sound came forth as he lifted her in his arms and held her. She lost herself in his kiss. Jael looked into the beautiful eyes she had so longed to see and touched his bearded face again.

He threw back his head and laughter echoed over the water. "You do not believe your eyes?" His voice was gentle. "'Tis true, my love – I am here with you." He drew back to look at her. "I'm wondering, though, how you came to be so far from home." He lifted a hand into the air. "Imagine my surprise when I saw you there, dancing upon the water's edge like a leaf upon the wind." He laughed merrily. "Do you even know how far you've come?"

Her power of speech returned at last. "I hardly know, my lord. I have not been so free of late."

He cast a rope over Sandelstar's neck and guided him back. Then he lifted Jael and set her upon Lodan. He climbed on behind her and urged Lodan forward.

"Young Will and the others have gone on, anxious for the sight of home. So long a time we have been away. What changes has time wrought, fair lady? Tell me of them as we ride."

It was difficult to tear her mind away from the spiritual pleasantries of such a blessed day to communicate worldly things. She wanted to enjoy the peace and tranquility in the warmth and splendor of his arms, but ere long the castle would loom ahead of them and there were many things he needed to know before his arrival.

She told him of all that had happened since he'd been away, with one exception. The unexpected joy he would receive when first she introduced him to his fine sons she held back like a special gift.

As she related the news of his father's illness, he leaned his head against hers and groaned. She turned her face to his and kissed him, doing her best to comfort him.

Adrina saw the riders before she heard the report. Her heart beat so fast in her breast as she watched their arrival, she could hardly breathe. Young Will rode with them. She heard his entrance into the castle and held back out of respect for his grandparents, but once he had broken free of them, she stepped out into the corridor.

He did not see her at first, for she hung back, shy of him. It had been so long she did not know whether he would still feel the same toward her. It soon became evident that no change had occurred except a strengthening of his feelings. He seemed to tower over her, this darker, larger Will. A scruffy beard covered his still youthful countenance, but his eyes were the same as his gaze pierced hers.

"Are you free, my lady?"

She blinked. Of course she was free. She nodded and dropped her lashes to hide her confusion.

He laughed. "You have not bound yourself to another while I was away?"

His meaning became clear and she lifted her eyes to his. "Nay, my lord, no other has shown an interest. It seems a learned woman has few suitors."

He picked her up in his arms and swung her about. "You shall have one now, for I will not wait long ere I make you my own." He kissed her quickly and let her go, before they could be observed. "I must away and see that my men are settled, but you will see me later, dear lady – that I promise you."

Adrina floated back to her room where she shut her door and leaned against it, closed her eyes and smiled. She touched her lips where he had kissed her and thus sealed his promise to her.

She was his.

Jael spent the evening caring for the twins and waiting for William to come to her. She had issued specific orders to everyone, "Do not speak of the children. After he has had the chance to settle in, I will introduce them."

William found her upon the great porch, where she stood looking out over the dark waters of the sea. "Here again, I find you intent upon the sea."

Jael turned to face him. He had bathed and cut away most of his beard, leaving only a well-tended chin covering. She blinked away tears at the sight. He was more handsome than ever. Still, his weariness was plain.

His brow furrowed as he continued, "I thought you may come looking for me, so long was I in conference, but I never discerned your presence." His strong arms encircled her. She had forgotten how wonderful it was to be held by him.

"I was ... otherwise occupied, my love."

He smiled down at her. "I have heard many things of you these last few hours, dearest wife, and I have come to the conclusion that I am not the only warrior in this family."

She savored the praise for only a moment, then broke free from his embrace and took his hand. "I have one more thing to acquaint you with and am quite anxious, so you will forgive me if I interrupt you?"

His eyes twinkled. "I am intrigued – what is it?"

"It is something you must see to believe." She drew him to the room once set aside for her when they first came to Coldthwaite. There, she dropped his hand, parted the bed curtains and drew out one of the children.

When William's gaze fell upon his eldest son, he seemed hardly able to take it in. His jaw dropped. "What is this?"

She smiled up at him. "Your son, my lord." She laid the sleeping child in his arms and reached for the lamp to light Freddie's face.

William's lips curved into a smile. "A son." His eyes found hers then returned to the boy in his arms. "And so fine a specimen, just look at these broad shoulders and fine hands. He will grow into a mighty warrior."

Jael laughed and shook her head at him. At Jonathan's insistent cry, William looked intently at the child in his arms and then at Jael. His brow furrowed.

"What is that?"

Jael set the lamp down beside William. "It is Jonathan," she said, as she parted the bed curtains to gather their second son in her arms.

William found the nearest chair and sat down heavily. "I thought that I had a great adventure. See what you have done in my absence." He shook his head. "My exploits pale in your shadow, lady – not one fine son, but two – and they are images one of the other!"

"You say it as though you had no part in it at all." She laid Jonathan back in his bed, kissed his brow and tucked the covers around him. "How like you they are."

He chuckled. "Twins in the royal house again."

"Aye, thus it was chanted in the streets – upon news of their birth."

He looked up. "Aye, I can fully believe it. It is too marvelous for me to take in." He nodded his head toward the bed. "So that is Jonathan, then who is this?"

Jael bent to brush Freddie's forehead with a kiss. "This is Freddie. William Ferdinand Horatio du Frain. I hope you do not mind the Ferdinand."

"Nay, 'tis fitting and I like it very well. Freddie is a good name." He handed Freddie back to his mother and she laid him beside Jonathan.

William stepped to the other side of the bed and bent over Jonathan. "This one is named for the Rogans, of course?"

"Of course – Jonathan Justus Rogan du Frain."

"Good strong names. Family names. I like that." He turned to her. "You have done well, Jael." He took her hand and led her outside, where she leaned against his chest and sighed. "I pray they may be assured of peace and may dwell in safety in this most beautiful of all places."

Out upon the waters of the sea, the moon shone full. Though the hour was late, she heard the coo of doves. They nested in the eaves of the castle.

"A Warrior King will come, who shall unite the divided kingdoms. Then peace shall reign though not without striving ... and when the time is fully come, a Rogan will sit upon the throne at Coldthwaite." – a prophecy of King George Horatio du Frain in the Third Year of his reign.

O tre mis corinor – Be settled (still) my friend

se din à domior – all is well

Se lunior le amistar – Watch over him: Se (Is) lunior (to watch) le (him) amistar (over)

mis corinor – my friend

Se dun mis corinor, se dun – It is good my friend, it is good

Lune de amistar à stordor – I have longed to see you: (to see over you with longing)

O tre mis corinor, se din à domior. Se din todor ànjes. – Be still my friend, all is well. You are in good company here.

Mis adone se lunior le amistar – Watch over my love: (My love, watch over him)

Se lunior se spare ... quon se din à domior ... aberono. – Watch; wait ... when it is all well ... open

Se abo se spare ... quon se din à domior ... veni – move, walk, go: (Listen; wait ... when it is all well, travel)

Se aberono hesperado ë porsè – Believing opens the door

This book, *A Gathering of Eagles*, is a work of fiction meant to inspire real belief. I pray the story blessed you and touched you. Perhaps you know a William or a Jael in your real life. Perhaps, like them, you have faced adversity and struggles of your own and relied upon your faith to see you through.

The characters in this book are works of fiction, but the telling of their story is meant to encourage and inspire. Believe the message of God's grace and determine in your heart to follow Him, no matter what the cost.

How well do you respond to trials and tribulation in your life? Do you realize the possibilities? Times of great distress can be stepping stones to the next level. Promotions usually come as a result of hard work and dedication. The pangs of childbirth precede the beauty of a new life, a fulfillment of many months of preparation. In this section, I have included what I pray are some thought provoking questions upon which you or a small group can meditate.

Newly wed and living in the farthest province of Coldthwaite, Jael is assured of God's presence in her life. The gift of God is so great in her, even her husband knows and trusts it. When she experiences a dark vision, he doesn't question, but sets off with his army in pursuit of the enemy she describes. Because of this trust, many lives are saved.

Read and prayerfully consider Psalm 30:1-5 in your favorite version of the Bible.

1. Yes, troubles come, but what promises do you see in these verses?

2. Do you think God means a literal night's passing in verse five?

When Jael sets off to bring aid to Young Will, she finds herself trapped beyond the avalanche. There is no return, and Young Will is nowhere in sight. This was not her plan. At this point, fear could easily put an end to her journey and snuff out the life she carries within her.

Read and prayerfully consider Psalm 121:1-2 in your favorite version of the Bible.

3. Who do you look to when all hope is gone?

4. Is prayer your first reaction in a time of crisis?

When Jael moves into the "spirit realm" she is hidden from sight and feels safe. Can we ever achieve such a state in our ordinary lives?

Read and prayerfully consider Ephesians 6:10-18 in your favorite version of the Bible.

5. What do you think this passage of scripture means?

6. Are we invincible in God's armor?

The saying, "You can run, but you can't hide," has its roots in scripture. Psalm 139 promises God's full time involvement in our lives. He knows our rising up and our down-sitting. Though we were to hide in the deepest regions of the sea, He would find us. As His children, even then, in the depths, we would see His hand guiding us. Kind of like Jonah in the belly of the whale—then waking up in the regurgitated stomach contents on the beach. Is there any denying God's presence in the situation?

7. How has God proven His presence to you?

8. Have you ever tried to hide or run from God's presence in your life?

Read and prayerfully consider Matthew 6:33 which reminds us to seek first the Kingdom of God. In the distressing time following King George's illness, Jael was presented with a choice. She could step in and take over as supreme ruler of the Kingdom of Coldthwaite. No one would question her actions. Instead, she chose to honor her father-in-law and in so doing, also honored God. Her actions brought ultimate respect from everyone around her.

She also fulfilled one of the most important of God's commandments, "Honor your father and mother..."

9. What does this say about Jael's character?

10. How important is our obedience to His commands, even when no one is watching?

This is sometimes the greatest measure of our integrity and our walk of faith—what we do when no one is watching, or how we behave when we have the freedom and the resources to do whatever we want. How differently this story could have ended, had Jael sought her own glory, rather than God's. Would William adore her and be proud of the woman she had become?

11. Are you sold out to God? Do you seek His Kingdom or your own desires?

"A Warrior King will come, who shall unite the divided kingdoms. Then peace shall reign though not with striving ... and when the time is fully come, a Rogan will sit upon the throne at Coldthwaite."

This fictional prophecy was fulfilled in Jael's lifetime, but was she the Rogan who would eventually sit on the throne at Coldthwaite? Or would there be another who would come after? Consider this in your own life.

12. Are you the end of the story, or the beginning of another, more important story?

Acknowledgments

To my Heavenly Father, who gave me life and light and love and a great big imagination, you have my forever love.

To Mom, who instilled in me a love for reading. Your quiet strength lends me strength.

Diana Scheich is a wonderful woman of God, a prayer warrior, a teacher, preacher, and encourager. She was one of the first to read this story. Her prayers and encouragement kept me going. Thank you, dear friend.

Another Diana, (Blaylock) was with me from the very inception of *The Lady of the Haven* and stayed with me until I wrote, "The End' on *A Gathering of Eagles*. Thanks for your friendship and encouragement.

My husband, Robert, my sons, Phil, Matt, and Todd – I love you with all my heart. Yulanda, Leigh Ann, Alyssa, Isabelle, Emily, Sophie, Teghan, Thomas, and Elijah, I love you and so appreciate your love and your prayers.

And last, but by no means least, thank you Gregg and Hallee Bridgeman of Olivia Kimbrell Press. I thank God for you. And thank you, Debi Warford for the drop-dead gorgeous cover designs! God bless you, dear lady!

About the Author

Born in the Pacific Northwest, Betty grew up in such exotic places as West Tennessee and San Diego, California. Today, she lives in Kentucky with her husband of nearly forty years. Now semiretired, Betty spends most of her time writing, studying about writing, and critiquing other people's writing. She's served as a deaconess at her church, sung in the choir for many years, sang, danced, acted in, and helped direct a very popular Christmas play for the last nine years. She loves to travel, watch movies, read, crochet, and spend time with her family.

They have three grown and married sons living in the area, along with three daughters-in-law, four beautiful granddaughters, two handsome grandsons, one very spoiled granddog, and a semi-famous grandcat named Smith Wigglesworth.

Besides her ACFW membership where she leads a critique loop, she writes on her own blog at www.bettythomasonowens.com and is a co-writer at www.writingpromptsthoughtsideas.wordpress.com. She remains active with Bluegrass Christian Writers.

Betty contributed to the collaborative romantic comedy novella, *A Dozen Apologies*, released on Valentine's Day, 2014. Watch for the first novel in her three-book Legacy Series, *Amelia's Legacy*, late 2014 with another publisher. The first novel in the Jael of Rogan series, *The Lady of the Haven*, is also available from Sign of the Whale Books™.

Of all the characters I've written thus far, Jael of Rogan is closest to my heart. I admire her single-minded pursuit of destiny, her humility, bravery, and steady faith in God. I want to be like her in so many ways. I hope she has challenged you to believe like her, that anything is possible as long as we have faith in our great God.

Betty Thomason Owens blog

www.bettythomasonowens.com

The Writing Prompts blog

www.writingpromptsthoughtsideas.wordpress.com

i. Psalms 29: 1-4, Young's Literal Translation (paraphrased)
ii. Psalms 30: 1-5, Young's Literal Translation (paraphrased)
iii. Psalm 29: 1, Young's Literal Translation (paraphrased)
iv. Psalm 139: 7-12, Young's Literal Translation (paraphrased)
v. Psalms 25:1-2, Young's Literal Translation (paraphrased)
vi. Ephesians 6: 10-18, Young's Literal Translation (paraphrased)
vii. Psalm 24 7-10, Young's Literal Translation (paraphrased)
viii. Psalm 121:1-2, Young's Literal Translation (paraphrased)
ix. Matthew 6:33, Young's Literal Translation (paraphrased)

www.ingramcontent.com/pod-product-compliance
Lightning Source LLC
Chambersburg PA
CBHW060426180626
46817CB00007B/2683